The new Zebra Regency Romance logo that you see on the cover is a photograph of an actual regency "tuzzy-muzzy." The fashionable regency lady often wore a tuzzy-muzzy tied with a satin or velvet riband around her wrist to carry a fragrant nosegay. Usually made of gold or silver, tuzzy-muzzies varied in design from the elegantly simple to the exquisitely ornate. The Zebra Regency Romance tuzzy-muzzy is made of alabaster with a silver filigree edging.

LOVERS REUNITED

"You really don't like me at all, do you, Francey?" Tony regarded her bitterly. "You have not forgiven me for my supposed transgression."

"It's of no account. My feelings are not the issue."

"I think they are. If we can't agree about my odious character at least we can observe a decent politeness in public."

"Yes, you are quite right. It's stupid to brangle about what happened six years ago. I fear we would never agree about that."

Tony appeared to be deep in thought. He resumed his pacing and then approached her. "You know, Francey, on one score we were always in agreement. Perhaps if I cannot persuade you to look kindly on my new career, I can remind you of our affinity another way."

Then to her astonishment, he took her in his arms and proceeded to kiss her with a gentle force. Tony's caresses had always stirred her to passion and she had not forgotten those embraces. Her arms crept up around his neck and she melted instinctively, once again the eager romantic girl caught up in emotions she had thought gone forever . . .

A Memorable Collection of Regency Romances

BY ANTHEA MALCOLM AND VALERIE KING

THE COUNTERFEIT HEART   (3425, $3.95/$4.95)
by Anthea Malcolm

Nicola Crawford was hardly surprised when her cousin's betrothed disappeared on some mysterious quest. Anyone engaged to such an unromantic, but handsome man was bound to run off sooner or later. Nicola could never entrust her heart to such a conventional, but so deucedly handsome man. . . .

THE COURTING OF PHILIPPA   (2714, $3.95/$4.95)
by Anthea Malcolm

Miss Philippa was a very successful author of romantic novels. Thus she was chagrined to be snubbed by the handsome writer Henry Ashton whose own books she admired. And when she learned he considered love stories completely beneath his notice, she vowed to teach him a thing or two about the subject of love. . . .

THE WIDOW'S GAMBIT   (2357, $3.50/$4.50)
by Anthea Malcolm

The eldest of the orphaned Neville sisters needed a chaperone for a London season. So the ever-resourceful Livia added several years to her age, invented a deceased husband, and became the respectable Widow Royce. She was certain she'd never regret abandoning her girlhood until she met dashing Nicholas Warwick. . . .

A DARING WAGER   (2558, $3.95/$4.95)
by Valerie King

Ellie Dearborne's penchant for gaming had finally led her to ruin. It seemed like such a lark, wagering her devious cousin George that she would obtain the snuffboxes of three of society's most dashing peers in one month's time. She could easily succeed, too, were it not for that exasperating Lord Ravenworth. . . .

THE WILLFUL WIDOW   (3323, $3.95/$4.95)
by Valerie King

The lovely young widow, Mrs. Henrietta Harte, was not all inclined to pursue the sort of romantic folly the persistent King Brandish had in mind. She had to concentrate on marrying off her penniless sisters and managing her spendthrift mama. Surely Mr. Brandish could fit in with her plans somehow . . .

Return Engagement

Violet Hamilton

ZEBRA BOOKS
KENSINGTON PUBLISHING CORP.

For Emily—The First Reader

ZEBRA BOOKS

are published by

Kensington Publishing Corp.
475 Park Avenue South
New York, NY 10016

Copyright © 1992 by Violet Hamilton

First printing: August, 1992

Printed in the United States of America

Prologue

Emerging from the colonnaded doorway into Oxford Street, Frances Lawton, accompanied by her mother, did not at first recognize the sultry brunette who had just alighted from her carriage.

However, Moira, Lady Stacy-Long, was not a woman to be ignored, and she tripped up to Frances and greeted her in honeyed tones, "Why, Francey, how nice to see you! Shopping, no doubt, for your trousseau. I have not yet had the opportunity to offer my best wishes on your engagement to Tony. How clever of you to annex London's most eligible bachelor, and in your first season."

To her fury, Francey, which was the name she preferred, felt a flush rising to her cheek at the innuendo in Lady Stacy-Long's tone. Determined not to be routed by this gazetted beauty, she thanked her prettily and introduced her mother.

Lady Lawton, recognizing in the lady a former *chère amie* of her daughter's fiancé, was equal to the occasion. "How do you do, Lady Stacy-Long. I am sure Francey is delighted that Lord Everely's friends are pleased with his engagement. I fear the Duke thought his son would never settle, particularly so satisfactorily. Tony and Francey have been friends since they were both in leading strings." Thus successfully depressing the spiteful beauty, she nodded graciously and shepherded her daughter toward the Lawton carriage which was approaching. Francey, in her turn, swallowed any unwise remarks and obediently followed her mother with no more than a murmured farewell.

Once inside the carriage Lady Lawton turned to her daughter with a smile. "You must expect to encounter such ill-bred remarks from some jealous women, my dear. Tony is a dear boy, with more than his fair share of charm. In the past he might have been a bit imprudent. Most young men are when they first come on the town. But all that will change now. I believe you have his complete devotion," Lady Lawton said with more conviction than she felt. She meant to discourage any wild ideas Francey might be entertaining.

"Lady Stacy-Long is perhaps not an acquaintance you should encourage," she concluded, revealing the doubt beneath her firm words. She had heard rumors about Tony's intimacy with the brunette.

"She and Tony are quite good friends, mama," Frances insisted, not completely mollified.

Although she would be loath to admit it, Lady Lawton felt more than a small glow of triumph from her daughter's success in capturing the affections of Tony. Granted Francey was attractive, a real beauty in fact, with smooth gold hair dressed in a manner to emphasize her high cheekbones and graceful neck. And her melting brown eyes, beneath strongly marked brows, so different from the usual blond's insipid blue, only added to her appeal. An elegant figure and a winsome personality made her a nonpareil. But her mother knew that she also had a hot temper and a willful spirit beneath her surface docility. Francey was capable of whistling one of the matches of the season down the wind if she questioned her fiancé's fidelity. So foolish. More experienced women realized that men behaved often in ways which were best ignored, that had little to do with marriage and a settled establishment.

"It behooves you to disregard any insinuations Lady Stacy-Long offers. Believe me, she is of no importance," Lady Lawton said firmly, hoping she was speaking the truth.

Francey nodded, acknowledging her mother's sensible advice, but her doubts were not completely laid to rest. She had been engaged but a month, the notice in the Gazette had appeared but three days ago, and she had not fully realized her good fortune.

"I think you should wear your beaded blue silk this evening. It flatters you exceedingly," Lady Lawton advised, adroitly changing the subject.

"Tony will be escorting you to the Granville ball this evening. It will be your first appearance together since your engagement was announced, and you must look your best, and do him credit." Lady Lawton was determined to distract her daughter's mind from the recent encounter with Lady Stacy-Long.

Unwilling to continue a discussion which was causing her discomfort, Francey obediently hailed the change in the conversation. The two continued on their way to the Mount Street house the Lawtons had rented for the season without any further reference to Lady Stacy-Long, although that lady continued to occupy more than a little of both Francey and her mother's concern.

Sitting before her dressing table later that evening while her abigail, Martha, arranged her hair, Francey stared critically into the mirror. She knew full well that she was considered an accredited beauty, but she put little stock in the compliments so fulsomely expressed by the various beaux who had courted her. Tony's opinion was the only one that mattered. She had loved him for years, ever since she had followed him and her brother, Robert, on their adventures in Dorset where the vast acreage of Tony's father, the Duke of Compton, bordered the more modest holdings of her parents. That Tony would ever return her regard seemed a miracle she found hard to believe, even though his passionate avowals had persuaded her to accept his proposal.

In her first daze of happiness she had paid little heed to the gossip linking his name with Moira Stacy-Long. Now she was forced to wonder if Tony's offer had been instigated by the Duke's desire that he wed, and with some suitable girl who would provide heirs to the title. Tony was the second son, but his brother Philip was a misogynist with no interest in doing his duty. The Duke liked Francey, thought her a taking piece who might lead Tony a dance, a situation he would enjoy, for the Duke thought his son a rapscallion without proper respect for his responsibilities. Marriage would settle him down. Francey, forced to examine the matter, realized she did not want to be married as a sop to the Duke's sense of fitness.

But it could not be true. She remembered with a blush her own frenzied response to Tony's lovemaking when she had accepted him. She could not deny that Tony had evoked feelings she had no idea she possessed, that she suspected few debutantes in their first season even imagined. She anticipated her wedding night with delight, not with the timid shrinking some of her friends had confessed they felt. How dispiriting to think that Tony might have been disgusted with her enthusiasm, even repelled by it. Naïve and protected though she was, she was not innocent of what happened in the bridal bed and she confessed to herself that the idea of Tony's initiating her into these mysteries excited her beyond belief. She was foolish to allow the snide remarks of a jealous cat like Moira Stacy-Long to disturb her. Tony loved her, Francey. He was not pretending an emotion he did not feel in order to placate his father.

Shaking off her forebodings she rose as Martha signified that her toilette was complete. Twirling before the large cheval glass in the corner of her bedroom, Francey acknowledged that she looked quite presentable

8

in her new beaded blue silk ball gown with its low bodice and slight puffed sleeves. She was going to enjoy herself tonight and not be affected by her silly imaginings. Picking up her long white kid gloves, and thanking Martha for her attentions, she skipped to the door, prepared to greet her fiancé.

Coming down the rather grand staircase a few moments later she saw Tony gazing up at her and could not repress a shudder of anticipation. In truth James Antony St. Leger Everely was a sight to cause any girl to experience a *frisson* of excitement. Tall, broad-shouldered, his figure well set off by the dark evening clothes, his chestnut hair carefully arranged in a *dégagé* style, Tony Everely had caused many girls to sigh languishingly after him. His grey eyes gleaming lazily below strongly marked brows now darkened with appreciation and a stronger, quickly masked emotion as he watched Francey approach.

When she reached the bottom of the stairs he drew her close. Ignoring the footman stationed by the entrance, he pressed a kiss on her welcoming lips. Then, drawing back, but still holding her by her shoulders he said, "I shall be the envy of every man at the ball this evening. You are dazzling, my lovely one."

"Thank you, sir. I hope I will do you credit," Francey murmured, her heart pounding. Oh, how irresistible Tony was, and what a fortunate girl she would be to become his wife.

"I hope you have saved me dozens of dances. Now that we are engaged, you cannot give me a paltry country dance or two, and then waltz off with Archie Pembridge and your other clamoring swains."

"Archie will not be there. I am afraid the poor boy is upset over my engagement and has gone to rusticate at Tonbridge Wells," Francey explained, giving a small frown. She had hated hurting Archie, whose devotion was only matched by his dullness.

"Just as well. I would be forced to call him out if he

9

persisted in pursuing you," Tony replied, only half in jest. He knew he had a formidable rival in the wealthy, if prosaic, young squire.

"Don't be absurd, Tony. I never cared for Archie except as a friend. He's a dear man, but not very exciting, I fear," she soothed, secretly pleased that Tony feared Archie's persistence.

"And I *am,* I hope. Well, this is no place to pursue that fascinating topic. Come, we must be off." Taking her silk cloak from the stolid footman, he draped her tenderly in its folds and offered his arm to escort her to the carriage. "I have already made my duty to your parents, so we need not delay. You kept me waiting quite long enough. Not the treatment to accord an impatient fiancé, my sweet," he reproved with a grin as they swept out the door toward the waiting carriage.

Once alone in the carriage, Tony gave every evidence of being a man who was desperately in love, gathering Francey into his arms and covering her face with kisses. For a moment she forgot the proprieties, as his roaming hand crept beneath her bodice evoking all kinds of tumultuous temptations. Fortunately their destination was a mere ten-minute ride or Francey might have abandoned all restraints under Tony's increasing ardor.

Panting a bit, she emerged from his embrace as their coach turned into Grosvenor Square, aware that she had behaved in a reckless wanton fashion under the demands of Tony's lovemaking. Surely she must accept that he loved her. No man could pretend such passion.

A bit flushed himself and aware that they had almost lost control, Tony tried to speak lightly, "Sorry, my love, if I was a bit rough, but you are enough to try the emotions of any man. I wish we were being married tomorrow."

"Oh, so do I," Francey assured him with an engaging lack of coyness. "But how do I look? Mother would never forgive me if I were to arrive at the Granvilles' in a state of disarray. Lady Granville is such a gossip. She would surely notice and bruit it about that I have been granting you unwarranted liberties," Francey said only half in jest.

"And so you have. Delightful they were too, but you look as charming as always, if I might just tuck this wayward tress back where it belongs," Tony said lightly, aware that emotion must be firmly harnessed and not allowed to get out of hand again. He did not want Francey to be the subject of gossip or conjecture, and if she arrived looking so obviously sated with lovemaking there would be a host of eager eyes to notice and tongues to comment.

Tony had been a popular target of matchmakers for some years, since he had first come on the town. He had treated all overtures, both from light skirts and well-bred debutantes, with lighthearted politeness, but refused to be committed. His few dalliances had been with matrons who knew how to play the game. He protested he could not afford to keep a Cyprian in the manner she would expect and had no intention of tying himself down in domesticity until he had sampled the delights of freedom.

If he had ever thought of Robert Lawton's little sister it was as an engaging and sometimes annoying pest who dogged his footsteps when he sought out her brother. When he came down from Oxford, lordly and rather insufferable, she had gone off to her school in Bath. It was a stunning surprise to recognize in the Incomparable of the season the former schoolgirl he had shunned. Tony went down before her like ninepins, furious not to have discovered his love before all the eligible and attractive gallants on the town had set themselves up as his rivals. He could not contemplate Francey Lawton as the wife of another.

To his dismay, his eventual impetuous proposal lacked the smooth address and savoir faire he had practised. Riding about the Compton acres on a brief trip to Dorset they had been caught in a sudden rain squall. Forced to take shelter for a brief time in an outlying barn, Francey had behaved with laughing indifference to the elements.

She looked entrancing even with her hair straggling in sodden strings down her back, and her wet habit clinging to her body, outlining every curve. Before he could help himself Tony had blurted out his proposal, and was both surprised and gratified by Francey's ecstatic acceptance. Now they were securely bound, with their marriage set for the last of June, a bare two months distant, with the enthusiastic approval of both the Duke of Compton and the Lawtons. Tony grinned as he helped a distracted and rosy Francey from the carriage. He wondered how he would be able to endure the succeeding weeks.

Lord and Lady Granville, receiving them at the top of the staircase at the entrance into the ballroom, greeted them kindly.

"There are several broken hearts among the young men waiting for Miss Lawton this evening, I vow. You have carried off a prize, Lord Everely," Lady Granville reproved him archly. A buxom matron in an overpowering display of diamonds on a cerise silk gown, their hostess liked to believe she was up on every *on dit*.

"Thank you, Lady Granville. I think I have and do not intend to mourn over my rivals," Tony replied smugly.

Francey smiled on their genial hosts but made no attempt either to agree or to demur. They entered the ballroom to be beseiged by a train of gallants, begging Francey for dances and bewailing her fate. Laughingly she parried their witticisms and agreed to some requests but Tony quickly commandeered her dance card and scrawled his initials over a large block of dances.

"Go seek some other partners, you rogues. The lady is pledged to me for this opening dance and several more, including supper," he warned with a half-ferocious leer. He then led her out onto the floor, brushing aside her protesting retinue.

"Very high-handed, my lord," Francey mocked. "I might have wanted to dance with one or another of those nice men." The movement of the dance separated them for a moment but when they came together again they

12

continued the conversation.

"I shall be a very possessive husband, which rather surprises me. It's considered very bad form to spend too much time with one's wife, you know. We will have to be unfashionable."

Francey, although she secretly agreed and was thrilled by his threat, was not entirely willing to play the complaisant fiancée. Tony was too accustomed to ladies who would readily grant his every wish, so subjugated were they by his charm. She might love him beyond reason but she had no intention of letting him glimpse the depth of her feeling.

"Heavens, we must guard against such a breach of manners. I will have to find a suitable beau to escort me about town so you will not win the reputation of a benedict, so damning don't you think?" she mocked. His answer was to draw her closer and for a shocking moment she thought he might kiss her right there on the dance floor, but prudence prevailed and aside from giving her an admonitory pinch, he grinned and let her go.

Supper was a very merry affair, with Tony and Francey basking in the congratulations of their friends and parrying some good-natured teasing. Flushed with the success of the evening, Francey wondered if her happiness could continue at such a peak. After a langorous waltz with Tony, following a lavish supper of lobster patties and cold pheasant, for which she had little appetite, she excused herself to her next partner, explaining that she needed a little respite from the excitement.

She slipped upstairs seeking a suitable retiring room, and as she looked down over the gallery was surprised to see Tony dancing with Moira Stacy-Long. As she watched, the couple left the ballroom by one of the French doors and wandered out onto the terrace. For a moment her darkest suspicions were aroused, and then chiding herself for her lack of trust, she tossed her head, turned her back and glided into a nearby room to rest and rearrange her hair. Still, she could not but wonder why Tony and the fascinating Moira needed to be alone, to hold a tryst away from the curious eyes that had watched their exit avidly. What were they talking about? Francey's worries deepened. Surely Tony was not deceiving her—playing the devoted lover to her and all the while continuing some liaison with Moira.

Chapter One

Beyond the *eau de Nile* silk-draped windows of the morning room, Lady Pembridge could glimpse the bare plane trees in her small garden as they stood shivering in the March wind. What a dreadful morning. She was grateful for the cheery fire in the grate, but not so grateful for the invitation list which faced her on the leather blotter of the cherrywood desk. She wondered, not for the first time, why she had decided to give this rout. Of course she had her reputation as one of London's most sought-after hostesses to consider, she conceded with a grimace. And she usually enjoyed giving parties, but on this bleak day the idea had lost its sparkle.

Perhaps she should abandon the party, pack up and travel posthaste to Dorset. London was not at its best right now and the season had yet to begin. Of course she could not be absent for the season. Why this sudden desire to escape from the social round? This depression was just a momentary aberration, brought on by last evening's extremely tedious dinner at the Seftons. Perhaps a ride in the park at an unfashionable early hour would blow away her unaccountable megrims. Throwing down her pen, she looked with distaste at the guest list her conscientious secretary, Maybelle Orton, had com-

15

piled, and rose to her feet, going over to the window where she pondered on her restlessness. Her brooding was interrupted by the entrance of her majordomo, the very correct Jepson, who announced a visitor. Before she could protest, he was followed into the room by Letitia Colgrove, obviously bursting with news.

"Oh, Francey, I am so glad to catch you at home. So exciting, you will never believe!" Letitia exclaimed, throwing off her bonnet and patting her ruffled hair, before settling down on a convenient chair.

"Perhaps some chocolate, Jepson," Lady Pembridge ordered, before dismissing the butler, and regarding the intruder with tolerant affection. Letty was an old schoolmate, and could not be gainsaid.

"How nice of you to call, Letty, to relieve my boredom on this unpleasant morning," she greeted her friend and joined her beside the fire. Letty looked enviously at Francey, sighing at the picture Lady Pembridge made as she settled serenely in her chair. Francey certainly had all the attributes of the classic blond beauty. In her simple morning dress of sapphire merino she was the epitome of fashion. Letty, on the other hand, was an appealing pint-sized brunette with a merry manner, who lacked the presence and elegant figure of her friend, a difference of which she was quite aware but rarely mourned. Letty enjoyed life too much to regret her deficiencies, and had little jealousy of reigning beauties.

"Now what is your budget of news. It must be dramatic to bring you out on this dreary morning," Francey suggested, smiling at the eager expression on Letty's face. There was no doubt that Letty had every *on dit* at her fingertips and was among the most blatant chatters of their set, but for all her tendency to gossip, Francey liked her, found her amusing in small doses, and was ready to indulge her passion for rumor and intrigue. Obviously Letty was bursting to reveal the latest item, and could hardly contain herself until the maid had brought the chocolate and Francey had poured out a cup.

"You will never guess who has at last arrived in London after an absence of lo these past six years. Tony Everely is home from Aix-la-Chapelle." Letty paused after a perfunctory gulp of chocolate, her eyes watching avidly for Francey's reaction.

"Well, I suppose he would return sometime. He could hardly stay on the Continent now that the Congress is finished," Francey replied calmly. "The Duke must be pleased. I am sure he missed him sorely."

"Is that all you have to say? Aren't you anticipating meeting him after all this time? He is still single, you know, and will be the target of every debutante once the season begins. And to think you could have been Lady James Antony St. Leger Everely, instead of just Lady Pembridge, a mere baronet's wife," sighed Letty. Then thinking that perhaps she had not been very tactful, as was often the case, she added, "Not that Archie wasn't a dear man, of course."

"Of course," Francey agreed dryly. "And I might remind you, Letty, before you go into paroxyms of mawkish nostalgia that I had good reasons for refusing Tony Everely, and those reasons still apply, even if I had any thoughts of placing myself in that unhappy position again. And I am sure he feels the same. You really must restrain your sentimental yearnings."

"I know it, but Tony Everely is so attractive," she sighed regretfully. Married to the staid, plain, but wealthy Mr. Colgrove, Letty often sighed for romance, although in her somewhat careless manner she quite liked her long-suffering husband.

"That was and probably still is one of his problems. He is quite incapable of being faithful to any woman. He should have been born a sultan. He needs a harem," Francey explained, a bit annoyed at her impressionable friend. Really, Letty was impossible at times, with absolutely no notion of how to go on. Then Francey smiled despite her annoyance. She could not be angry at Letty for long.

"And you would not like the role of chief concubine," Letty responded, eyeing her friend mischievously.

"A waste of my talents, Letty dear," Francey grimaced. "Although the idea has a certain piquancy."

"But what about Oliver Fanshawe?" Letty persisted. "Are you considering him as your next husband?"

"I am not considering a husband at all. I much prefer my single state."

"With the tidy income Archie left you, I suppose you can do as you please," Letty agreed, sighing a bit for such a luxury. "You don't have to bow down to any man's hand."

"True. And this past year has proved very pleasant, but I do occasionally miss dear Archie. He was a very nice and undemanding man."

"But not very exciting," Letty complained, remembering Francey's acquiescent husband.

Refusing to be drawn, Francey smiled and kept her own counsel. Despite her insouciant manner, Letty could often prove very perceptive. Archie had not been exciting and his devotion, welcome at first, had often been a trial.

"But enough of this idle chatter about men. What do you think of a Roman breakfast instead of a rout? I am committed to some entertainment to repay various invitations," Francey explained.

"Novel. I rather like the idea of sprawling on the floor munching a meal," Letty agreed. "But now I must dash. I have an appointment with Mme Héloïse to fit a new gown and you know how irritable she can be if one is the least bit late. I have ordered quite a dashing Hussar's outfit, all the rage," she confided.

The picture of her plump friend festooned in braid and epaulettes was almost too much for Francey, but she did not voice her objections. Letty, try as she might, would never be among fashion's leaders. She refused to see that every style was not suited to her figure.

Parting, with a promise to meet again soon, Letty

rushed off to her appointment, leaving behind a reflective Francey. Not for the world would she have admitted to her inquisitive friend how much the news of Tony Everely's arrival back in London had disturbed her.

The object of Francey's and Letty's lighthearted discussion was finding his homecoming less agreeable than he had thought. In the ducal mansion in Grosvenor Square, his father, Philip Eustace St. Leger Everely, fifth Duke of Compton, eyed his second son with a combination of pride and disgruntlement. There was little in Lord James Antony St. Leger Everely's appearance to cause criticism. Tall, with broad shoulders set off to best advantage by Weston's latest midnight blue superfine coat atop creamy kersey pantaloons and shining black Hessians, his chestnut hair carefully combed *à la* Brutus, his grey eyes gleaming lazily below strongly marked brows, he cut a handsome figure, which any father might applaud.

"Well, Tony, you have at last seen fit to honor us with a visit. I thought you would spend the rest of your life on the Continent, a pesky place, and not much better since Waterloo, I vow," growled the Duke, whose somewhat ferocious mien hid a kind heart and loyal disposition. His son favored his father in looks and it was evident that in twenty years Tony would have the commanding presence and thick greying hair of his parent.

"It's good to be back, sir, but I enjoyed my stay at the Congress, and perhaps, did some useful work," Tony suggested modestly.

"You could do a more useful job here, taking up your responsibilities," the Duke demurred.

"And what would those be, sir? I understand Philip is minding the estates with unusual acumen," Tony offered, not at all intimidated by his father but conscious of the direction that the Duke's conversation might be taking.

"I want you to get married and provide me with an heir," the Duke countered baldly. "Philip will never do his duty. He manages the estates well enough but he will never marry. It's awkward, but Philip does not seem to like the ladies," the Duke admitted gruffly. Not for the world would he admit, even to Tony, that his eldest son had a penchant for his own sex rather than for the most luscious debutantes paraded for his delectation, or even ladies of a different and less respectable sort. It was an interest that the Duke could not understand, and Philip's tastes were a sore trial to him, although he never mentioned them.

Tony, not one whit embarrassed by his father's allusions, still thought it best not to admit that he was aware of his brother's preferences. He neither protested nor agreed that it devolved on him to solve the dilemma.

The Duke hesitated, not knowing quite how to broach the dearest wish of his heart. But as he was not a man to flinch before an awkward task, he plunged into the matter.

"You might not know that Francey Lawton is now a widow. Poor Archie Pembridge died of pneumonia contracted after a miserable day hunting in the rain. A good fellow, but not up to Francey's weight. She has become quite a hostess on the London scene. We rarely see her in Dorset these days." He paused, not sure how to proceed, for Tony showed no reaction to this news.

Amusement masking his annoyance, Tony realized that he must give his father some answer. "I hardly think she would welcome my entrance into the lists for her hand. We parted on a very acrimonious note as I remember," he offered lightly.

He did not want to anger his father, but his own reaction to the Duke's efforts at matchmaking was justifiable irritation. Thoughts of Francey and their one-time engagement had been successfully buried and he did not like this attempt to revive them.

"Well, if you are looking for a bride, you could do

worse. I always liked Francey. Lots of spirit that girl," the Duke muttered, a bit nonplussed by Tony's indifference. But determined to press his case he continued, "Of course there is a whole bevy of delectable girls on the London scene. I am sure you will find someone who meets your rather strict standards."

"I am not really inclined to marriage, sir," Tony explained casually, hoping his father could be distracted from this distasteful idea.

"Now, look here, Tony. You have a duty to me and the title. I discount Philip. Do you want the title and estates to go to that rubbishy cousin of yours, Colin St. Leger?" he argued.

"Oh, Colin is not too bad. At any rate surely there is no immediacy to this marriage business. I am only thirty, you know, lots of time," Tony soothed his irate sire.

"Maybe for you, my boy, but not for me," the Duke insisted, even though he looked the picture of health. He was not accustomed to having his orders disobeyed, and did not take Tony's refusal in good part.

"Nonsense, you're good for many more years. You could marry again yourself," his son suggested only half in jest. The Duke was a hearty sixty-two and had been a widower for twenty years. Not that he did not enjoy the company of women. Tony remembered some high-steppers who had enjoyed his father's protection. Naturally he would not remind the Duke of these past excursions into the muslin company.

"Don't be ridiculous, Tony. I have done my duty to the Compton title. Now it's your turn. Choose some nice little gel from this year's crop of eligibles. All I ask is that she come from a decent stable," the Duke urged somewhat coarsely. He was apt to speak of breeding in terms of horses, which his son believed he thought more of than women. But Tony was not concerned with brood lines or his abilities as a sire. Graver matters had compelled him to seek his father's assistance.

Ignoring the Duke's suggestion, Tony rushed into

speech. "Sir, I have a more important duty to the Compton title now. I have just come from witnessing the deplorable scene in Skinner Street, the unjust hanging of that poor fellow John Cashman," Tony spoke with unusual passion and was about to continue when the Duke interrupted him.

"One of the Spa Fields rioters. Deserved what he got," the Duke had little patience with disturbers of the King's peace.

"That was not really proved. He was arrested for breaking into Beckwith's gun shop. And the poor fellow had every reason to be desperate. His treatment by the Admiralty was scandalous. Wounded nine times in the service of the King and then denied his pay and prize money. He had a starving mother and a host of brothers and sisters. If ever there was a case for clemency this was it, and the crowd thought so too. In a very ugly mood. And if we do not take care, give these poor devils some work and cheaper bread there could be a revolution. I want to enter Parliament and secure some relief for the Army and Navy veterans. It's disgraceful that they should return to such deplorable conditions." Tony surprised himself and his father with the sincerity and strength of his views.

"Parliament, I see. Well, what can I do to help you achieve that." The Duke agreed quite mildly, impressed by his son's fervor.

"The only way to help these poor fellows is with a voice in the Commons. I know you have a borough in your pocket, down near Poole, and that the member died recently. I want that seat," Tony insisted, with a force of conviction his father had rarely seen in him.

"It's yours, my boy. But in turn remember I would like you seriously to consider this marriage business. You cannot be effective in politics without a wife. And she must be an experienced hostess, not some drab little debutante without a notion of how to go on," the Duke argued, unwilling to surrender completely, and quite prepared for some trading on the matter of the seat in Parliament in exchange for his son's marriage. If he did not agree with Tony's politics, he could only applaud his determination. "Francey is an accomplished hostess. But you are perfectly right about her. She wouldn't have you," he concluded slyly, knowing his son would take up the challenge.

Tony frowned but refused to be drawn. He bade his sire a terse farewell, promising to see him at dinner. Thankfully, he was living in rooms at the Albany, and if his father continued to press him on this marriage he could curtail his visits. Rankling, that remark about Francey. Damned stubborn girl she had been, unwilling to listen to reason. She would have made an uncomfortable wife and he was well out of that engagement. Six years had passed and both their situations had changed. Still, it would be interesting, in view of his father's challenge, to see if she were susceptible to a light flirtation. There was little danger he would fall into her trap again, but it might be entertaining to send out a few lures.

The Duke knew his son well, and as he watched Tony run down the steps of the mansion and jump into his curricle, he chuckled. Guile was more persuasive than coercion. He had learned that a long time ago. Tony would not be able to resist chasing after Francey Lawton just to prove to his father that he could still attract the girl, even if marriage was out of the question. And the Duke was not sure that it was. Francey was a spirited filly despite her facade of cultivated indifference. Tony needed a wife who would not allow him license to go his lazy arrogant way without interference. If he would pursue a career in politics, he needed a knowledgeable wife. It should be amusing to watch the tempestuous exchanges between the pair. Tony could do with a lesson.

Chapter Two

Lady Pembridge's arrival in her box at the Drury Lane Theatre on the arm of Sir Oliver Fanshawe that evening was the occasion of some comment. The cynosure of all eyes, she knew she looked her best in a gown of cerulean silk beaded in seed pearls which also dressed her hair, arranged *à la* Sappho. Around her neck lay a parure of diamonds and pearls and more of the jewels fell from her ears. All the theatre boxes were filled, for Edmund Kean was appearing as Hotspur in *Henry IV*.

Francey greeted her guests, Lord and Lady Holland, Lord Melbourne and Lord and Lady Cowper with serene aplomb. If she was conscious of having captured several of the social lions of the day as her guests she showed little evidence of it. Rivals insisted that the secret of her success was her apparent indifference to the most magnificent personages of the *ton*.

She believed that the enviable position she had acquired in that closed society was due to her wealth and her refusal to play by the rules. She entertained whom she wished and paid no heed to gossip. The Hollands, for example, were not received in many of London's most august houses, but Francey found them amusing and intelligent and paid no heed to the scandal which had dogged them since the then Lady Webster's shocking elopement with a man younger than herself after the birth of an illegitimate son. Lady Cowper, as well, had been for years conducting a discreet affair with Lord Palmerston, Secretary of War, and Lord Melbourne was the victim of his imprudent marriage to the notorious Caroline Lamb, whose affair with Byron had caused tongues to wag for years. Francey's own reputation was impregnable. Not a hint of gossip followed her career as one of London's reigning beauties despite the fact that she was eagerly pursued by a host of gallants.

The betting at White's was that she would eventually accept as a husband her favorite escort, Oliver Fanshawe. However, the *ton* had not forgotten her brief engagement to Lord James Antony St. Leger Everely and waited to see how his arrival after this long interval would affect her. If she were aware of this interest it did not appear to disturb her, although she could not but notice the whispers which heralded her entrance into the box. Smiling graciously on her guests, she settled herself in the front of the box, after allowing Oliver to divest her of her satin pelisse lined with ermine.

Turning to Fanshawe she thanked him graciously and began to chat with Emily Cowper seated beside her. Lady Cowper was among her favorite people, a good-tempered, small merry woman, who looked on the foibles of society with a mild eye.

"You are looking in fine fig tonight, Francey," Lady Cowper complimented her hostess. "I suppose you realize everyone is watching to see how you greet Tony Everely, whose homecoming has excited all kinds of speculation in mothers with marriageable daughters."

"Rumor is the curse of society," Francey agreed calmly, not even to Emily Cowper would she admit any trepidation in confronting Tony.

Although Emily Cowper would dearly have liked to hear exactly why Frances had broken off her engagement to Lord Antony and then quickly accepted Archie Pembridge, she did not probe further. Lady Pembridge, for all her amiability, did not reveal her secrets. Unlike her good friend Letty Colgrove she was not a rattle.

Before Lady Cowper could ask any further questions the curtain rose on the first act of *Henry IV*, saving Francey from her kindly interrogator. For her part, Francey thought Edmund Kean a bit long in the tooth to play the youthful Hotspur. But she could not deny the dramatic impact of his entrance nor the passion of his first speech:

> My liege, I did deny no prisoners.
> But I remember when the fight was done,
> When I was dry with rage and extreme toil,
> Breathless and faint, leaning upon my sword,
> Came there a certain lord, neat and trimly dress'd
> Fresh as a bridegroom . . .

Despite the tales of his drunkeness, lechery and ungovernable tempers, or perhaps because of these unlovely characteristics, Kean continued to be a favorite both with the pit and the boxes. Francey found him crude, coarse and unhandsome, but she admired his force and realism. These qualities were unhappily lacking in many of the men now gracing London's drawing rooms.

Often as she enjoyed the company of Oliver Fanshawe, he did not inspire excitement. His was the popular pose of boredom and he deplored the expression of any sincere sentiment. He could be amusing, attentive, complimentary and courteous, but Francey, darting a sideways glance at him sitting in a negligent slouch, suddenly wondered why she had allowed him so much license. He had a certain attraction, a lean stylish figure, and a not unhandsome face—although his hard agate blue eyes were set a bit too closely together, and his mouth had a sensual curve that hinted at appetites not denied. But nothing in his character or in his appearance stirred her to any but the most tepid emotion.

Sometimes she yearned for the tension, the warmth, the thrilling anticipation which she had felt as a debutante. She pulled herself up sharply. That had been the disastrous period of her engagement to Tony, hardly a time to remember with nostalgia. She pulled her mind back from such restless yearnings, wondering what could have induced such thoughts. No doubt, the return of the gentleman who had caused her such anguish. Well, she would not entertain them a moment longer, and so she concentrated her attention upon the stage, where the talent of Kean and the action of the drama soon captured her entire imagination.

When the curtain descended at the end of the first act, Oliver turned to her and asked if she would like to promenade in the halls.

"Kean is so fatiguing, I feel I need a little respite," he urged. "Of course the fellow is brilliant. Hard to think of his equal," he said, following the popular line. Since the retirement of Charles Kemble, Kean had dominated the London stage.

As they rose to leave the box, Francey suddenly felt a spurt of irritation at Oliver. Why could he not say something original, or even enthusiastic? She fanned herself energetically, and took his arm reluctantly. They began to stroll about the corridor, stopping to greet friends and to exchange remarks about the performance. Just as Oliver suggested they might return for the beginning of the next act, they were halted abruptly by a gentleman emerging from an adjacent box.

"If it isn't Lady Pembridge! How lovely you are looking, Francey, not at all matronly, although it must be all of six years since our last encounter," Tony Everely bowed with a mocking grin toward Francey who made no move to extend her hand. If she were surprised or embarrassed by this meeting, she showed no evidence of it as Tony's eyes raked over her, daring her to flare up over his remark about her age.

"Hello, Tony. You are looking well. I suppose the Duke is pleased to have you back," she returned in a bored tone, then as if remembering what was due to politeness, she added, "Do you know Oliver Fanshawe?"

"Yes, good evening, Fanshawe," Tony greeted him curtly, not at all impressed with this apparent tulip of the *ton*. What he had heard lately about Oliver Fanshawe had not pleased him.

"Is this your first glimpse of Kean? A most interesting actor," Francey offered in the cool social tones she used with chance acquaintances.

"Ah, Francey, what a distinguished ornament of society you have become! I am most impressed. And very happy to have met you here. I was planning to call, you know," he responded, ignoring her reference to Kean but implying that he did not approve of her current role.

She succeeded in keeping a tight grip on her temper. Bandying words with Tony in the halls of Drury Lane would neither add to her consequence nor prove her indifference to his jabs. Ignoring the wicked light she saw in his eyes, she turned to Oliver, who had remained silent through this exchange. "Shall we return, Oliver? Good evening, my lord," she dismissed Tony glacially, adding to his amusement, and swept away on Oliver's arm, not at all confident that she had won that passage at arms.

Seated once more in her box, but this time toward the back, having relinquished her former seat to Lady Holland, she looked across the body of the theatre. It was as she had suspected. Tony was the guest of the notorious Mrs. Marlow, a widow whose lifestyle was supported by mysterious means, and who managed to hang on at the fringes of society by virtue of her cousin's position, and her own undoubted charms. Francey could not gainsay the lush attractions of the lady, who possessed an abundance of attributes gentlemen found so alluring. Of middle stature, and a bit plump of figure, she had a pair of speaking blue eyes and a mass of black wavy hair. She knew just how to appeal to men's conceit, and how to enhance their own opinions of themselves as dashing fellows. She was wearing an especially lavish necklace of rubies which complemented her satin gown, with a décolletage low even by the lax standards of the day.

Francey wondered if the jewels were a gift from Tony. What a devil he was. Obviously he had not abandoned his pursuit of women, despite his long stay on the Continent. On the contrary, his sojourn in European capitals had probably improved his technique and increased his conquests. He had lost no time in meeting the *risquée* Mrs. Marlow. How right she had been to have broken that engagement six years before. She would have been that pitiable case, a jealous, humiliated and abandoned wife.

Wrenching her mind away from this picture with some effort, she was ashamed to realize that much of Kean's energetic performance had passed her by. Hoping that no one had noticed her distraction, she glared fiercely at the stage as if daring Mr. Kean and the assembly to question her lack of attention. For the rest of the play she appeared wholly absorbed in the antics of Prince Hal and Falstaff and the maneuverings of Hotspur. She did not give even a surreptitious glance to the occupants of Mrs. Marlow's box.

After the final curtain, Francey and her companions repaired to the Clarendon where Lord Holland had bespoken a supper. If Lady Cowper had noticed Tony Everely's presence in the threatre, she had too much tact to mention it, and the party enjoyed their lobster patties and champagne in an atmosphere of much jollity.

Whenever the Hollands gathered a group about them, the talk was bound to be of politics. Tonight they debated the injustice of the Corn Laws, Princess Caroline's shocking behavior, and the recent riots in Lancastershire, where the workers were attacking the factory looms. Francey contributed her bit to the dialogue, but she noticed that Oliver Fanshawe had little to say. She suspected the Hollands were far too liberal for his High Tory tastes, but he was either too polite to argue or too indifferent to the plight of the dispossessed weavers. She had often suspected that Oliver cared for little besides his own comfort. It did not endear him to her, for Francey

29

had very enlightened ideas which included reform of the franchise and alleviation of the plight of the poor. On the way back to her Bruton Place house she chided him for his lack of interest in these problems.

"My dear Francey, the Hollands with their prosing on about politics can become very wearisome," Oliver drawled as their coach made its way through the dimly lighted streets.

"I find them provocative. They stir me up to think about something besides the endless talk of clothes, parties and love affairs," Francey insisted, giving him a severe look.

Realizing that perhaps he had spoken too harshly, Oliver, as usual, tried to trim around, avoiding any controversy. "I'd rather talk to you, my dear, about love affairs," he suggested in a warm tone, moving close to Francey and putting his hand over hers.

Determined not to allow him any further license, still Francey allowed the hand to remain, peering out the window to see that they were within a few streets of approaching her house.

"I have a great deal of a particular nature to say to you, Francey," Oliver pressed her hand and looked at her with meaning. His usual pose of cynicism had been doffed for an effort at sincerity, and Francey thought it did not become him. She was inclined to giggle when meeting his eyes, but realized that would never do.

"Have you, Oliver? That sounds intriguing, but I am much too tired to listen to any confidences tonight. I am afraid you must postpone whatever you mean to say for a more appropriate time," she insisted as the coach rolled to a stop. It was her coach, and she intended to give the orders. Her footman hurried to let down the steps, and Francey turned to Oliver with a kindly, distant smile. "Thank you so much for escorting me this evening, Oliver. No doubt I shall see you soon. John will take you on to wherever you wish to go, White's perhaps. I know you gentlemen can stay up to all hours, but alas, we poor females must have our rest," she spoke with a certain forced gaiety. Really, she sounded like the veriest ninny, eager to escape the clutches of some ravening beast who had designs on her virtue. Oliver had only the most honorable of intentions, she was sure. But she did not want to hear a proposal of marriage this evening.

He escorted her to the door, his dignity not allowing him to press his attentions before the servants, but he bowed over her hand and promised silkily, "You may escape tonight, Francey, but there is always tomorrow. And you cannot put me off indefinitely, my dear. Matters have gone too far for that."

Francey bade him a cool goodnight and swept into her house. She did not like Oliver's threatening tone. She might find him acceptable as an escort but that did not allow him to assume proprietorial rights. Oliver Fanshawe would have to be discouraged, and smartly. She had no illusions that he cared deeply for her. She would not be breaking his heart. Francey had quickly learned that her wealth and position made her a target for fortune hunters and hangers-on of which Oliver Fanshawe was among the least objectionable. It was after an episode like the one just past that she especially missed the stolid, comforting and devoted presence of Archie Pembridge who had protected her from such unpleasantness. Well, she was more than capable of dealing with Oliver should he decide to propose.

As she trudged upstairs to her bedroom, she suddenly giggled. Perhaps she was wrong and he was preparing to offer her carte blanche. But, no, he was on the lookout for a rich wife, and had no doubts that whomever he selected would fall in easily with his wishes. Wasn't he in for a surprise?

Much later, after her faithful abigail, Martha, had tucked her into bed and opened the window as Francey insisted, although her maid clucked over the injurious properties of the night air, Francey lay sleepless. This was a rare condition, and she suspected that the brief meeting with Tony Everely was more the cause of her insomnia than Oliver Fanshawe's dramatic warning. The wind stirred the trees outside her window, and occasionally she heard the wheels of a late carriage rumble over the cobblestones. Despite her efforts, memories of her first season, when she had made her bow to society, and accepted Tony's proposal, drifted across her consciousness.

What a silly naïve girl she had been. And how besotted with Tony. Of course her reputation as an Incomparable had turned her head. She recalled the legions of young men who had tried to win her. But there had never been anyone for her but Tony, whom she had known and loved all her life. He had caught her young and she had never been able to shake off his mesmerizing influence. It had all seemed so perfect. Her parents were thrilled at Tony's interest and the Duke encouraged their affair.

It had been obvious from her first country assembly that Francey would take, for all the young men in the neighborhood beseiged her. No doubt she had been flattered and had come to expect adulation as her due. Of course, Archie Pembridge had always hung doggedly about, waiting for any crumbs of attention Francey might accord him, hoping beyond hope that his persistence would win the prize. But Tony had swept into London late in the season and within a few days all rivals were pushed aside. She had not even tried to play the aloof beauty, but had gone down beneath his charm without a struggle.

His proposal in that musty barn had lacked the address she had expected, Francey remembered, but had been persuasive for all that. And she had been such a little gullible fool. She should have questioned that Tony, well aware of his suitability, his need to marry, his father's approval, had decided to take the plunge into parson's trap. Despite the ardor of his lovemaking, which certainly spoke of experience, she should have had doubts, especially since once she had accepted his proposal he took her love for granted. She sighed with disgust at her naïveté, remembering what he had said later in the Mount Street house her parents had rented in London.

"Well, Francey, you seem to have all the beaux of London at your feet. Not at all good for your character, you know, this power over the poor fellows. I will put a stop to that, so do not think after we are married you can wind me around your finger and continue to flirt and dally. I will have a faithful wife, and must be certain of your love," he said in a stern way.

She hesitated, not knowing quite how to answer. Surely Tony must know that when he was around she didn't even see other men. She loved him more than she could admit. In her shyness and awe at her good fortune in attracting him, she could not imagine such behavior. Every bone in her body trembled when he was near and when he kissed her she was lost to all propriety. She should have known, Francey concluded after more experience, that Tony's heart was never really engaged.

He wanted a docile wife to satisfy his father's wish for an heir, but had no intention of altering his life in any way to accommodate the inconvenience of such an addition. But there had been no doubt that she was truly and deeply in love with this grand and glorious young man who embodied all her dreams. Her parents' pleasure and the envy of less fortunate girls only increased her own euphoria when the engagement was duly announced in the Gazette. Tony pressed for an early wedding and the ceremony was set for June, just two months away.

The short period of the betrothal had not proved easy for the couple. Tony dutifully escorted her to balls, routs and the theatre when he was in London, but he spent an increasing amount of time in the country, hunting and fishing, well able to bear these absences from his fiancée. That he was enjoying other pursuits, Francey never suspected until the night of the Granvilles' ball. Some of her spiteful and ungenerous fellow debutantes had been

33

eager to point out to her that Tony was not of a faithful disposition. He had the reputation of cutting quite a dash with the ladies. Then there was a long-time association with Lady Stacy-Long, a fetching brunette who enjoyed men's company and Tony's most of all, so the *on dits* went. At first, Francey discounted much of the gossip, but on the night of the Granville ball her doubts were reinforced and she had proof of Tony's faithless nature beyond argument.

She had not seen him for several days when he appeared that disastrous evening to escort her to the ball. His passionate kisses in the carriage had soothed all her niggling feelings of unease that had surfaced under Moira Stacy-Long's snide remarks. That was why what followed had been so shocking. After she had returned to the ballroom she could not see Tony anywhere, and when her partner—what had been his name, oh yes, a young Guardsman, Peter Ramsay—had suggested a stroll onto the terrace she had eagerly agreed.

Beyond the terrace they had come upon Tony and Moira clasped in what could only be called an enthusiastic embrace. Francey had given one agonized gasp and then prevailed upon Peter to take her away. Tony, cursing under his breath, had started after her, but she refused to wait, and he could hardly chase her across the dance floor. He should have followed her home and made his explanations immediately, but foolishly he waited until the next forenoon to make his appearance, thinking to give her temper time to cool. That was not his only mistake.

The scene which followed, Francey remembered now with disgust, was as dramatic and violent as any heroine could wish.

In a rage, and convinced that Tony had cared very little for her, according to the romantic notions she then held, Francey had lost her temper, all her doubts and uncertainties bursting forth in an uncontrollable surge of emotion. Tony stood quietly waiting for her to simmer down, prepared to let her have her say. Finally, she finished her tirade and to her mortification felt she had behaved in a hoydenish fashion which her mother would decry.

"If you will stop ripping me up, you little shrew, I will tell you exactly what happened. I had been able to assist Moira in some trifling matter and she was just expressing her gratitude. It was unfortunate that you wandered upon us and mistook events," he explained calmly.

"If you are implying that I followed you, you could not be more mistaken. But this incident with your Moira only substantiates all I have come to believe about you. You are a lecher, a libertine, a chaser after every available woman, and incapable of being faithful to any. You never cared for me. I just suited your need for a conformable wife. Our engagement is at an end," Francey concluded grandly, almost without knowing what she had said. What she wanted, of course, was for Tony to sweep her into his arms, plead with her to accept his excuses, make undying promises of fidelity and to behave like a knight from some gothic tale. Instead he lost his own temper, and called her a demanding, selfish, spoiled chit with no notion of how to go on, which would certainly alter when he had charge of her.

But Francey, furious and ashamed, and convinced he had never loved her, had the bit between her teeth and rushed toward disaster. "You will never have charge of me, Tony Everely. Please send the announcement that our engagement is at an end to the Gazette immediately. I never want to lay eyes on you again," she cried in a fury and swept from the room.

Chapter Three

If Lord Antony had any intention of renewing his relationship with Francey, he must have abandoned it after their cool meeting at the theatre. She was not put to the trouble of refusing to receive him, a decision which caused her little satisfaction. When you have made up your mind to ignore a man and he does not offer the opportunity for you to snub him, it is very lowering to the spirits. Francey attended all her usual haunts, as well as some exclusive dinners and even a ball in the week which followed their encounter, but Lord Antony was nowhere to be seen, a situation which irritated not only Francey but some of London's most notable hostesses.

By a determined effort Francey put the disturbing episode behind her and entered into the social round with every appearance of enjoyment. She was not so successful in ridding herself of Oliver Fanshawe. Having decided that Oliver was becoming too insistent in his attentions, Francey tried to put some distance between herself and that persistent gentleman, but he continued to pursue her. Finally, accepting that she must tell him that she had appreciated his company but believed they were becoming the object of undesirable gossip, she agreed to an interview.

He arrived soon after breakfast, an unfashionably early hour, but Francey saw no reason to postpone what she sensed would be an unpleasant scene. She had no idea how unpleasant it would become.

"My dear Francey, how kind of you to see me at this gothic hour," Oliver greeted her, bending over her hand with smooth, practiced skill.

Before she could offer any excuse for avoiding him, he continued, "I fear I have offended you in some way, since you have been avoiding me."

Unable to deny the truth of this, Francey wisely did not argue, but indicated that Oliver should be seated. Watching him cautiously as he positioned himself on a settee, she carefully moved to a chair opposite, folded her hands and waited for him to have his say. If she was apprehensive, she did not show it. For the first time she noticed a certain obsidian cast to his eyes, and the obstinate set of his lips. Here was a man accustomed to having his way, and if he could not get it, he might turn ugly.

"Ah, I am correct. You have taken me in dislike. Most unkind, dear Francey, and I cannot imagine what has induced this change of heart. We appeared to be getting along famously, and moving toward more than friendship."

"No, Oliver, we were not. Perhaps I have been unwise to have allowed matters to drift along without making my feelings plain. I have enjoyed your company, and you have made a most acceptable escort. But I greatly fear you have read more into our acquaintance than it warrants. If I mistake your reaction pray excuse me." Francey looked straight into his eyes, making as plain as possible that she did not want the conversation to go further. A gentleman of sensitivity would have understood, but Oliver Fanshawe, if he had such an understanding, refused to honor it.

"Francey, you must know, I have come to care for you deeply, and I want to marry you. You could not have mistaken my intentions, which I have made quite plain, not only to you, but to all of London."

"I have lately come to realize that you might be intending to offer for me. The fault is mine that I did not make my own feelings clear sooner. I do not want to marry you, Oliver. I am not in love with you, and I fear we should not suit." Francey spoke plainly, but feared Oliver would not easily accept her decision.

"Come now, my dear, we are not children who dream of romance and happy endings. Marriage is a matter of common interests, common goals. I assume you want to have children and to continue your success as one of London's most brilliant hostesses. You will find a husband a great deal of help and not too demanding for the life you want to lead."

Francey, swallowing her disgust at this cold-blooded proposal, had no illusions as to what Oliver expected from such a union—a wife whose fortune would be at his disposal, an opportunity to continue his extravagant lifestyle with no reason or inclination to adapt to any requirements the future Lady Fanshawe would have the temerity to suggest. Whatever kindly feelings Francey might have entertained for Oliver based on their past association fled in that moment.

"I hardly think your idea of married life offers me or any woman much chance of felicity, Oliver. In fact I find it quite insulting. And I wish you would leave now. You have made it quite evident that your regard for me is based mainly on my competence. Even if I cared deeply for you, which I don't, I would find your proposal soulless and demeaning."

Oliver flushed, then paled, fury for a moment overcoming his smooth address. Then, seeing that he had mismanaged the business, he played his strongest card. "Don't be too hasty, my dear. I am reluctant to threaten you, but I should tell you I have some rather revealing letters of yours which I doubt you would want publicized."

Francey, knowing that she had written no such letters, laughed in disbelief. "Are you trying to blackmail me,

Oliver, into marriage? I regret I must disoblige you. I have written no such letters, so you are wasting your time, and I must say, have done nothing to improve my opinion of you."

"I thought you might try that tack, and so I have brought one of the letters with me. They are quite explicit and revealing. I had no idea passion of that sort lurked beneath your cool facade, my dear." Certain now that he held the upper hand, Oliver removed a letter from his brocaded waistcoat and passed it across to her. "Do not destroy it. It will avail you nothing for there are several others, even more lurid."

Francey took the letter, holding it gingerly. Oliver had not understated the passionate outpouring, the admiration and despair of a young girl writing to her idol. Francey recognized both the handwriting and the sentiments. Her sister, Flora, at seventeen, just before her debut had imagined herself in love with Byron, one of a host of silly girls intrigued with the notorious poet, now living in exile in Europe. But his notorious past had not been forgotten, and the memory of it was stimulated by Caroline Lamb's publication of her *roman à cléf*, *Glenarvon*, and by the whispers about a child born illegitimately to a Miss Clairmont. If Flora's letters were published now, or even a hint of their existence suggested, her happy life with Roland Courtland and their two children would be forever tarnished. Francey doubted that Byron had ever been Flora's lover, but the letters could be easily misinterpreted. Francey must not let Oliver know that the letters, signed only with a scrawling *F*, were not hers but her sister's.

"I wonder how you came by these pathetic little outpourings. Really, Oliver, you are quite the cad, threatening me with such a weapon. I am tempted to echo the Duke of Wellington and say, 'Publish and be damned.' What would you do then, I wonder?" Francey was holding her temper in check, but Oliver recognized the scorn in her voice and wondered if he had just made the greatest mistake of his life.

"You cannot take that chance. Your reputation would be ruined, like Caroline Lamb's, and you would find no man to marry you, no drawing room in which you would be welcome, and no decent woman to speak to you," he said with some relish.

"It's true women have little recourse in these matters. But then they also have little recourse in marriage when all their property comes under the control of their husband and he squanders it away. I am faced with two equally disagreeable prospects, it seems. I must either wed a man I distrust and dislike or become a social pariah. An invidious choice. And certainly not one which I can decide in a moment. You will have to give me time to debate the matter." Francey spoke evenly, apparently unmoved by his threats or sneers. Then she stood up. "I think this interview is concluded."

"Just a moment, Francey. You are not dictating the terms here. I have accepted an invitation from the Howards and shall be out of town for a few weeks. That should give you enough time. But I am in little doubt as to your decision. Believe me I regret having to force you to this pass, but you shall wed me." Oliver spoke with more assurance than he felt, for Francey's reaction to the letter had not been at all what he had expected.

"I will leave you with that specimen just as a reminder," he jeered. "Your servant, ma'am." He bowed and left the room unhurriedly, yet aware of Francey's assessing eyes following him to the door. He felt he had both Francey and her fortune within his grasp, but some nagging suspicion that she might solve her dilemma dogged him as he made his way down Bruton Street.

He had disliked forcing her with the letters, but his debts were mounting. If he did not want to end up like Brummel pigging it in some hovel in Calais, Oliver must retrieve his fortunes. Once the engagement was announced his creditors would wait patiently for their money.

She must marry him and she would. No respectable woman would allow those letters to be circulated. He had been fortunate to secure them, as part of a gaming debt, settled by Byron before he went abroad. The poet had not wanted to let them go, and he had regretted confiding their contents to Fanshawe in a drunken state. Well, they had served their purpose. Before the month was out the unassailable Francey and her tidy income would be his.

Francey had no intention of wedding Oliver Fanshawe, not even to save her sister from scandal, but she was not quite sure how to proceed. There was little point in revealing Oliver's chicanery to poor Flora, who would only wail and moan, and beg Francey to save her. It was best that Flora and her Roland know nothing of this matter. Oliver had mentioned an invitation from the Howards. That would take him to Yorkshire for at least two weeks, and perhaps more. Entertainment at Castle Howard was lavish, and Oliver was enough of a snob not to wish to offend the family by a hasty leave-taking. She would have time to make a plan.

However if Oliver delayed his departure or decided not to go, she would have to leave London herself, so as to avoid any possibility of running into him. Only that morning she had received a pressing invitation from Ian and Ariel Montague to visit them at their Gloucestershire estate. Ian had only recently come into the title upon the death of his father, and the new Earl and Countess of Dursley were spending the best part of the spring in the country while he settled estate matters. A visit to Ian and Ariel would remove her from both Oliver Fanshawe's threats and the chance of encountering Tony Everely, both possibilities equally repugnant.

Francey found she was quite disgusted with men, their arrogance, insensitivity and belief that the world, and women, were ordered for their convenience. Tony Everely had thought her foolish and naïve to object to his

41

flirtations while he was engaged to her. Oliver Fanshawe had seen nothing objectable in marrying Francey for her money, which he needed to support his own hedonistic life. Only Archie had proved to have the qualities prized in a husband—devotion, fidelity and consideration—and yet poor Archie had been so dull.

Perhaps the fault lay with her, Francey concluded. The attractive men were selfish and unwilling to compromise within the bounds of domesticity, while the other men lacked excitement. What she needed was to spend some time with happily married couples who managed to combine romance, respect and rapture in their unions. The Montagues were just such a couple and Francey determined to leave forthwith for Gloucestershire.

Riding through the fresh countryside toward Dursley Hall, Francey was refreshed by the sight of hawthorn trees coming into bud and occasional clumps of daffodils and crocus blossoms. She was reminded of how long it had been since she had last visited the Pembridge estates in Dorset—or her parents, who lived nearby. They rarely came to London now, for her father suffered from gout and her mother would not travel without him. It had been too long since she had seen her brother and his wife and their son. And then there was Flora—but Francey pushed the thought of her sister to the back of her mind. When this visit with Ian and Ariel was finished she would journey down to Dorset.

The Pembridge estate was a tidy manor house with several hundred acres of land, and since it had not been entailed, it had come to her upon Archie's death eighteen months ago. They had been happy, she told herself, the only shadow on their marriage the lack of children. Francey had greatly desired a child, and Archie a son, but it was not to be. If she married again, of first consideration would be that the man she chose would have the right qualities to make a good father. Certainly few of the men who pursued her in London fitted that criterion.

Well, she need not think about it now. Feeling more cheerful as the miles lengthened behind her, Francey looked forward to her sojourn with the Montagues and their two engaging children. Young Ian must be four and Elizabeth turning two. How fortunate their parents were! But their marriage had begun under the most ominous circumstances and had struggled through a spy chase, danger, and Ian's wound at Waterloo. They were in safe harbor now, but it had been a tempestuous voyage. As the carriage turned into the long drive leading up to Dursley Hall, Francey anticipated the meeting with pleasure.

Her welcome was all that she could have wished. Both Ian and Ariel were on the steps to greet her, and Francey stepped down to receive a hearty hug from her host and an equally enthusiastic embrace from Ariel.

"Ariel, you look marvelous. Rusticating obviously agrees with you. I feel a veritable hag in contrast." Indeed, Lady Dursley was a striking woman, statuesque, with unusual green eyes, and heavy black hair pulled into a severe chignon which suited her classic features. Her husband, tall and tanned, with a soldierly bearing, had attracted many a feminine eye before he had married Ariel in Vienna, five years ago.

"Ah, Ian, still a heartbreaker. I can see that marriage has not tamed you," Francey teased as they all walked toward the drawing room.

"Don't you believe it, my dear. I am a true benedict, not allowed off the leash for a moment."

Ignoring her husband's effort to rouse her into some imprudent reply, Ariel shepherded her guest into a chair by the fire. "I will take you to your room in a moment as I know the journey must have been wearying. We will catch up on your news later. I cannot believe that we have at last lured you from the heady delights of London to relieve our tedium."

"I doubt the tedium. I am the one who has found the usual social round productive of ennui. A brisk series of country pleasures will restore me, as does seeing you both. It has been so long. Since before poor Archie died," Francey remembered sadly.

"You have been out of black gloves for months now, Francey, but I know you have not forgotten," Ariel eyed her friend with compassion. "Perhaps becoming one of London's most sought-after hostesses has distracted you a bit, but I know it is no substitute for a loving husband and home."

"As usual, you are correct, Ariel. But enough of my troubles. Will you be entertaining a house party during my visit?" she asked, hoping that there would not be a large company which would require her to exercise her social skills.

"We will have you to ourselves for a few days but on Friday the Glendennings and a few others are expected. You remember the irrepressible Alistair and Verity, I know. They have been on a visit to her mother in Devon, and are stopping here on their way home to Northumberland." Ariel hesitated for a moment before plunging into a delicate subject.

"We would have asked Oliver Fanshawe, but I gathered you needed a respite from his company."

"What my dear wife is too tactful to say is that I can't stand the fellow, one of those poodle-faking idle men about town, and a fortune hunter beside. I hope I have not offended you, Francey," Ian added a bit tardily.

Ariel shook her head in mild reproof, but Francey only laughed. "What I admire in you, Ian, is your forthrightness. I think I agree with you about Oliver, and I would not want his company on this visit."

"Capital!" Ian applauded, then turning to his wife mocked, "And how do you like being used as a bolt hole, madam, a convenient haven for Francey here, who can't bear to give the fellow his *congé*."

Francey, used to her host's acerbic turn of phrase,

wondered what he would think if she confided how she had spoken her mind to Oliver, and how he had responded by trying to blackmail her. Well, she might seek the Montagues' help and advice but not immediately. She had some plans of her own for dealing with the meretricious Sir Oliver.

They went on to talk of other matters, and Francey failed to realize that Ariel had not elaborated on her guest list beyond mentioning the Glendennings. A clever strategist, Lady Dursley had learned long ago not to display her hand too early. If she had mentioned one of her other guests, Francey would have been quite capable of ordering her coach and departing forthwith. Ariel had warned her husband, who scorned such ploys, not to give the game away.

After a few moments Ariel escorted Francey to her room, and saw to it that her guest had all that was necessary for her comfort. Leaving Francey to rest and superintend the unpacking, Ariel reminded her that they would be having an early and informal dinner. Francey insisted she be allowed a visit to the nursery to see the young Montagues before their bedtime and Ariel promised her that such a treat was in store.

Hurrying downstairs to catch her husband before he left on some estate business, Ariel was just in time, for he was standing in the hall slapping his crop impatiently against his knee while awaiting his horse.

"There you are, Ian. Off to Farmer Griffith's, I suppose. I just want to remind you not to mention Tony Everely's arrival to Francey. She's sensitive about him, and I suspect vulnerable too. I wonder if we were wise to invite him," Ariel said as a frown marred her brow.

"As I recall," her husband replied dryly, "we did not invite him. He invited himself when he learned Francey was coming." Ian did not like the secrecy of the business.

"According to his letter they met in London and quarreled. No doubt if he had not had to journey to Dorset on Parliamentary business he would have mended matters. Francey and Tony should have married years ago. They are both so strong-willed and stubborn. Instead Francey rushed off in a pique and married Archie. Now she might do the same with that wretched Fanshawe creature."

"Yes, it was convenient of Archie to put his spoon in the wall before Tony came home. Just in time for the true lovers to have a reconciliation and live happily ever after. Really, Ariel, it sounds like some silly novel, and I only hope you will not regret this meddling," Ian warned, but alleviated the severity of his remarks by placing a consoling kiss on her cheek before walking to the door where his horse awaited him. He turned to see her watching him warily and gave her that brilliant smile which had first charmed her and then won her heart.

"Don't fret, my dear. I will be as close as a clam, and aid and abet you in all your schemes." With a wave he was off upon his ride, leaving Ariel with a warm reassurance. Her marriage had turned out so happily— she wanted Francey to enjoy the same communion and passion she shared with Ian. Still, Ariel would not have interfered if Tony had not written and begged her to help. He must want to restore the old relationship. She only hoped Ian's warning about meddling was not apt. Tony was due to arrive late on Friday, just in time for the dinner she had planned. She must keep Francey occupied and unsuspicious until then. After that it would be up to Tony to win her over, if that was what he intended.

Chapter Four

Friday morning dawned bright and clear, more like May than late March. Francey arrived back from a long walk with the nursery party—young Ian and toddling Elizabeth—cheerful and a bit windblown, to find several carriages in the drive. Bidding an affectionate goodbye to her small friends and their nursemaid, Francey hurried around to the back entrance of the Hall, not wanting the arriving guests to see her in such disarray. It would be just as well to meet them at luncheon.

Dressed in a becoming cherry and cream redingote gown, she descended sometime later to find the drawing room full of people. Ariel hurried up to her, eager to introduce the newcomers. Francey knew two of the couples, but an elderly *grande dame* was a stranger to her. Ariel shepherded her friend up to the formidable lady.

"I do not believe that you have met my great aunt, Elsbeth Hecuba Clifford, Francey. Aunt Elsbeth, this is our great friend, Frances Pembridge," she made the introductions smoothly, but Francey sensed Ariel was discomforted by her relative's presence. And well she might be. Francey saw an imposing lady of some sixty years, a massive figure in black tafeta with pince-nez about her neck, which was festooned with depressing jet jewelry. Lady Clifford eyed her with black deep-set eyes which missed nothing. Her greying hair was bundled tidily into a severe style, and she generally gave an impression of overweening curiosity and disposition to take umbrage easily.

"I had no idea dear Ariel and Ian were having a house party or I should not have intruded. I wanted to break my journey to Bath where I am going to take the waters, as my health has been so indiffernt this winter. I understand you are a widow and from London," Lady Clifford sniffed.

The tone of the woman's remarks immediately made Francey feel both as if she were a scarlet woman and as if she were guilty of Archie's demise. Behind the lady's back Ariel had raised her eyes in an expression of deepest chagrin, and Francey could barely suppress a laugh. Poor Ariel, being burdened with such a relative and her unexpected descent on what Ariel had hoped would be a cheerful party.

"Delighted to meet you," Francey murmured mendaciously. "And, yes, I am both a widow and from London, which I trust will not completely damn me in your eyes." She would not be intimidated by this rather nasty old woman.

"London is a sink of vice, and not at all the place for attractive young women in mourning for their husbands. You're not wearing black, I see," Lady Clifford came back sharply.

"Come now, Aunt Elsbeth, that is not fair. Francey's husband has been dead for more than eighteen months. She misses him, of course, but life must go on," Ariel tried to smooth matters tactfully. Seeing that Francey was about to burst forth with a demur, Ariel continued hurriedly. "But I must finish the introductions. Will you excuse us, please." Taking Francey's arm, she dragged her friend from Lady Clifford's company.

"Isn't it dreadful? We had no idea she was coming. Of course if she had written we would have put her off, but what can we do? Ian thinks it's amusing, and he will tease her unmercifully until she departs in high dudgeon. But we have a more cheerful group to alleviate her ghastliness. You remember the Glendennings," she said as they approached an attractive couple drinking sherry by the windows.

"Of course. How nice to see you again, Verity, and Alistair, too," Francey welcomed these old friends with a sigh of relief. Alistair gave her a warm kiss and Verity a gentle hug.

"This is a treat, Francey. Really my first outing since Alan's birth and I must say it is lovely to put aside maternal affairs and indulge myself. Good for Alistair, too. We have been rusticating for the past year, and I am sure he has been bored to death. And he missed Ian. They are old friends, as you know. But come, Francey, tell me all the London gossip. It's been ages since I was there, and I want to hear all about the latest *on dits* and the fashions. You look so smart, I do feel antiquated." Verity sighed, not looking the least dowdy in her green cashmere traveling dress. She was a sparkling redhead with a pair of speaking hazel eyes, and it was easy to see how she had captured the volatile Alistair.

"Nonsense. Whatever you say about the constraints of country living, you seem to have thriven on it. How I envy you your baby! Archie and I regretted we had none. You are to be congratulated," Francey sighed, thinking of what she was missing.

"I know you miss Archie. He was such a dear," Verity pressed Francey's hand sympathetically, and was about to continue, when she looked up, her eyes on the door, and gave a gasp. Francey, her back to the entrance, saw her friend's face reflect her astonishment. She turned around and barely repressed a gasp herself. Standing with Ian, looking every inch the aloof Corinthian, was Tony Everely.

Ariel was too clever a strategist, and too accomplished a hostess, to ask Tony to escort Francey into dinner. That honor was reserved for Alistair, and Tony was paired with Verity. Since his arrival had barely preceded the announcement of dinner, there was no time for Tony to approach Francey. Appalled at his appearance Francey gave no sign of her consternation, but accepted Alistair's arm and chatted gaily, applying her skill in masking her reactions. She did not gull her escort for a moment. He looked at her mockingly as they strolled into the dining room.

"Quite a surprise, old Tony showing up here. Did you know he was coming?" Alistair asked. Famous for his forthright speech and penchant for blurting out what should best be kept quiet, he could not quite hide his amusement at this contretemps.

"Not at all. I knew Tony was home. I saw him at the theatre last week," Francey replied smoothly as Alistair seated her. Then she looked up at her partner with a devilish glint in her eye and reproved him. "I hope you were not in on this plot, Alistair. You have a reputation for bearding lions in their den."

"Whatever do you mean, Francey? How would I learn all these intrigues, isolated in the country as I have been?"

Unconvinced, Francey contented herself with raising a wry eyebrow at Alistair, and dipping into her mulligatawny soup, as she listened with every appearance of interest to Alistair's shocking tales of his stay in Devon with Francey's mother, a lady of clinging ways and enjoyment of ill health. Inside, however, she was stunned by Tony's arrival and she wondered what it meant. Surely Ariel must have realized that she did not want to meet that arrogant rogue again. Fortunately he was seated far down the table with Ariel's aunt on one side, and it served him right too if that formidable lady quizzed him about his doings. Francey was determined to carry off the encounter with aplomb, but she had difficulty stilling the frantic beating of her heart.

Oh, why did he have to disturb the even tenor of her life? She would not fall victim to his specious charms this time. She was no gullible girl now but a sophisticated woman with a great deal of experience in dealing with libertines and deceivers. He would not lead her down that path again. She laughed at herself. He probably cared nothing for her now, if he ever had, and she was a looby even to think his arrival here concerned her.

Pushing aside her doubts and confusion she discovered that she had quite a good appetite for the salmon and lamb which followed the soup. By the time the *crème à l'anglaise* was placed on the table she had managed to engage her other neighbor, the local vicar, Mr. Upton, in a sparkling dialogue about the problems of his parish. Adept at drawing out shy and insecure guests within moments of their greeting, she had completely charmed the vicar, a man of scholarly habits and little social grace.

"I applaud your efforts to establish a parish school, Mr. Upton, and I wish you all success with inculcating the rudiments of learning in your charges. I remember my own schooldays with much enjoyment, and your insistence on including girls in your teaching is admirable. So often young women go into service without any knowledge of sums or even unable to read the simplest primer. It is shocking."

"Thank you, Lady Pembridge, for your kind words. Many have criticized my efforts as radical," the vicar beamed, delighted with this *soignée* lady from London.

"Doing it too brown, Francey. Stop charming the poor vicar. He is absolutely *boulversé* by your charms. You are a minx," Alistair whispered in her ear. "Surely there are more suitable targets for your flirtations."

"Not you, Alistair. Verity would scratch my eyes out. How she endures you, I cannot fathom," Francey teased as she rose to accompany their hostess from the dining room.

"Now, Ian, no lingering over the port. Miss Ainsworth has promised to sing for us, and you won't want to postpone that treat," Ariel insisted as she shepherded her ladies from the room.

In the drawing room Francey decided she would not

take Ariel to task for adding Tony to the house party, and instead she would ignore the whole regrettable matter until she had decided how to deal with this disturbing development. Not for words would she admit she found Tony's presence upsetting. Settling herself by the charming Miss Ainsworth, she engaged her in light conversation, unwilling to surrender to the chaotic emotions Tony's unexpected arrival had caused.

Damn the man, she said to herself, as she complimented Miss Ainsworth on her gown, he wants to challenge me. His consequence will not allow any woman to deny him. Well, he had met his match in her. She would not allow him to lure her into a flirtation, raising hopes which he had no intention of fulfilling. She had gone that route before. No, cool indifference was the manner to adopt. If he tried any of his famous ploys with her, she would receive them with a smile of contempt, and ignore any efforts to charm her into slavish adoration again.

For all Francey's resolutions, she had to steel herself not to look up when the gentlemen joined them. But she was aware of Tony's entrance, even if she refused to meet his glance. He confounded her by not joining her, and she was left to reflect that she might be concerning herself for naught. Perhaps he no longer had any interest in her. Whatever she and Tony had shared was long gone, and she would be wise to remember it.

She smiled entrancingly at Hubert Lancing, a bluff squire and neighbor of her host, who settled beside her on the settee and asked her if she enjoyed riding. She bent all her attention on the middle-aged squire until Miss Ainsworth honored them with some lovely ballads from Tom Moore's *Irish Melodies*. She did notice that Tony was quick to offer his services in turning the pretty brunette's pages at the pianoforte. Naturally, he could not resist trying his amatory skills on such a likely victim. Watching Tony bending over the singer, thoroughly captivated, Francey reminded herself that his behavior was now no concern of hers.

Satisfied that she had made a wise decision, Francey managed to avoid him for the rest of the evening, but she was grateful when several of the guests signified that they would depart. Arrangements were made for further meetings and the party was deemed a success. Verity and Francey walked upstairs together, but her friend was too diplomatic to refer to Tony's unexpected arrival and they parted for the night with little discussion.

In her room, Francey answered her abigail's few questions with an abstracted air. Never had she been less inclined to talk. Despite her good intentions, she felt long-suppressed emotions, feelings she had believed forgotten, nagging at her. But at last she was ready for bed. Dismissing her maid she settled herself by the fire. She knew sleep would be a long time coming.

Her first instinct, to tell Ariel in the morning that she must return to London, she abandoned. She would not run away from this unexpected meeting. As her thoughts scurried this way and that, she did not hear the slight tap at her door. But finally she indicated that the visitor could come into the bedchamber. As she expected, it was Ariel.

Her hostess gave her a rueful look and rushed into speech. "I am sorry if Tony's appearance startled you, Francey. I know it was unfair not to warn you, but he particularly asked me not to when he begged for the invitation." Ariel looked unusually uncomfortable. A woman of equable temperament, she did not normally allow herself to be placed in situations that she could not control, but she was a bit apprehensive that her friend would be angry, or even threaten to depart in a huff. Francey had expected to have a restful visit, a respite from her hectic London life. The last thing she needed was a bitter exchange with Tony Everely.

"And why did he beg for an invitation? I am sure he is in great demand by hostesses. You are honored, Ariel," Francey said, a bit caustically.

"I think he wanted to see you in an intimate setting, away from all the false inanities of London salons. He must want to be reconciled, Francey, or he never would have been so insistent," Ariel pleaded, knowing that she had been forced into a difficult position. "If his joining our party causes you discomfort I shall throw him out tomorrow," she promised with a tentative grin. "But I really think he wants to be friends. I understand your last encounter was inconclusive."

"He cannot bear the idea that any woman is not enslaved by his powers of attraction. I was the one who got away, and a good thing too. He was not fit to put on Archie's boots," Francey replied fiercely.

"Perhaps he has changed—realized that he cannot go on his merry way philandering and breaking hearts," Ariel offered.

"He did not break my heart, only gave me a deep disgust. But I believe he wants to charm me into forgetting that, and then when he has me completely fascinated, he will walk away. Well, I will not play his game this time, Ariel, and you should not have become implicated in his nasty schemes."

"Oh, Francey. I do apologize. And you are quite right not to accept his expressions of contrition, if that is what he intends. I just thought you were so well suited."

Realizing that she was making too much of the affair, and not wanting Ariel to think it mattered one way or the other, Francey laughed a bit hollowly. Picking up her brush she gave her hair a few hard strokes and with her back to Ariel tossed off a disclaimer. "Obviously we were not suited, and never will be. But I do not want to refine on the matter. I will behave with chilling propriety and not cause any upset. I can see you could not resist Tony's blandishments. Few women can."

"He may have changed," Ariel persisted weakly.

"I doubt it. But let us not discuss it anymore. I am fagged to death, and a good night's sleep will put the business in proper perspective. Don't worry, Ariel. I will create no tempestuous scenes."

Not completely reassured, Ariel decided against championing Tony any further and bade her friend an affectionate goodnight. Francey continued absentmindedly to brush her hair, irritated that her anticipated respite in the country should be troubled by this unexpected contretemps. Well, she would not allow Tony to disturb her visit. Resolutely she climbed into bed, and doused her candle, banishing all thoughts of Tony Everely, Oliver Fanshawe and the problems both these gentlemen offered. To her surprise she dropped off to sleep immediately, exhausted by the experiences of the day.

Saturday morning dawned clear and brisk, good weather for Ariel's plan for her guests to make an expedition to the ruins of an old priory and a Roman fort. Arranging the disposition of journey required some tact. She and Ian would preforce have to take Aunt Elsbeth with them. Francey had signified she would travel with the Glendennings, and several of the gentlemen had agreed to ride. In all, the party, with the addition of some neighbors, numbered a round dozen. They started off smartly after a leisurely breakfast at which Francey had appeared in sparkling spirits, treating Tony with reserve and fending off his efforts to engage her in conversation. He received these rebuffs with uncharacteristic meekness.

The weather continued to cooperate and the company had a healthy trek through the ruins, some of the ladies sketching the rather uninspiring views from Uley Tumulus, a long barrow 180 feet long. A lavish luncheon was unpacked in the grounds of a former Dominican priory and Ariel congratulated herself upon the way all seemed to be progressing happily. But soon after luncheon the sky turned threatening and Ian suggested that they ought to return home. Tony Everely, who had been balked in his intention to wrest Francey from her companions for an intimate chat, decided that more drastic measures were called for. Enlisting Verity's aid, he persuaded her to allow him to take Francey up in his curricle where he would have an uninterrupted opportunity to plead his case.

"I don't know, Tony. Francey was most insistent on riding with us. I don't think she wants to be alone with you and I must honor her wishes," Verity protested, her romantic heart touched by Tony's sincere efforts to mend matters with his former fiancée.

But Tony was more than equal to Verity's doubts. "It is ridiculous for us to be at odds, Verity. We shall be meeting constantly in London and the gossips would delight in thinking we are still harking back to that broken engagement. I just want to put matters on a friendly footing. Francey had every reason to be annoyed with me. I behaved badly but she leaped to the wrong conclusions. I should have allowed her to cool down a bit, but we had a devil of a row and I stormed off in a fury. I have a terrible temper," he explained disarmingly.

He did not quite know why he was so determined to make his peace with Francey. She certainly had dealt a blow to his self-esteem by rejecting him so harshly and then rushing off to marry Archie Pembridge. He would have denied that he wanted to bring her around to her former satisfying state of abject love, but he did not like this coolness between them. Certainly marriage was not on his mind, but his father's challenge had irked him. Naturally he did not reveal his rather disreputable motives to Verity who would have rung a peal over him, but he used his considerable charm to enlist her aid.

The company prepared to depart, rather hurriedly, eyeing the deepening clouds. Francey had wandered off to explore the inside of the Abbey and she was not aware of the leave-taking. She stood examining an ancient tablet commemorating Alfred the Great, England's savior, who had been born not too many miles away, when she felt a strange tingling, a sudden awareness that recalled past sensations. She turned, not surprised to find Tony viewing her with a satisfied grin. She had always felt that *frisson* when Tony entered a room. It left her feeling vulnerable, not an emotion she wanted to entertain for a moment, remembering whither it had once led her.

"It's coming on to rain, I fear, Francey, and most of the party have left while you were dreaming over tombs and tablets. I volunteered to escort you back to Dunsley Hall," he offered, knowing his mocking words would annoy her, but unable to help himself. There was something in Francey's assessing gaze which raised his temper. She looked at him rather as if he were a doubtful bargain she had decided not to accept.

"Have the Glendennings left already? How mean of them to forget me! I thought you had brought Miss Ainsworth. Base of you to desert her," she said in a tone of reproof, and looking very unwelcoming.

"A charming girl, but a bit tiring. After all, I accorded her some hours of my time this morning. Now I must share my sparkling wit, spread it around, so to speak, and you are the fortunate recipient," Tony teased, wondering why he was behaving so inanely, but there was a cast to Francey's expression that boded ill for any flirtatious wiles.

"Thank you," Francey answered wryly. "Had we not better make a start? I don't fancy a drenching." She started up the nave, uncaring whether he followed, determined to behave with cool friendliness. Inside she was throbbing with anger. She suspected that Tony had arranged this embarrassing tête à tête for some peculiar reason which she feared could only rebound on her head. She had once known him so well and she doubted he had changed. Whatever it was that he wanted of her it would give her great pleasure to deny him.

"Just a minute, Francey," he stopped her with a gentle hand on her arm and turned her to face him. "You know we cannot go on in this stupid fashion. I don't want to ride back to Dunsley Hall for the next hour with your vinegary face and resolute back lowering the atmosphere. You look as theatening as the weather."

Despite herself Francey felt a reluctant smile overcoming her best intentions. "You are quite right. I had hoped to avoid you as much as possible on this visit for I can see no reason for us to attempt friendship. However, it would require a great deal of discipline to remain silent and disapproving all the way back to the Hall. I will endeavor to put aside my contempt, dislike, and general feeling that your absence is to be preferred always to your presence, and behave in a ladylike and acceptable fashion," she promised, delivering these outrageous words with disarming sweetness.

"You are a shrew, Francey, but if we must brangle let us do it here. I will be at a great disadvantage trying to manage my horses together with a railing female once we are on the road."

"A railing female! What a quaint term! If telling you that I have forgotten your caddish behaviour of six years ago is railing, then so be it. I know it is a wound to your vanity, Tony, but you cannot always emerge the victor in these inconsequential affairs of the heart." Francey knew she was losing control of the situation, and on the verge of giving in to all her past resentment and humiliation when she had determined to adopt an air of serene indifference. Why could she not react to Tony with the cool composure she adopted toward other men?

"I would not call an engagement an inconsequential affair of the heart, my dear," Tony flushed. Her hit had gone home.

"I am not your dear," Francey responded, irritated by his effort to put her in the wrong.

"You were once. And let me warn you, Francey, that you will not be any man's again if you behave in such a sharp-tongued fashion," Tony said, reproving her with a lazy grin. "Actually I wanted to explain, if you can manage to listen at last, how you misunderstood that situation with Moira Stacy-Long at the Devonshires' ball."

"Does it really matter after all this time?" Francey tossed off the disclaimer as if it were of no account.

"I think so. You misread the situation. I dislike tattling on a lady, but I am afraid this time I will have to sacrifice honor to prudence. Moira had lost a great deal of money in a bad speculation and she was in deep trouble. She had pawned the family diamonds to a nasty money lender in Hatton Gardens and her husband was beginning to suspect her lame excuses. I was able to retrieve them for her and she was merely showing her gratitude, a bit effusively I will admit."

"Yes, quite enthusiastically as I remember." Francey leaned against a convenient arch, eyeing Tony sceptically. Why was he making so much of that long ago contretemps? "You do not deny, I suppose, that your relations with the lady were far from platonic."

"No, of course not. But that was before we became engaged and that had nothing to do with you. I was a very pattern card of fidelity after the banns were called," Tony insisted impatiently. "You were in such a passion you would not listen and I was to blame for not persisting in trying to put the affair right."

Francey wondered why, after all these years, he was trying now. She admitted to herself that she had behaved poorly, but not for the world would she let on to Tony that at one time she would have welcomed this overdue explanation. Now she looked at his excuse more cynically. He had some devious reason for trying to mend their relationship and she did not trust him. One of the reasons she had been so upset at the time was that she had doubted Tony's love for her, but she had been so besotted with *amour* that she had lept into his arms, overcome by his proposal. She would not be so credulous now.

Tossing her head, she adopted a casual air. "Well, it is of no account now. Probably if it had not been Moira

Stacy-Long, some other lovely would have provided an equally good excuse. I think you were happy to be relieved of our engagement, and certainly Archie was a far better husband for me—kinder, more devoted and faithful. Fidelity would have proved tiresome for you, and I would have demanded it. Then there would have been scenes and you would have disliked the whole business." Her tone was brisk and matter-of-fact, revealing none of the wistful hope she had once entertained of sharing loving companionship with this maddeningly attractive man.

"Quite right. I am sure Archie made an impeccable husband, although you undoubtedly kept a firm hand on the marital reins. But I agree that all of this is long past. I only wanted to clear the air in the expectation that we could progress to a different footing now. It really is too boring to be arguing and exchanging recriminations every time we meet. I hate giving the *ton* reason to gossip, and I am sure you do too, for from all I hear, you are a top-of-the-trees hostess whose invitations are sought after by the most august personages." From Tony's manner of expression Francey realized that he did not think much of her current status. Then, before she could take evasive action, he raised her chin with a gentle hand and looked candidly into her eyes.

"Please, Francey, let us make our *pax*. I promise to behave with every degree of circumspection in the future." Then as if afraid he had let down his guard, he returned to that lazy mocking humor which she found so annoying. "Well, perhaps not *every* degree of circumspection. You were always an engaging poppet, but now you are much more, a fascinating and provocative woman. Obviously some man completed the education I had barely initiated, and I doubt it was poor old Archie."

Refusing to let him see how wounding she found his careless words, Francey shrugged. "That is none of your business. However, I accept your olive branch, albeit grudgingly. Once I trusted you too much, Tony. I shall not make that mistake again." Unwilling to have him see that the conversation had upset her in any way, she settled her bonnet firmly on her head, retying the ribbons quickly. "Now, do you think we can travel back to Dursley Hall before the weather puts us at risk. We shall be quite a pace behind the others as it is," she protested, walking briskly up the aisle. She had endured quite enough of this painful delving into the past and she wanted no more of it.

Tony shrugged his shoulders in a gesture of defeat, realizing that she had not accepted his story. If he had found her appealing enough six years ago to consider matrimony, how much more intriguing she was today. Was it ignoble of him to pursue her from rather dubious motives? Was it just his father's assertion that she would have nothing to do with him which forced him to put his chances to the test? He had been uncommonly attracted to her long ago. Was that attraction reviving, intensifying now because she seemed impervious to his lures?

Was he responsible for her wary outlook, her cynicism? If so he regretted it, for that young Francey—eager, admiring, unquestioning—had been very loveable. Now she thought him unreliable, a libertine, a rubbishy fellow not worth her time. He would be wise to avoid her, relegate that old fiasco to the past where it belonged. There was certainly a host of more amenable lovely ladies about. But Francey intrigued him. She should not be allowed to shrug him off so easily.

He followed her up the aisle, hurrying to overtake her and open the heavy door that led out of the Abbey. Ahead lay a two-hour ride and he would make the most of the opportunity to breach her defences.

Chapter Five

Francey had been quite correct in her warning about the weather. The afternoon now lengthening into dusk had turned ominous. Dark clouds scudded across the sky, hiding the sun which earlier had shone with such brilliance. As Tony assisted her into the curricle she wondered if they would make it back safely to the Hall. How foolish to have delayed so long in the Abbey, missing her ride with the Glendennings, although she suspected Tony had arranged it so that they would leave without her. She made no attempt at conversation as they set off down the road at a spanking pace behind Tony's matched greys. Stealing a glance at her averted face, Tony decided he would be wise to concentrate on his horses. The lady was not in a receptive mood.

After a half an hour of wordless travelling, a few drops of rain began to fall, increasing Francey's somberness and not adding to Tony's joy. Neither of them relished arriving at the Hall sodden and miserable both from the elements and from their strained relationship. Francey also realized, even if Tony did not, that the less charitable members of the household would look at their tardy arrival with suspicion. Somehow, whenever she became involved with Tony her normally serene life turned chaotic. This promised respite at the Montagues' had turned out to be a disaster.

Now the rain was coming down much more steadily, and she thought she heard Tony curse under his breath. He disliked exceedingly a situation which he could not control, provoking a small secret smile from Francey which did not go unnoticed.

"I am glad you find this weather so amusing, Francey. But when you are sniffling and sneezing because of your exposure to the elements, don't blame me."

"You may be master of your fate, my lord, but you are not master of the weather. Don't be so childish. Of course I don't blame you for the rain. It looked a cloudless perfect day when we started and even after the picnic it was delightful. We should not have stayed so long in the Abbey, prolonging a meaningless conversation. Instead we should have left when the others did," she reproved him, pleased that he was discomfited. They now entered a gloomy patch of road, overhung with dense trees, dripping with water, which did little to improve their mood.

Suddenly the curricle lurched and the lead horse stumbled. Tony cursed in earnest then, pulling strongly on the reins to keep the horses under control and bringing them to a stop.

"Damn it. I believe a wheel has come loose. Here, Francey, hold these while I see," he ordered brusquely, tossing her the reins and jumping down onto the road. Certainly the curricle had veered dangerously to one side. Only with difficulty did Francey hold the horses, which responded nervously to this unexpected accident. Tony soothed them easily, running a hand over their flanks. Then he strode around to the back of the curricle, now listing badly to the left.

"Yes, as I thought, the wheel has come off, split at its seams. I wonder how that could have happened. Someone will answer for this," he growled, thoroughly put out by this disastrous turn of events. Here they were some twenty miles from Dursley Hall, in the driving rain, with no sign of habitation. His attempt to put matters right with Francey had led to catastrophe.

But for some reason Tony's ill-humor and frustration cheered Francey. She looked down at him and said quite matter-of-factly, "Well, we shall have to try to find some shelter. We cannot let these poor horses shiver here in the rain. And I could do with some warmth and even a cup of tea. There must be a farmhouse or some dwelling nearby."

Tony looked up at her with a grateful grin. "You are a Trojan, Francey, not to wail and have hysterics as most women would."

"Well, what cannot be helped must be endured. What do you suggest?"

"Perhaps we can abandon the curricle, ride the horses, and search for some good Samaritan who will take us in. You used to be able to ride quite well. Are you up to scampering onto the grey's back, riding without a saddle, or are you too much of a fine lady now to attempt such a feat?" he challenged, knowing she would rise to his dare.

"Of course not. Don't be such a nodcock. Riding bareback is greatly perferable to wilting here, even though I am not dressed for the occasion." She tossed Tony the reins and jumped down from the curricle unaided.

"Champion. Let us get moving," Tony ordered and steadying one of the greys, helped Francey up on his back. Perforce she had to ride astride, hitching up her bedraggled skirts, and grasping the reins which Tony shortened for easier handling. Within moments he had mounted the matching grey and they trotted off down the road, if not in good spirits then at least resolved on their course of action.

At Dursley Hall the company had assembled, happy to be indoors before a warming fire in the drawing room. Ariel, gathering her guests together for tea, scones and seed cake, suddenly realized that two of the group were missing. Tony and Francey had not appeared. In all the confusion of the hurried return from the picnic she had not sorted out the traveling arrangements, although she had concluded that Francey had ridden with the Glendennings. As Verity approached her hostess, ensconced behind her silver tea service, Ariel mentioned the missing Francey.

"Is Francey ill? She has not come down for tea?" Ariel asked her friend, conscious of her duty to hospitality.

"I have no idea. She was to ride back with Tony. Is he about somewhere?" Verity had been having a few doubts about the wisdom of allowing her friend to be commandeered by Tony, but she had been no proof against his persuasive arguments.

"Oh, dear. I have a lowering feeling about this. Could they have had an accident? The rain is coming down quite hard now. Perhaps they had to take shelter somewhere," Ariel beckoned to her husband in need of some reassurance. He strolled over to her side, noticing at once that her usual calm demeanor was disturbed.

"You want me, my dear?" he asked.

"Ian, where is Tony? He and Francey were to drive back together and I don't see either of them. Could you ask Perkins if they have returned. Don't make a fuss. If they are marooned somewhere because of the rain and Aunt Elsbeth finds out about it, she will create a fuss. You know what a tartar she is about observing the proprieties."

"I saw Francey going into the Abbey before we left, but I did not notice whether Tony followed her. Oh dear, I do hope they have come to no harm," Verity offered, concern darkening her charming face. Ian left on his errand and the two friends continued to murmur softly to one another. Fortunately Lady Clifford was engaged in conversation with the vicar, who had dropped in for tea, and who now looked harrassed under her catechism.

Verity looked in Lady Clifford's direction and sighed. Her mind followed Ariel's train of thought. If Tony and

Francey did not appear, the formidable Aunt Elsbeth would begin asking questions and casting aspersions. Any hint of scandal would delight her. Both women looked up anxiously as Ian reappeared.

"Neither Tony nor Francey have returned. Francey's maid has been creating in the kitchen, an hysterical type who fears her mistress has come to some dire end," Ian reported ruefully. "I suppose we ought to mount a search in case there has been an accident." A man who always preferred action to indecision, Ian went across the room to enlist Alistair's aid. Within moments the two left the room, no doubt to organize a search party. Unfortunately Aunt Elsbeth now sensed some kind of drama in the air and confronted her niece with probing questions.

"I understand that Lord Everely and Lady Pembridge have not returned from the picnic. Surely Lady Pembridge realizes how unseemly it is to be absent, and with a man of that sort, for all this time. I thought she was riding in your carriage, Lady Glendenning," she accused Verity.

"Francey and Lord Everely are old friends. They were to ride back together. We are only concerned that they may have suffered some mishap," Ariel explained, hoping to quiet her aunt's suspicions.

Verity, who longed to ask Lady Clifford what she meant by referring to Tony as "a man of that sort," wisely held her tongue, realizing she would only add fuel to that harridan's nasty conjectures.

"Ian and some of the men are mounting a search party. I believe we must await their findings. I only hope no misfortune has befallen Francey and Tony in this storm. They have probably stopped at some farmhouse to take shelter from the rain. Tony was driving his curricle and they would have suffered a bad wetting if they had tried to continue their journey. As it was we all just reached home before the storm broke, and they were some time behind us," Ariel explained struggling to hold on to her composure. She knew only too well where her aunt's probing was leading.

"Humph," snorted Lady Clifford. "And why should they have been delayed? I think your friend is no better than she should be, dallying with that libertine. I know all about these Londoners, fast women and immoral men. You should choose your friends more carefully, Ariel. It doesn't do to relax standards." Lady Clifford's nose was twitching with pleasure. There might be the makings of a scandal here and she intended to see that the miscreants received what they deserved.

But Ariel was not prepared to allow her aunt any more license.

"You are quite wrong, Aunt Elsbeth, in assuming a situation for which there is no proof. You must not malign my friends if you expect to be welcome in this house. Ian will not stand for such allegations," she said sharply, daring her malevolent relative to continue her prying.

Lady Clifford, sensing that she had perhaps been too precipitate, retreated somewhat. "I meant no harm, Ariel, my dear, and regret that you should feel forced to use such language toward me. However, we shall say no more about it and I shall keep my thoughts to myself," she sniffed and sailed out of the room.

"Miserable woman! I will not have her here again. Even if she arrives uninvited, she will be shown the door. I never heard such puerile nonsense. It's so worrying. You know Francey hoped to have a quiet visit, and enjoy her respite from the hectic social round in London. Now Tony has embroiled her in what could become a very awkward situation. I should never have let him come here." Ariel was truly disturbed, visions of all kinds of disaster clouding her mind, including her own responsibility for any fiasco.

"Don't be goosish, Ariel," Verity said. "I am sure your explanation is the proper one. They have sought shelter in some farmhouse. Ian and Alistair will find them if an accident has befallen them, which I doubt. And I bear some blame for allowing Tony to escort Francey back here. Really, it is too bad of him to lead Francey into a scrape."

The friends commiserated with each other but eventually left the drawing room to wait for news and dress for dinner, which had been delayed. The gentlemen had ridden off in the driving rain to see what they could discover but they returned within a few hours to report no sign of the missing pair. They had discovered the wrecked curricle on the road and stopped at several farmhouses without locating Tony and Francey. Where could they be?

The couple had not been able to reach a farmhouse because Francey's horse had cast a shoe. Instead they stumbled upon an abandoned keeper's hut, with a ramshackle shed where the horses could be protected from the rain, now coming down with fierce intensity.

Francey, wringing out her dress and unfastening her shoes, which were a sodden mess, looked about the hut with a slight grimace. Not the most salubrious of sanctuaries, but welcome for all that. She looked up as Tony joined her after seeing to the horses. Although equally drenched by the downpour, somehow he managed to look unruffled and thoroughly in command of the situation. Annoying man. Probably only too used to being marooned in the midst of a storm with a willing lady. How unfortunate that his companion this time was such a reluctant one. She chuckled a bit at the thought.

"I am happy that you find our plight so amusing, Francey. You don't seem to realize that we might have to lay up here for hours, waiting for the storm to abate, and then I will have to lead that grey back to the Hall. He can't be ridden without his shoe. Damned nuisance."

"Rather more than a nuisance," Francey said scornfully. Obviously Tony was more concerned for his horse's welfare than for hers.

"Well, I can't see what else we can do but stay here until the rain stops. I wonder if they will miss us at the

68

Hall," he cast a wary look in Francey's direction. She had not yet taken in the awkwardness of their position.

"I am not blaming you, Tony, for this disaster. And, yes, I know just what you are thinking. Our absence will certainly be remarked upon, and we can only hope that those remarks will be charitable. I suspect Ariel's Aunt Elsbeth will believe the worst and enjoy doing so. What a tartar that woman is!"

"Not a pleasant type. But you do realize how damaging this enforced intimacy could be to your reputation?" Tony asked, a wicked twinkle in his eye. "I have you quite at my mercy."

"I suppose you have, but I am not without certain resources, so don't become too confident. I wish there were some way we could light a fire. I am sure I will catch pneumonia in these damp clothes," Francey returned prosaically, determined not to allow his teasing to affect her.

"You really should remove them," he continued, hoping to cause a blush or at least a furious reaction.

Francey gave him a speaking look and then replied calmly, "Yes, I know, but I think in the circumstances I will have to take the safer option, a risk of pneumonia."

"Francey, you wound me. I gather you don't trust me and believe I would take advantage of you." He grinned, wondering what she would reply to such an outrageous threat.

"This is hardly the setting for a passionate seduction scene. We should both find it vastly uncomfortable to carry on in any fashion amid these wretched surroundings." Francey turned her back on him and began to take the pins out of her hair, not seeing any anomaly in this intimate task after her practical words.

"Oh, Francey. There is no one like you. What other woman would treat me to such a scathing putdown. Very off-putting, but let me assure you I might yet triumph over the tawdry accommodations." Tony did not quite know why he was teasing Francey so, for in reality he felt both helpless and irritated. She might pretend that the gossip provoked by their enforced isolation in this hut would be of no account, but he knew society. A story about this regrettable episode could ruin her reputation for in these matters the woman was always blamed, and the gentleman, if he failed to make the *amende honorable*, rarely suffered equally.

Francey had no doubt about the aspersions which would be cast, but she would not admit to Tony that the possibility of scandal worried her.

"I suppose we can sit on these chairs. They look a bit fragile, but then I am feeling fragile too. We shall suit each other," she said sitting down gingerly. "Ignoring your previous suggestions, have you any idea how we shall pass the time?"

"I suppose chatting about our future does not appeal to you," Tony offered.

"We do not have a future," Francey occupied herself in tidying her hair with a comb she had taken from her reticule.

"Oh, I wouldn't say that, Francey. Now that I am going into Parliament, I shall become an ornament in the fashionable salons, of which yours, I understand, is one of the most eminent. Surely you will not bar the door to me?" he asked wryly.

"You are going to be an MP?" Francey abandoned her comb and looked at him in surprise.

"Is that so remarkable? I have a political agenda, and the only way to accomplish my aim is to enter the government."

"From a safe borough, no doubt."

"Yes, I have been down in Dorset paying my political dues. Aren't you interested in my efforts?" he asked sardonically.

"I'm not sure. Somehow I don't see you as a champion of the people."

"You wrong me, Francey. Actually I hope to influence legislation, and get the Poor Law annulled, as well as the

70

Corn Laws. Our lads who served so bravely are having a difficult time of it. Even in London you must have noticed the rebellion and the unhappiness, not to mention the deplorable condition of the returned veterans." Tony spoke with conviction, not showing his annoyance at Francey's suspicion of his motives.

"Of course, I have noticed. I work in a refuge for abandoned wives and children. But somehow I thought you would continue in the Foreign Office, a pillar of the diplomatic corps." She spoke with some cynicism.

"You really don't like me at all, do you, Francey?" Tony regarded her bitterly. "You have not forgiven me for my supposed transgression."

"It's of no account. My feelings are not the issue."

"I think they are. If we can't agree about my odious character at least we can observe a decent politeness in public."

"Yes, you are quite right. It's stupid to brangle about what happened six years ago. I fear we would never agree about that."

"I may yet redeem myself in your eyes," Tony suggested.

"Is that important to you? I would have thought you had more pressing concerns," Francey said a bit cynically. Tony's sincere professions about his political intentions impressed her despite her distrust of him, but she was even more amazed to find her own opinion of him mattered so much.

He did not pursue the argument, but rose and walked restlessly around the room, irritated by her response. Her good opinion of him was becoming a nagging obsession.

After a rather long silence Francey suggested they assess their position. "Has the storm abated at all? I really think we should consider how we can return to the Hall."

Tony appeared to be deep in thought. He resumed his pacing and then approached her. "You know, Francey, on one score we were always in agreement. Perhaps if I cannot persuade you to look kindly on my new career, I can remind you of our affinity another way."

Then to her astonishment, he took her in his arms and proceeded to kiss her with a gentle force. Almost without her volition she found herself responding. Tony's caresses had always stirred her to passion and she had not forgotten those embraces. Her arms crept up around his neck and she melted instinctively, surrendering with delicious abandonment. The past receded and there was nothing but this moment in the dim dirty hut. Once again she was the eager romantic girl caught up in emotions she had thought gone forever. Tony's kiss deepened and there was no sound but the tender murmurings of two lovers lost to all but the present rapture.

Chapter Six

"The storm has passed, Ariel, and I think it's safe to start another search for Tony and Francey. I am a bit worried, however, for I thought they would have either sent a message if they had found a refuge or returned by now. Alistair and I and some of the men will ride out again," Ian told his wife as they tried to entertain their guests in the drawing room. Dinner had long since ended and the absence of the missing pair was becoming a subject of overriding concern. Ariel had tried to pass off the questions and suggestions with nonchalance, but she found that the situation was taxing her best efforts, particularly with Lady Clifford's sly comments. Ariel wanted to save Francey's reputation but now she cared more for her safety.

"Yes, you must find them. They could be lying injured somewhere in the storm. I am convinced that Tony would somehow have contrived to escort Francey back here if he possibly could." She was genuinely worried.

But before Ian could marshall his forces, the door opened and the truants appeared, looking very much the worse for wear. Francey's hair had escaped its confines again and was tumbling in careless disarray around her shoulders, and her skirts were muddied and torn. Tony looked damp but still in command of the situation. They were the cynosure of all eyes.

Rushing across the room to her friend, Ariel exclaimed with relief. "Oh, Francey, are you all right? We have been so concerned." She ignored the exclamations of her other guests.

"We are sorry to have caused you concern, Ariel. But we had an accident with the curricle, and then one of the horses cast a shoe. We had to wait the passing of the storm in a rather ramshackle keeper's hut, then lead the horse back here. It was quite a fraught experience." Francey tossed off her explanations carelessly, as if the whole affair had been the merest mischance. If she was aware of Lady Clifford's raised eyebrows and the other guests' knowing looks, she did not appear concerned.

"We are dashed hungry, having missed dinner. And Francey needs a hot bath if she is not to suffer from pneumonia." Tony's insouciant attitude had a certain possessive quality which reinforced Lady Clifford's suspicions. That redoubtable dowager hurried up, intent on probing every facet of the couple's mysterious absence.

"You have been gone some hours. We were quite worried that you might have suffered some grievous harm, but on the contrary you appear to have enjoyed yourself," Lady Clifford's dark eyes took in every aspect of Francey's dishevelment with satisfaction. Here were the makings of a glorious scandal. The woman looked a veritable wanton with her hair falling about her and her dress disturbed.

"On the contrary, Lady Clifford. It was most uncomfortable. And if you will excuse me I will remove myself and try to repair the damages. I am dripping all over your nice carpet, Ariel. I do apologize." Francey ignored the dowager's piercing stare and turned to Ariel. "I knew you would be worried, otherwise I would have gone directly to my bedroom. Please make my regrets to your guests, Ariel." Francey realized she had made a mistake in rushing into the drawing room to satisfy Ariel's fears. But if she had tried to sneak upstairs without an explanation, that might have worsened matters further. She suspected that Lady Clifford would make the most of this regrettable incident, but she was too tired and upset to care.

"Of course, Francey, and I will order a bath and some food. Come along. You must be fagged to death." Ariel took charge, casting a meaningful glance at her husband, whom she left to repair the damage of this untoward occurrence as best he might.

Ignoring Tony, Ariel and Francey departed, leaving behind a company torn between the necessity of observing the proprieties and the desire to speculate on Francey's fate. Ariel decided her own reservations about the incident could wait. For now her duty as a hostess was to see to Francey's well-being. But she rued the day she had been persuaded to allow Tony Everely to join this house party. What would be the outcome of this contretemps she could not imagine, although she had little doubt that Francey's reputation would be torn to shreds by the implacable and inquisitive Aunt Elsbeth.

"Well, Lord Everely, you have thoroughly compromised Mrs. Pembridge. I expect you know that," Lady Clifford rushed to attack Tony once Francey and Ariel had left.

"I would like to think so, Lady Clifford," Tony replied outrageously, completely routing that prying old woman, who had little recourse but to sniff and mutter her shock and disgust.

Ian, sensing a dramatic scene, hurried to the rescue. "Come on, Tony. What you need is a tot of brandy and some food. You will excuse us, I know, Aunt Elsbeth." And in a cowardly fashion he pushed his discreditable guest toward the door. In the hall he turned to Tony in dismay.

"That's torn it, Tony. The old harridan will make a meal of this unfortunate occurrence. You and Francey have been closeted for hours in some lonely hut. You know what she will make of that." The two friends crossed to the library, where Ian quickly provided the promised brandy that Tony downed gratefully.

"She will tell everyone that Francey is a fallen woman, no better than she should be, and that I should do the honorable thing and marry the chit. Well, I have every intention of doing just that, so her guns will be spiked." Tony confided cheerfully. His sudden volte-face surprised Tony as much as Ian.

"Do you really want to marry Francey?" Ian asked a bit dubiously.

"If you recall, I have always wanted to marry Francey. She was the one who decided I would make a poor husband."

"She may still believe that. And she still may not have you," Ian said bluntly. "This is a devil of a mess. I only hope you did not contrive this accident to get your way. I wouldn't put it past you. And furthermore, it's quite unfair to Francey."

"How suspicious of you, Ian. As if I would do such a heinous thing. No, it is just my good luck. Francey will marry me, if she wants to save her reputation. It's all turned out for the best," Tony explained smugly.

"I wonder. I suspect you had some such idea in the back of your mind when you foisted yourself on us. I really object to being made use of in this way, Tony." Ian was genuinely disturbed, for Francey's position was not an enviable one, and he disliked the thought that their invitation had resulted in such a dilemma. Of course, she would have to marry Tony, no matter how she felt.

"You refine too much on it, old man. You will see. Now how about that delayed dinner. I could eat a horse," Tony insisted blithely, obviously pleased with himself and events.

Ian laughed hollowly. "You are a devil, Tony. I am certain that even if Lady Clifford had proved a charitable old lady, you would somehow have managed to direct matters to your advantage."

Despite himself Ian could not be too censorious. Tony

76

appeared quite happy to enter the parson's noose, and if he decided to make Francey happy no doubt he would be successful there too. Unjust, perhaps, but that was the way of the world. Ian himself had experienced a similar forced union and had lived to bless the necessity. He hoped Tony and Francey would be as fortunate, but there were nuances here he did not quite understand. Shrugging off his unease, he rang the bell for his butler, deciding that his responsibility for the moment was to see that Tony had his dinner.

When Francey awoke the next morning after her ordeal, which had been exhausting both physically and emotionally, she felt rested in body but not in mind. The events of the previous afternoon and evening could easily be banished. She did not really worry about Lady Clifford's insinuations, although she had no doubt that the lady would enjoy embroidering the story of Francey's hours in the hut with Tony wherever she could do the most harm. If Francey spent a month or so in Dorset with her family, by the time she returned to London some new scandal would have replaced the suppositions. As cowardly as it seemed, she really had no interest in facing the sly glances and whisperings and trying to ignore the slurs on her reputation. By retreating to Dorset she could avoid a great deal of trouble.

Reminded of Tony and those intense embraces in the hut, Francey blushed. What had she been thinking of to allow such intimacies? She could not deny she had responded to Tony's practised kisses, and that was the problem. Those kisses had shown a wealth of experience. Obviously a host of women had enjoyed his lovemaking and she did not want to join their number. She found Tony's intentions toward her mystifying. Did he want an affair, as a revenge for the broken engagement? She did not think he was that spiteful—but perhaps he hoped that she would fall in love with him again and he would then have the pleasure of rejecting her. Her first instincts had been wise. Keep a safe distance from Tony. If it were not for the fact that it would appear to be an admission of guilt, she would fly to Dorset this very day. Oh dear, what should she do?

Before she could marshall her thoughts and plan some dignified retreat from her dilemma, her breakfast tray arrived by the hands of her scowling abigail, Martha, who had been with her since girlhood.

"You are looking gloomy, Martha," Francey said as the maid plumped up the pillows after setting down the tray across her mistress's knees with more force than necessary.

"And who wouldn't, hearing all those nasty tales belowstairs about your goings-on? It's more than a body can stand." Martha drew her mouth down, emphasizing the lines about her thin lips. She stood accusingly before Francey, her hands behind her back, and inspected her mistress as if she had some dangerous disease.

"I have no idea of what you are talking about, and I must say, you should be ashamed to listen to gossip about me," Francey reproved, hoping that an immediate attack would distract her abigail. She should have known better.

"You spent hours alone in a hut somewhere with Lord Antony, when you should have known better, having had some reason to suspect that he meant no good," accused Martha, not one bit intimidated by Francey's attempt to chastise her.

"It was not my fault that the curricle was wrecked, or that it rained so hard, or that the horse lost a shoe. I suppose you would be happier if I had stayed out in the storm, suffered a thorough drenching, caught pneumonia and died," Francey retorted, annoyed to realize that she was justifying herself to Martha.

"Doesn't matter who is to blame, although it would not surprise me if that dratted lord had planned the whole business. He has always meant trouble. Now you are in a right pickle. What your ma will say I shudder to think.

Probably say I should have taken better care of you," Martha sighed deeply, feeling the weight of her responsibilities. "You always were pesky. How the late master put up with your goings-on I will never fathom, but then he was a saint."

"Really, Martha, Archie was no such thing. And as I recall, he had very little to endure from me. You are making a great deal of an unfortunate mishap. Servants will gossip, and so will their employers, but I refuse to feel guilty about an accident I could not have prevented."

"You should never have agreed to ride in Lord Tony's curricle." Martha was determined to have the last word, and Francey had to agree she was correct. But it did no good to think of that now. And if the servants were gossiping already, the sooner she left Dursley Hall the better. No doubt Lady Clifford's maid, as vinegary as her mistress, had spread the word in the servants' hall. That miserable old woman had little charity. She enjoyed thinking the worst of everyone.

"That will be quite enough, Martha. No, go away and leave me in peace to eat my breakfast." Uncaring that she had deeply offended her abigail, who stalked from the room, Francey turned to her meal with determination. But before she could take the first bite of her shirred egg, she noticed an envelope tucked under the toast rack. it was unaddressed. Abandoning the egg, she quickly ripped open the letter.

My dear Francey,

I think we had better meet and talk over our plans. The announcement of the wedding should not be postponed. Will you meet me in the folly at 11 o'clock. If you don't come I will be forced to fetch you, causing even more tittle-tattle.

Your faithful and loving servant,

Tony.

Ha! Faithful and loving indeed. How dare he make these assumptions—that she would come when he ordered, and even more arrogant, that she would consider renewing that old engagement.

Summoning Martha back to help her dress, Francey continued to tell herself that she would not go to the folly at 11 o'clock. Still, she was dissatisfied with every dress in her wardrobe, causing Martha to mutter beneath her breath and finally complain outright that she was behaving in a rag-mannered fashion.

"Quite right, Martha. I am the veriest pudding heart, with no gumption, as you would say. Come, the aquamarine sarsanet will do very well." As Martha buttoned up the back of her frock, Francey heard a soft knock on the door. At her bidding the caller to enter, Verity poked her head in and then sidled through tentatively.

"If you are not in the mood for visitors, just say so, and I will take myself off. But I thought you might be brooding up here and I have been ordered to rout you out by Ariel."

"Brooding?" Francey asked as if having no idea of what Verity could mean. Then she shrugged, wincing as Martha pulled the comb through her hair.

"Afraid to show her face, is that it? And no wonder," Martha interrupted. Then, realizing she had gone too far, backed away. "There you look a treat anyway." And she scuttled out of the room before Francey could reprimand her. Verity and Francey laughed, sharing the same thought.

"If you have to face your accusers 'tis best to be dressed to the nines," Francey conceded, knowing that was what Martha had intended.

Verity ignored Francey's poor attempt at levity. "It's monstrous that society insists women are ruined if they spend a few hours alone with a man. And the man never suffers any criticism. It infuriates me."

"The way of the world," Francey agreed cynically.

"It seems to be the way of Lady Clifford's world. I'd

like to catch out the old terror in some grave misdoing. She's a nasty spiteful harridan, absolutely gleeful about the supposed moral transgressions of London women. Of course Tony, being a Duke's son, comes in for far less of her invective. One would think you were the most scarlet of creatures who had lured Tony into that hut by the fellest of designs." Verity was up in arms at the unjust innuendoes involving her friend. "But, Francey, what will you do?" she finally asked.

"What is it that gamblers and disgraced clubmen do? I'll go on a repairing lease to the country," Francey explained.

"Do you think that's wise? Wouldn't it be better to face down the cats, ignore their slights? It isn't as if you were some timid debutante who would have to wear the willow for this one unhappy incident."

"No, I am much worse, a gay abandoned widow, who does not show proper respect for my poor dead husband by wearing black gloves for a decade." Francey hesitated. "Really, Verity, I don't know what to do. I think Tony believes he must marry me," she blurted out her suspicions, no, her certainty. "Here, look at this note. He acts as if the whole matter is settled."

Verity glanced at the strong black strokes of the note, realizing how the arrogant tone would have annoyed Francey. Even if this pair did marry, what chance of happiness did they have, with all these problems in their past and forced to the altar by convention, not love? Whatever advice she gave was sure to be wrong.

"You must do what you think is right for you, not be persuaded by convention or social pressures, or the ill-natured remarks of catty old ladies. It's difficult being a woman alone and unprotected, but an unhappy marriage could be worse. I wish I had the answer," Verity said. Giving Francey a comforting hug, she reminded her, "You know that Ian and Ariel, Alistair and I will stand by you whatever you decide."

Ariel indeed was reassuring when Francey cautiously

descended downstairs. It was approaching 11 o'clock and she had still not decided whether to meet Tony in the folly. Ariel tried to cheer her with the news that she had asked Aunt Elsbeth to take her leave.

"Ian spoke quite strongly to her, telling her she had outstayed her welcome and in the future would be wise to bridle her tongue. He can be quite ferociously haughty and frightening when he feels an injustice has been done. Unfortunately we cannot be sure she will hold her tongue, although she looked almost cowed when she went to pack."

"Well, she has done her damage, but it is not wholly her fault. I am certain the story of our disastrous escapade would have made the rounds eventually. I suppose I had better agree to this interview with Tony. He behaves as if the matter were all settled and we shall wed," Francey confided.

"Do you have no feeling for him, Francey? I feel so guilty in allowing him to come here. But somehow I felt he really still cared for you and wanted to chance his hand again, hoping you could be reconciled. You did love him once," Ariel suggested warily.

"Yes, I did love him once and he betrayed that love. No doubt he would enjoy the opportunity to have me at his mercy again, but this time I am forewarned. I suppose I must remarry sometime, and the world would say I am clever to have captured such a nonpareil," Francey agreed bitterly.

"Oh, Francey, what a coil." Ariel had no comfort to give, only support. But Francey left to meet Tony feeling somewhat heartened by her friends' loyalty if not by their suspicion of Tony's motives, which she shared.

Chapter Seven

Some hundred years ago a besotted Lord Dursley had built the folly for his frivolous wife, twenty years his junior, in an effort to keep her intrigued with country life. His present had not been well received, as Lady Dursley had eventually run off with a neighboring peer, abandoning both folly and husband. Ian and Ariel had restored the small classic structure which lay on a slight rise some five hundred yards from the Hall. They often chose it for intimate conversations away from domestic cares.

As Francey approached the folly she hesitated. It was not too late to turn back. But Tony must have sensed her reluctance for he stood in the entrance by one of the Doric columns and watched her coming, as if daring her to change her mind. Evidently he had come to the rendezvous from a morning ride, for he was dressed in breeches and boots, with a trim black coat, looking every inch the fine gentleman.

"Good morning, Francey. You look entrancing. Obviously your outing did little harm," he said as he took her arm and escorted her into the folly toward the banquette which lined the far wall. Enough of a diplomat to sense her antagonism, he knew better than to show any satisfaction that she had accepted his invitation.

"I have not suffered pneumonia yet," she replied shortly.

"You were kind to grant my request for this private talk."

She forbore reminding him it had hardly been a request, more of a threat. "Yes, well, here I am, and I think I should tell you your matter-of-fact acceptance of a wedding between us is not so justifiable." She edged away from him on the seat. Tony's overpowering personality was suddenly too intrusive, recalling memories best forgotten.

"Come, Francey, let us be practical. It is true that we could probably ride out any scandal, especially if you disappear into Dorset as I suspect you are planning, but then you will miss the season, perhaps sacrificing your position as one of London's leading hostesses."

"You have maggots in your head if you think my standing in London society is of such overriding import to me, Tony. I am not that light-minded. Besides I like Dorset," Francey said mulishly, realizing she was behaving with less than her usual assured sophistication.

Tony looked rueful then admitted, "Really, Francey, I am also thinking of my own position. The by-election is in two weeks. No doubt I would be returned whatever I did, on the governor's orders, but I do not want to begin my political career under a cloud. It would not look well to pose as a social reformer when my own morals are suspect, you know," he added with a certain ingenuous simplicity.

"Of course, I knew you must be more concerned with your own situation than mine. You have an overweening conceit, as I recall."

"Oh, Francey, what can I do to alter your harsh opinion of me? I am just trying to be honest and persuade you that this marriage will be of benefit to us both. After all, you'll want to remarry someday. You desire children, I suppose, and you can't wish to pose as a sorrowing

84

widow forever, not that you don't look quite lovely in the role."

"What is the benefit to me, besides avoiding a silly scandal? I will be left with an unfaithful husband who will expect me to play the adoring wife while he flirts with every attractive woman around, probably keeps a mistress and makes me an object of scorn."

Tempted to make an imprudent reply, Tony held his words back before they could ruin his whole campaign. "I can hardly act the libertine if I hope to have a political career. Be reasonable, Francey. I need your help in this effort to achieve some of my goals for the poor wretches who are suffering from the effects of the war, the Corn Laws, the enclosures and all the other disturbing social ills."

Francey was impressed despite herself. Tony appeared to be quite sincere. "Will marriage help you achieve these noble ends?" she asked caustically, unwilling to admit that she was slowly being persuaded into a course she had rejected vehemently just an hour or two before.

"Of course. You will be the perfect political hostess, managing a glittering salon which will attract all the august personages I wish to influence. You see, I really cannot do without you," he pleaded with an engaging grin.

"I don't believe I want to be married just to preside over a political salon," Francey protested. "And the scandal, vexing though it is, would not persuade me."

"Do you want me to appear as the worst sort of cad, who compromised you and then refused to make the *amende honorable?* That is really mean-spirited of you, Francey."

"Somehow I seem to be on the defensive, as if by refusing to wed you I am behaving in a very cavalier fashion. I want to marry for love, not just to avoid scandal."

"You married once before without love, why can't you

85

do it again," Tony offered wickedly.

Francey gasped. How unfair of him to refer to her union with Archie in those unflattering terms, although there was more than a germ of truth in his accusation.

"How dare you impugn Archie! I was very fond of him and we were very happy together. He was a model of fidelity," she insisted, returning to the shoals on which her engagement to Tony had broken.

"I am not impugning Archie, a fine fellow indeed, but be honest, Francey. You were not passionately in love with him." The more Francey balked, the more determined Tony was to marry her.

"You are not trying to make me believe that you are in love with me, are you Tony?" Francey asked sceptically, but aware that she would have hailed such an avowal with pleasure. Not for the world would she admit how much she wanted Tony to say that he still cared for her, and that he had not forgotten what they had once shared.

Tony, unsure of his feelings and chary of exposing himself to ridicule, hesitated just too long. "We are both adults, Francey, and know that marriages are arranged for other reasons than love. Indeed, the happiest unions are often the result of shared interests, children, property, all the matters which people of our position must consider. You know how my father feels. He would welcome you as a daughter-in-law. He wants me to be married because it looks as though Philip will remain a bachelor and there must be heirs to the title, although I will not insult you by implying that you might consider a coronet as some inducement. There must be some arguments I can use which will persuade you that you too will reap benefits from our marriage."

Francey, if disappointed in this sober analysis, refused to show any sign of her repugnance at this practical list of advantages.

"Of course I know I must remarry. It is not comfortable being a widow in the circles in which I move, and I am having a certain amount of difficulty right now with Oliver Fanshawe. And I do want children, eventually." She cocked her head on one side and regarded Tony in an assessing fashion.

"Judging my merits and trying to decide if the risk is worth it, Francey?" Tony asked bitterly. He had hoped for a more enthusiastic reception, but he was not surprised that his proposal had inspired no other reaction than the one which Francey had revealed. However, he realized that he must show more warmth of emotion than this, even if his pride rebelled at exposing himself to ridicule.

Raising her chin with one hand and looking at her with all the force he could muster, he said, "You are a very attractive woman, who would have no trouble marrying a score of better men than I. But we have a certain affinity, and believe me, Francey, I do not intend this marriage to be one of mere convenience. Who knows, if we work at it, we might find again that passion and excitement which I once hoped would be ours. Please do not refuse me."

Overcome by a mixture of emotion, Francey could only nod her head. She would marry Tony and pray that someday his prophecy of emotions deeper than mere affection and respect would emerge from this problematical union. She was not willing to admit that he had again enthralled her with his unique blend of charm and passion. She could not give him any quarter in their contest, for he would then dominate her and she would be helpless.

"For someone who has just agreed to an honorable proposal of marriage you do not look overjoyed. In fact you appear to regard me as an unwise purchase that you might yet return to the shop," Tony said facetiously.

"I have every reason to view the whole business warily. You do not inspire confidence." Francey knew she was behaving ungraciously but could not prevent her reaction.

"If I cannot reach you one way, there is always this," he conceded and took her in his arms. "Don't fight me, Francey." His kiss was warm and drugging, driving all idea of struggle from her mind and heart. In his arms she felt secure and sheltered, a false conception, but as his kiss deepened and his hands moved with familiarity over her acquiescent body she surrendered to the desire he could always evoke. He was the first to break the embrace, causing her to blush with mortification.

"Don't be ashamed of your response to me, Francey. If we can meet on no other ground, at least agree that you do not find me repulsive," he pleaded, as if unsure of her reaction. But he could be in little doubt that she welcomed his caresses, and that was a victory she could not deny him no matter how chagrined she felt.

"You make love with expertise, Tony. I have never found you wanting in that department, but there is more to marriage than the pleasures of the bed." Francey had no illusions about what lay ahead.

Tony laughed hollowly. "You are a worthy opponent. We will just have to try our best. And now I think it would be prudent to return to the Hall and make our announcement. I am sure our friends will be delighted and our enemies confounded."

As they left the folly neither of them was completely satisfied, but neither was willing to make the move which would expose their vulnerability. Walking slowly toward the Hall they discussed quite amicably when the ceremony should take place.

"A special license, I think," Tony persisted. "And we can be married in London as soon as possible. We must decide what you will do with your house on Bruton Place, for we shall be living in Grosvenor Square. That is if you agree," he proposed diffidently.

"I can rent out the house. There are always people who want a place for the season. When is the by-election?" Francey considered the problems ahead, but decided to

88

e practical. She had made her decision and must do her
est to make this marriage work.

"In a fortnight. And we must go down to Dorset. No
ime for a wedding trip, I fear, but I promise to take you
o Venice when Parliament recesses."

As they entered the Hall they met Lady Clifford
reparing to depart, her boxes packed, and her hosts
peeding her off.

Tony could not resist the opportunity. "Dear Lady
Clifford, you will be happy to see that I took your advice.
rancey has consented to become Lady Everely. I know
hat will give you pleasure." He grinned outrageously
nd waited for that spiteful lady to congratulate him.

"She could hardly do otherwise," Lady Clifford
napped back, furious that she would be denied a scandal.

But Ian and Ariel more than made up for her caustic
omment. They embraced Francey and Ian shook Tony's
and vehemently. "We are so pleased, Tony. It was
lways in the cards."

"I was not so sure. But she could not resist me in the
nd."

If the Montagues sensed that Francey had reserva-
ions, they did not show it. Bundling off Aunt Elsbeth,
vho departed from the Hall in deep dudgeon, they spared
o more time for their difficult relative and insisted that
he engagement be celebrated forthwith.

As the quartet walked toward the drawing room, Tony
aised an eyebrow at Francey. "Ian and Ariel have no
loubts that our union is blessed by the gods. We must
ot disappoint them, Francey."

Tempted to demur, she kept her own counsel and
eceived the good wishes of the company, who gathered
o wish them happiness. If only she could believe that
Tony felt more for her than a need for a suitable and
complaisant wife.

*   *   *

They were married ten days later in a quiet ceremon[y] at St. Margaret's, with the Duke signaling his delight, an[d] then were on their way to Dorset. They spent thei[r] wedding night at the Compton hunting lodge in Surrey[.] Tony insisted he did not want to begin their married lif[e] in some posting inn, no matter how luxurious an[d] comfortable. He had made every effort to see that thei[r] accommodations were all that she could have wished. I[f] Francey had felt any apprehensions about what la[y] ahead, she need not have feared. Tony was a tender an[d] considerate, if silent, lover, and as she had half feared, h[e] drew from her a passionate response. She lay awake for [a] long time considering what a barren union it would be i[f] no words of love were exchanged in their nightl[y] encounter. She had wanted to receive him coldly but tha[t] had proved impossible. He was a devil, luring her int[o] giving him all he wanted. If he had behaved with smu[g] satisfaction the next morning over their late breakfas[t] shared with friendly intimacy she would have bee[n] furious, but he was careful not to make that mistake.

Regarding her over the coffee cups, he smiled at th[e] picture she made in her ivory and lace dressing gown[.] "You are a sight to delight the eyes, Francey. I am goin[g] to enjoy having you for a wife. And it is up to me to se[e] that you find equal satisfaction."

"Time will tell," she responded a bit ungraciously. I[f] she were to admit how she had thrilled to his caresses an[d] had been overwhelmed by his lovemaking, he would hav[e] won all he wanted without a struggle. He did not deserv[e] such a victory. They had made a marriage of conven[i]ence, and Tony found it convenient to have an eager an[d] affectionate bed partner. If she had hoped for more sh[e] must contain her longing.

"You have a reputation as an excellent lover, and I ca[n] now testify that it is well deserved. But as I warned, ther[e] is more to marriage than expertise in bed," Francey refused to allow him more than that.

90

"I am happy to have given satisfaction ma'am. You are an amazing woman, Francey, but then I always knew that if you would have me we would make a fine match of it." And with that he went on to discuss his political ambitions, enlisting her advice and opinions.

Francey could not but admire his ambitions and promise to give her own enthusiastic cooperation. If she sighed for a more romantic outcome from their wedding night, Tony would never know how his casual acceptance had hurt her.

The newlyweds' reception in Dorset was gratifying. At Compton Towers, the seat of the Dukedom for four hundred years, Tony's elder brother gave his congratulations with enthusiasm and relief. A wan, indeterminate copy of his dashing brother with thin features and pale eyes, Philip Everely hailed the marriage as a heaven-sent escape from the entreaties of his father. Philip cared nothing for women but since Francey represented no threat to his bachelor existence he welcomed her as his sister-in-law with pleasure. He had always liked her and now she was his savior. The tenants, too, appeared pleased that Master Tony had at last settled down and was prepared to do his duty to the estate and the title.

Some days later Francey and Tony drove over to see her parents, whose acres bounded the Towers. Mr. and Mrs. Lawton were more than happy to see Francey wed to her erstwhile fiancé. They had liked Archie Pembridge but had sensed Francey's unhappiness over her broken engagement to the Duke's son. Mrs. Lawton, in particular, found the situation satisfying. She had liked neither Francey's status as a widow nor the rumors she heard about the sophisticated life her younger daughter was leading in London. A round, cheerful woman with little pretension to looks and even less sensibility, she was content to live quietly with her husband, enjoying country pleasures.

Francey's brother Robert, home on leave from the

Navy, was visiting as well with his wife and small son. Christina Lawton's somewhat vapid blond looks and inane conversation drove Francey to distraction, but Tony won great favor in that corner. Few women could resist him when he turned his fabled charm upon them, and Robert's wife was no exception. Francey, annoyed by her sister-in-law's flirtatious antics, wondered what her brother had been thinking about to marry her. She knew they had met in Portsmouth on one of his leaves, and that Christina's father was an Admiral. Robert's first love was the sea and Francey sometimes wondered whether his ambitions for his career had influenced his choice. But all told, she was fond of her brother and had the happiest memories of their childhood. Tony and Robert had always been the best of companions and this, at least, had not altered.

However her family's bland acceptance of her marriage irritated Francey. They appeared to find nothing untoward in her taking Tony so suddenly, having once so soundly rejected him. But in this she misjudged her father. Drawing his daughter away from the family group after luncheon, he took her into his study for a private chat.

"Are you happy, Francey? I always knew that Archie was your second choice and you probably should have married Tony years ago despite his suspect ways. I believe he has decided to abandon those junketings which caused you such distress. He seems devoted, but are you certain this time of his fidelity?" Francis Lawton faced his daughter, his hands behind his back, looking at her searchingly from deep brown eyes like the ones she had inherited. This daughter, his namesake, had won his heart when she was but a babe and he could not bear to see her suffer any pain. He respected his son, was proud of him, and had a great deal of affection for Flora, Francey's elder sister. But this one, his youngest child, had always inspired a special fondness.

"We shall go on all right, Papa. Events conspired to bring about our marriage and I am not discontented. I had to marry again someday and at least I am aware of all Tony's faults. Better the devil one knows, as they say," Francey spoke lightly, unwilling to tell her father the reason for the hasty ceremony.

"I would not force your confidence, Francey, but you may depend on my support in whatever you do. If Tony does not behave, he shall answer to me." Francis Lawton might be immured in the country but he was not unaware of the temptations offered by the social set in which his son-in-law and daughter would be moving.

"Oh, Tony has decided to become a model citizen. He is entering Parliament and is determined to become quite popular in political circles. Don't worry, Papa. After all, Tony is considered a catch."

Francis Lawton was not impressed, but realized he would get little more from his reticent daughter. She had never been one to parade her emotions, cloaking her deepest feelings in a merry carefree facade. He could only pray she would find happiness.

"Remember, Francey, I love you and will always welcome you home if life's troubles become too pressing."

"Oh, Papa. You are a darling." Francey gave her father a reassuring kiss, knowing how angry and hurt he would be if he learned the real reason for the marriage. To have his daughter an object of scandal would be more than he could bear. She must spare him that.

Sensing that the interview was becoming too emotional, Francey tried to lighten the atmosphere with a teasing reference to his added pounds. "You must let up on the Madeira, Papa, or you won't be able to mount your favorite hunter next fall."

"Quite right, my dear. I will heed your words." They parted with affection, Francey much cheered by her father's offer of love and support.

Tony, not unperceptive, queried her later as they were returning to the Towers about her interview with her father.

"I have the feeling your father does not wholly accept me as a son-in-law," he said casually, keeping his eyes on his horses.

"Of course he does. Papa worries too much. He wonders if you will make me happy, a condition much valued by fathers when marrying off daughters."

"Are you happy, Francey?"

"So far, I see you as a most obliging husband."

"Not exactly an overwhelming endorsement, but all I can expect for the present, I suppose. I hope you are not pining for some other fellow, Oliver Fanshawe, for example." Tony had hesitated a long while before bringing up the matter of Oliver. He had no idea of Francey's real feelings for the man, although she had implied that he had become a problem.

"I have been meaning to talk to you about Oliver. He really is the most utter cad." And Francey proceeded to tell Tony of Oliver's attempt to blackmail her into marriage with some incriminating letters of her sister's.

"Not surprised. The fellow is under the hatches and always had a nasty streak. I will handle him when we return to London and I am certain you will not be bothered by him anymore." Tony was pleased that she had confided in him and that she relied on his protection.

"One of the most pleasant aspects of marriage is having a husband to attend to these annoying problems," she agreed, finding that indeed the protection offered by her new husband was strangely comforting. So they continued in companionable silence toward the Towers with much still unresolved. But the first steps toward a more rewarding relationship had been taken.

Chapter Eight

Some six weeks later Francey sat in the morning room of the Compton mansion on Grosvenor Square checking an invitation list for the ball which would introduce the newlyweds to society. She remembered with a rueful smile the last time she had been engaged in planning a party, a rout which had never taken place because she had gone to Gloucestershire to visit the Montagues. And look what had happened then. Despite her resolutions to have nothing to do with Tony Everely, she was now his wife, the marriage a matter of convenience. It appeared to be to Tony's convenience much more than to hers.

Since their return from Dorset she had seen very little of her husband. He had escorted her to a few engagements, quelling any rumors about the suddenness of the match by acting the devoted bridegroom, but then he had been off to Poole for the by-election. Not that he had needed to campaign, for the Duke's influence had secured the seat. Francey had suggested she might accompany him to the constituency but he had not thought that necessary. Instead he had taken his new Parliamentary secretary, Captain Sidney Portman.

Her hopes that the marriage would take on a deeper meaning during those first days in Dorset had not been fulfilled. Her relationship with her enigmatic husband had not improved. Of course it had not worsened either.

It had simply settled into an even tenor, as if they had been married for decades not weeks.

Still, she had little reason to complain. Tony had dealt with Oliver Fanshawe very competently. He admitted that much of Oliver's threat had been dissipated by the marriage. Fanshawe, afraid of social ostracism by the powerful Comptons, had sulkily vanished from the scene, no doubt on a repairing lease to the country, there to plan a strategy for winning another well-dowered bride. Really, the man was impossible, the veriest cad. Francey sighed gratefully remembered how she might have married him instead of Tony.

Well, idling here repenting of her past and sighing over her blasted hopes for the future would not finish this list. Her secretary would be coming soon after luncheon to address the invitations. And Francey must see to it that this affair became one of the most successful balls of the season, a veritable squeeze, with all the most respected members of society, including the most influential politicians, as well as a goodly number of wits and fashionable types to enliven the proceedings. Dutifully she returned to Maybelle's list, inscribed in neat copperplate script, but before she had gone any further than the *G's* there was a tentative tap on her door.

On her bidding the visitor to enter, she repressed a momentary burst of irritation when she saw that it was Tony's secretary. Really, she was most unfair. Captain Portman was unexceptional, correct, polite, grateful and awesomely intelligent, so Tony informed her. He was a man of average height, with indeterminate brown hair worn severely cut *en brosse*, light blue eyes of a startling intensity, usually masked by heavy lids, and an erect soldierly bearing. There was little in his appearance to inspire distrust. On the contrary he embodied the most desired attributes of an officer and a gentleman. Why was it, then, that Francey found him so annoying?

"Good morning, Lady Everely. I am sorry to disturb you, but Lord Everely has just remembered three more guests he wishes added to the ball list. I hope this will not disturb your arrangements," Captain Portman said in his well-modulated voice, which never seemed to raise or lower a tone. Francey doubted that he ever gave himself over to the normal passions suffered by lesser men.

Giving the secretary a cheerful smile, Francey assured him it made little difference. "Since the list is already at four hundred I suppose a dozen or so more can hardly matter. But Captain Portman, I do wish you could call me Francey, or if that seems too informal, Frances. Lady Everely is too off-putting. I am sure you call my husband Tony." Francey had decided to deal with Captain Portman by assuming a friendliness she did not feel. She hoped to rectify the fault which was entirely hers, as the poor man had done nothing to deserve her aversion.

"That is quite kind of you, Lady Everely, but I would not be comfortable assuming such intimacy." Sidney Portman's implied criticism made Francey feel she had committed some glaring social solecism. Oh, well, she had tried.

"If that is all, Captain Portman," she signified that the interview could now end, and he bowed and left the room, in no way discomfited. No, indeed, Francey fumed. She was the one to feel that uneasy emotion. She would make no further overtures but if Tony continued to sing Portman's praises, she would speak her mind. Although that might prove to be difficult as she so rarely saw her husband.

Sometimes Francey wondered if he threw himself into his Parliamentary duties to escape his marital responsibilities, then chided herself for doubting Tony's convictions. He did feel strongly about the unjust treatment suffered by the veterans and was bending every effort to bring them some relief.

Her own drawing room was becoming quite a political salon and reflected these interests. A few dandies and Corinthians gathered at her Wednesday at-homes but they were vastly outnumbered by serious statesmen such as Castlereagh, Sidmouth, Palmerston, even Liverpool, the Prime Minister. The Duke of Wellington often dropped in to confer with his former aide, but these stalwarts of the Tory party did not like some of the conversation they heard from reformers like Brougham, Grey and Durham—Whigs concerned with Catholic emancipation, education bills, prison reform and the abolition of slavery, all of which were anathema to the conservative Iron Duke.

Some violent discussions ensued and Francey was hard put to keep affairs on an amicable footing. Now, of course, all political matters, even such vital concerns as food shortages, unemployment, and unrest in the Midlands, had given way to the scandal about the Prince Regent's wayward wife, Queen Caroline. Henry Brougham was her greatest defender, saying with some justice that she was no worse than her dissolute husband. In truth even the monarchy itself appeared endangered, for poor old George III was dying and his heir had never been more unpopular. Francey was not alone in wondering if the country would escape revolution.

Shaking off her mood, she returned to her ball list, pushing aside the thought that they had no business engaging in such frivolity while the populace was starving. Within a matter of moments she had completed her task, and was feeling eager for a brisk ride to dispel her malaise.

Just as she was about to repair to her bedroom to change, Jepson announced Sir John Fitzhugh Lennox, who entered the room fast on Jepson's heels. "Fitz" never stood on ceremony, relying on his ebullient personality, his long-time friendship with Tony, and his admiration of Francey to secure a welcome at whatever hour he wished to invade the Grosvenor Square house.

"Your servant, Francey. You are looking deuced attractive this morning. And where is that elusive husband of yours? He should be here with you gazing besottedly at the prize he has won. It was a victory which caused mourning in half the bachelor establishments in London," Fitz mocked, bowing over Francey's hand.

"You are the most complete rattle, Fitz. I think Tony is at the House, conferring with Sidmouth. He is about to be named assistant Home Secretary, you know. It's a rather impressive feat having just entered Parliament," Francey announced with a certain pride.

"How the fellow stands all those prosy bores, I can't fathom. Sidmouth is such an old woman and a mean moralist besides," Fitz objected, while taking Francey's invitation to sit beside her on a nearby settee.

"Lord Sidmouth has the responsibility for protecting us all, and I suppose the Luddites and the northern riots have unnerved him," Francey explained.

"Well, whatever, let's not talk about dreary politics. I came to ask you to drive with me this morning. It's quite a jolly day," Fitz asked. Sir John Fitzhugh Lennox was welcome in London's most august houses for his merry manner, his willingness to oblige, and his impeccable taste. Hostesses who worried about their gowns, their guest lists, their menus, even their abigails, consulted him, certain of obtaining reassuring advice. Although not really handsome, a slight man with thinning brown hair and light blue eyes which looked on society's foibles with a tolerant air, Fitz cut a figure of some note. A determined bachelor, with rooms at the Albany, where he lived in sybaritic comfort, he fought off all efforts to lure him into the parson's mousetrap. "Can't afford a wife, my dears," he would explain to those of his friends who had taken the plunge and wanted him to join them. Tony twitted him on his valuing his freedom too dearly and not wanting to confine his attentions to one woman.

Actually Fitz was not much of a womanizer, but preferred to be on terms of friendship with a score of matrons who did not threaten his liberty. He was the perfect extra man at every dinner party, for he could be called upon in any emergency, was punctilious in dancing with wallflowers, chatting up ancient aunts, and patiently listening to debutantes' endless diatribes against faithless men. Francey quite enjoyed him and since her marriage had found Fitz a most devoted *cicisbeo*. Since even the most jealous husband could not object to Fitz's presence in milady's boudoir, his informal comings and goings in the Everely *ménage* caused no comment. Not that Tony showed any signs of becoming the jealous bridegroom, Francey admitted.

"Oh, Fitz, I have a host of tiresome errands to do, books to exchange at Hookam's, a few trifles elsewhere, and a visit to the milliner's. So boring for you," she protested with a smile. "Otherwise I would enjoy a tool about the park."

"Think nothing of it. I will accompany you and relieve your tedium. And I am a dab hand at millinery. Why you might make a disastrous purchase, a depressing straw bonnet or some other equally grievous mistake without me to advise you," he replied cheerfully. "I am at your service."

"Thank you, Fitz, you are the most obliging man. I will just get my bonnet and shawl and be with you in a trice." And true to her word Francey did not keep Sir Fitzhugh waiting. Within the quarter hour they drove off in Fitz's spanking black curricle—he deplored the more rakish red vehicle some young bloods were sporting as being bad *ton*. Thus when Tony arrived home hoping for a few moments with Francey, he learned that he had been superseded, and not for the first time.

Upon informing Lord Everely that milady had departed with Sir Fitzhugh, Jepson received in return a bland smile. Within moments Tony was ensconced in the library, going over his speech on veterans' pensions with Sidney Portman. His maiden speech on relieving the plight of the veterans some weeks ago had been received with gratifying approval. Political insiders speculated that despite his rather liberal views Tony Everely was a coming man. Even Wellington, renowned for his conservative stance on all matters of the public welfare, conceded that Tony had a just cause in trying to help the Waterloo veterans, numbering a quarter of a million. But the Iron Duke had no patience with rioters, and Liverpool's government had already begun preparation for meting out severe punishments for any further assaults against His Majesty's government. Tony was trying, with some success, to steer a perilous course in finding supporters for his measures without antagonizing those whose assistance was vital to his cause.

Of great help to him in this endeavor was Francey's ability to attract the powerful to her at-homes, to her dinners, and now to this ball. Tony belatedly realized that he had seen very little of his wife in the six weeks since his marriage. Until now he had been fully occupied with his political goals, but in the past few days he had realized that his marriage needed attention.

Francey had done her part. As a hostess she had few equals. She managed by a combination of tact and charm to attract all the most suitable figures to the Grosvenor Square mansion, which she ran impeccably. What worried Tony was her attitude toward him, and he admitted that much of the fault was his. He had hoped the intimacy of marriage would bring them to a closer understanding, to a realization that beneath the conventions they could rediscover the love which had marked the early days of their engagement years ago. He knew he had been distracted by his political responsibilities, and certainly Francey seemed to share his desire to shake up the Tory establishment, to bring some relief to the poor and distressed who were fast becoming sullen and angry.

No one could ask for a more obliging wife, but Tony wanted more. What they shared in bed never translated into a closeness or even an obvious affection in the daylight hours. If Francey still felt any love for him, she hid it under a sophisticated, casual manner which he could not fault. How could he say to her, "Do you love me still Francey, or is this marriage just the convenient charade we both pretended it would be?" Pride kept him from pleading for more than she was willing to give. It was paltry of him, but somehow he could not make the first move.

He sighed, then turned back to the speech. They could not go on this way, but he did not know how to break the impasse. If Francey should become pregnant, perhaps . . . he dreamed, but then shook off the thought. That was no answer. If only they could go off alone, to Dorset perhaps, where they had begun their marriage under promising auspices. But that was not possible now, with the vote on the Veterans' Relief Bill coming up in the House and this wretched ball in less than a fortnight. His father and brother were coming to London for the occasion and they must not find anything in this marriage to criticize. Francey would have to improve her acting, begin to pay him such attention as befitted a bride, he decided moodily. He would suggest that his father expected to find them behaving as if they were enjoying the intimacy shared by loving newlyweds. If she could not feel the proper emotion, she must try to give convincing evidence that the Everelys were in love.

Having worked himself into a bad temper and shifted the blame for affairs onto Francey, he was not at all pleased to join his wife at the luncheon table an hour or so later and to find the company augmented by Fitzhugh Lennox. Damn it, the fellow lived in Francey's pocket these days. Not that there was anything to take exception to in Fitz's manner. Tony greeted him cordially. It would be bad *ton* to be discourteous to the harmless Fitz.

Surprising Francey, Tony gave her a hearty kiss, before holding out her chair. "Good afternoon, my dear. Have you had a successful morning and has old Fitz here played the cavalier to your satisfaction?" Tony asked in what he thought were nonchalant tones, but Francey immediately bridled.

"Fitz is a charming companion and seems to have time to waste on us more frivolous members of society," she spoke sharply, then felt ashamed. It was not part of the bargain she shared with Tony that he neglect his Parliamentary duties to idle at her side. And she must not appear to regard his neglect as troubling her. "But I quite understand that the government takes precedence. Certainly the veterans depend on you, Tony. How is the bill coming?"

Accepting her honorable amends Tony grinned a bit ruefully and replied, "Slowly, I fear. Not too many enthusiastic supporters in the House, but the Duke will talk them around. His prestige is still immense."

"And a great boon that he has decided to give up the Army for politics," Francey insisted, aware that not everyone agreed that the Duke would win the success in Whitehall that he had achieved on the battlefield and at the conference tables of Europe.

Before the discussion could continue they were interrupted by Captain Portman, who slipped into his seat with a murmured apology. Francey endured his presence at luncheon, and was relieved that he did not appear at dinner. She knew she was being unreasonable, for naturally Tony wanted him on hand during working hours, but she found the secretary an inhibiting figure, and it became impossible to engage in any personal conversation when he joined them.

The party talked commonplaces until the end of the meal, when Francey left the gentlemen to their port after bidding Fitz an affectionate farewell and thanks for his attendance on her errands. Tony, who had hoped to lure his wife into a *tête à tête*, accompanied her to the door. "Will I see you at dinner tonight, Francey?"

"Have you forgotten? We are promised to the Egertons. I understand that Peel will be among the guests. I am sure you want to have a few words with him," she answered more brightly than she felt. She was rather provoked that Tony only wanted to escort her when a political aim could be answered.

"Yes, of course," he agreed cheerfully, although for

once he wanted to damn the Egertons, Peel, politics and the whole business which prevented him from enjoying a close relationship with his wife. "There is something I want to talk to you about, but it will have to wait, I regret. Portman, here, wants to put the finishing touches on my speech."

"I quite understand," she replied and glided from the room, leaving her baffled husband to curse at another missed opportunity. Well, he was a cad to complain. She never did, and she accepted his preoccupation with a tolerance which was perhaps excessive. She might prefer his absence to his presence and that was beginning to worry him.

Once this damned bill was passed he would try to spend some time with her to mend matters. They could not continue in this stilted false manner. His concern about the state of his marriage was beginning to override any satisfaction he might feel about the progress of his political career. And he wondered why he had embarked on either course. The afternoon with Captain Portman and the veterans' relief bill did not go smoothly.

While Tony Everely was working to alleviate the plight of the veterans, and to put his marriage on a more acceptable footing, events in the country were conspiring to thwart his intentions in both directions. Henry "Orator" Hunt and his Lancashire weavers continued to spread agitation in that county. In the Midlands some of the workers began to drill on the hills. Violence was in the air, solidifying the Tories' fears of an uprising. The harvest that fall had been bad and hunger was rampant. The repressive Corn Laws added to the problem, for the people could not buy cheap bread while artificially high prices were favoring the landowners and keeping foreign grain out of England. A savage penal code, decried by the Radical Whig reformers, exacerbated matters. The members of the House of Lords were so worried for their heads, that they repealed the Commons' law abolishing the death penalty for five shillings worth of shoplifting. Wellington joined the Cabinet as Master General of Ordnance and began to complain about the "mischief and embarrassment" in the country. It appeared unlikely that the summer would bring relief to the populace or the politicians, and in Windsor, George III, in his eighty-first year, sank steadily toward death.

Chapter Nine

On the night of the Everely ball, Francey faced he[r] mirror with some satisfaction. Downstairs all was i[n] readiness for a most successful evening, and she now ha[d] nothing to do but don the new ball gown laid out by he[r] abigail across the four-poster bed. A rather darin[g] concoction, Francey thought, of sheer silver gauz[e] plainly cut with no embellishment, but enhancing he[r] figure, which had grown a bit slimmer over the pas[t] weeks. She sat in her chemise as Martha brushed he[r] blond hair into a glossy sheen before cleverly twisting i[t] into a Grecian knot which would not detract from th[e] simplicity of the gown. Not for Francey the curls an[d] elaborate coiffures of less self-assured ladies.

She stood to allow Martha to carefully draw the gauz[e] gown over her head. Francey nodded as she faced th[e] glowing figure reflected in the cheval glass. She ha[d] achieved her aim. Elegance and sophistication was th[e] note to strike. Turning away she opened her jewel box t[o] consider which gems would complete the picture, bu[t] before she could make a choice Tony entered from th[e] adjoining room.

She could see that he wanted a private moment, so sh[e] dismissed Martha with a warm smile of thanks and face[d] her husband.

"Words fail me, madam. You are a sight to behold," h[e]

106

bowed gazing at her with warm admiration which evoked a similar response from his wife.

"You look quite handsome yourself, sir," Francey praised. And, indeed he did, the very epitome of the fashionable gentleman in his austere black evening coat with the *de rigeur* white satin knee breeches, his cravat—tied in the intricate *trône d'amour* knot—emphasized with one simple diamond stickpin. Tony never overdid his dress, never sported the flamboyant brocaded waistcoats favored by some dandies.

"In short we are a handsome pair," he quipped, then stepping closer he grasped her by the arms. "I promise not to disarrange this stunning picture," and kissed her warmly, causing her heart to pound with ardor. Tony rarely made such gestures outside the marital bed, and she did not quite know how to receive this passionate embrace. But before she could make any response he drew away and she noticed he was carrying a flat velvet case.

"I know you have some exceptional jewels, Francey, but I rather hoped you would wear the Compton diamonds tonight. Father drew them from the bank earlier this week and Turner cleaned them. He would be honored if you would wear them and so would I," Tony said tentatively. Francey noticed that he waited, almost apprehensively as if this were some sort of test. She was not about to fail it.

"Of course, I will be thrilled, and diamonds are just the touch my costume needs. Do let me see," she agreed, agog with anticipation, as eager as any woman to wear magnificent jewels that were a gift from her husband.

And the Compton diamonds were justly famous, a delicate parure with matching tiara and earrings, set in a light filigree. Tony clasped the necklace about her throat, his fingers lingering on her creamy skin, and then offered her the tiara. "I would not presume to upset that glorious hair." Francey placed it carefully on her head, and then twirled before the mirror and her lord.

"You look the perfect duchess," Tony complimented, "and will be the envy of every woman here tonight, just as I will be the envy of every man."

"Thank you, sir. You turn a graceful compliment," Francey replied lightly, afraid of revealing too much. If Tony was disappointed he did not show it as he offered his arm to escort her from the room. When they approached the door, he suddenly stopped and surprised her with his next words, "I want to thank you, Francey, for all you have done to make tonight and indeed these past weeks so successful. I have been a bear, I know, but now that the veterans' bill has passed the House I want to concentrate on my wife." Again she had an impression that he was waiting for some overture from her.

"Tony, it is marvelous that you have persuaded the government to reward those poor fellows. They would never have been given a penny without your efforts," she acknowledged, avoiding any personal discussion in a cowardly manner. But they could hardly begin a discussion of their personal affairs when four hundred guests awaited them below. It was so like a man to choose a moment when, as a hostess, she was thinking of all sorts of domestic matters, like the arrangement of the lemon trees, and whether the decorations would be effective.

"Well, after all, the prize money from Waterloo was pretty paltry, privates receiving only two pounds ten shillings. They cannot survive for long on that. But who knows what will happen to the bill in the Lords. Those old men are terrified of giving anything to anybody. They should follow the Iron Duke's gesture. He returned his prize money of sixty thousand pounds to the treasury." Tony was well away on his pet subject and seemed to have forgotten his tentative efforts to engage Francey in some intimate talk. Just as well, she thought.

"Well, since the Duke is expected for dinner and we must be on hand to greet him, I think we had better make our way downstairs. I am not unaccustomed to entertaining, but this is my first big party in Grosvenor Square. I

don't want to embarrass either you or your father."
Francey could not but remember that one of the reasons
for this marriage had been her skill as a hostess.

"You could never do that," Tony answered a bit
abruptly, conscious that he had somehow not achieved
the response for which he had hoped. "Come, you are
right, and we must make our entrance." He offered his
arm and they walked into the hall toward the magnificent
stairway designed by Robert Adam with its graceful
soaring curves and delicate handrails. As they walked
down the stairs Francey noticed the Duke and Philip
waiting at the bottom, gazing at them. She hoped they
looked both admirable and amiable, for she would not
want to shake the Duke's innocent delight in this
rekindled romance, no matter how disillusioned she
might feel herself. Then she shook off her unease. She
was in danger of becoming a cynical mean-minded harpy.
When she reached her father-in-law, and received his
careful kiss on her cheek, she was startled to see tears in
his eyes.

"How lovely you look, my dear, in Mary's diamonds,
but of course, they are yours now, and she would be so
pleased. Such a fine job you have made of the house. And
about time to see it decked out for a festive occasion. I am
going to enjoy myself."

"I hope so, sir. But I have had card tables put up in the
library. After you have done your duty toward the
dowagers, you can settle down in there with a few
cronies."

"Do my duty, don't like the sound of that. But you are
the general, my dear, and I will obey orders. You, too,
Philip, my boy." The Duke was in a relaxed mood, happy
with the marriage, pleased with Francey's ability as a
chatelaine, and ready to entertain and be entertained.
Even Philip looked a little less harassed, although
Francey knew he hated these occasions. Before she could
reassure him, Jepson, puffed with importance on this
grand night, announced the first of the dinner guests and

the evening began.

They sat down thirty to dinner, with the Duke of Wellington on Francey's right and the Duchess given the seat of honor next to Tony at the other end of the table. Francey knew she had the best of it, for Kitty Pakenham Wellington was shy, badly dressed and dull of conversation. Rumor, later spread by that prolific diarist, Charles Greville, insisted that the Iron Duke was disgusted with his marriage, and had begun a flirt with Harriet Arbuthnot.

Poor Kitty, Francey thought, as she chatted easily with Wellington, well known for his attraction to politically aware and attractive matrons. Once sprightly with an exquisite figure and glowing complexion, over the years Kitty's looks and temperament had deteriorated. She disliked political talk and the Duke was not fond of the domestic circle, preferring to pass the time among his officers in the camaraderie of the staff tent. However, since his return from the Continent he had made an effort to restore some semblance of harmony to his marriage, and the Everelys were among the first to welcome the Wellingtons together.

"It is an honor to have you here, sir. And the country is well served to have you join the government. Are you finding the climate in Whitehall less exciting than that of Paris or Vienna?" she asked carefully.

"Since there seems to be no war on the horizon, I must fight my battles in Whitehall, Lady Everely. But your husband, too, has made the change and is finding that the new arena has challenges undreamed of in staff headquarters, I vow," the Duke threw the conversational ball back to her.

However, Francey was too skilled a hostess to criticize either the government or specific members, although she knew Wellington favored stringent repression of civil violence and did not share Tony's concern for the veterans of his "infamous army."

By the time the braised turbot had been removed for a

baron of beef, Wellington had indulged in a light flirtation and insisted that his hostess save him a waltz. He was a skilled performer, and gossip had it that at one time all of his officers had to be proficient on the dance floor or they could not be considered for a staff appointment.

Francey gave a swift survey to the rest of the table before turning to her other neighbor, Lord Castlereagh. The table was covered with an antique lace cloth, set with candelabra gleaming between Sèvres bowls of yellow and white roses. The effect was simple yet elegant, she thought, but she realized only the women would notice. As long as the men approved of the wines—Tony had ordered a rather rare claret—and were given good beef, they never commented on the arrangements. Conversation with a witty and good-looking woman also was among their demands, and she had chosen her guest list with extreme care. All in all, the dinner seemed to be progressing well, although Kitty Wellington appeared *distraite*, having to talk with the Home Secretary, Lord Sidmouth. Still, the real test of the evening lay ahead.

Francey, like most accomplished hostesses, could carry on a conversation while mentally reviewing her arrangements, with no guest the wiser, but she was startled out of her concerns about the ball by Lord Castlereagh's next remarks.

"Lord Everely is most fortunate in his bride, my dear. I am sure you are the greatest help to him in this new career he has chosen. And I am convinced you will be a soothing influence on his more radical views."

Francey was surprised, for Lord Castlereagh rarely made personal remarks. He was noted for his reserved, aloof manner. She remained silent, waiting for Castlereagh's next words. He hesitated, as if reluctant to say more, but his serious impression emphasized the importance of his warning. "Your husband is an astute young man but perhaps overpassionate in his concern for the less fortunate among us," he explained diplomatically. And Castlereagh had a great deal of experience in expressing unpleasant ideas tactfully.

"I believe he is worried about the mood of the country," Francey explained cautiously.

"Yes, we all are," Castlereagh said abruptly. "The Duke does not think appeasement is the answer. Your husband is at odds with him there, not a tenable position for a rising statesman."

"Of course we all admire the Duke and must listen to his counsel, but don't you worry that violence begets violence?" Francey asked boldly.

"The country is on the verge of revolution, and severe measures are necessary to quell insurrection," he replied just as shortly. But realizing that the Everely dinner table was perhaps not the proper place to be exposing his views, he offered her his somewhat wintry smile. "But enough of these grim forebodings. I am sure that the softening effect of marriage to such a charming and clever woman will ameliorate his views."

Francey thought no such thing, but did not propose to argue the matter with the noble lord. She agreed with Tony, not with the Duke nor with Castlereagh, but she had no intention of taking issue with him over the compote of pears now being served. She changed the tenor of the conversation by making an innocuous remark about Caro Lamb's novel, and Castlereagh politely followed her lead. But she was not to forget his warning. He had implied that Tony's radical views could cause trouble.

Some hours later, standing at the top of the long stairway to receive her guests with Tony, the Duke and Philip, Francey was able to bask in the knowledge that her ball was already proving to be a great success, a veritable squeeze, in fact. The stairs were crowded with the *ton*, all of the first stare. The Devonshires, the Seftons, the Count and Countess Lieven, the Norfolks, and even a royal Duke had seen fit to honor them.

Frederick, the Duke of York, had recovered from the

scandal which had forced him to retire as commander in chief of the Army when it was discovered that his mistress had been selling preferments to officers who wanted promotion. Always the most affable of the royal princes, and his father's favorite, he was regarded affectionately both by his brother the Regent and by the King. His attendance at the Everely ball was a signal honor.

The only sour note in the triumphant reception of the parade of worthies was the sudden appearance of Oliver Fanshawe. His name had not been on Francey's invitation list, and she did not like the fierce frown her husband gave her when he noticed Sir Oliver. That gentleman, impervious to snubs, bowed low over her hand.

"So kind of dear Lady Sefton to include me with her guests. I realize you thought I was out of town, or I would have received a card," he murmured intimately and outrageously to Francey.

"Indeed, Sir Oliver," she replied in glacial tones, and looked over his head to the Earl of Uxbridge, who followed him, greeting that gentleman with enthusiasm. Sir Oliver raised an eyebrow but had no choice except to move along the line, encountering the Duke and Philip, and then hurrying past Tony's cold nod into the ballroom.

Francey suspected that Tony would have some hard words for her, but she did not intend to take his strictures meekly. She had not asked Oliver to the ball and his effrontery was beyond bounds.

Her reflections on Oliver were soon rudely interrupted. The crowd had thinned somewhat but a ripple of excitement now passed among the guests waiting to be received. Francey noticed that the commotion below stairs was disturbing the even flow of guests, and some were even turning away to discover the source of the commotion. Breasting the tide, a harried footman managed to reach Tony and whisper into his ear. Tony, turning to his family, muttered an excuse.

"Some rumor about Liverpool. I must see to it," and he hurried down the stairs, brushing aside questions and attempts to halt his progress. When he emerged at the foot of the stairway and crossed the marbled entrance hall he was met by a few startled servants, and the sight of the imperturbable Liverpool handing his hat and gloves to a minion, while trying to soothe an agitated Lady Liverpool.

"What's the trouble, sir?" Tony asked.

"Some poor fool tried to attack me outside your door, but no harm done. The runners carried him off. A bit mad, no doubt, screaming curses at me. Really, I must apologize for taking you away from your guests for such a trifling matter," Liverpool explained coolly.

"Come my dear," Liverpool turned to his wife, who appeared a good deal more agitated than her husband. "We must not keep the Everelys waiting, or hold up proceedings." He shepherded his wife toward the stairs, prepared to greet his hosts as if nothing untoward had occurred, although there had been an attempted assassination.

Tony, querying his servants, discovered that a disgruntled, hungry millworker, among the crowd of watchers in Grosvenor Square, had tried to attack the Prime Minister with a cudgel but had been apprehended by the Bow Street runners Tony had hired for the occasion. While Tony's sympathies were with the poor disenfranchised people who must view this extravaganza as an arrogant insult to their plight, he could not condone attacks on Liverpool.

Returning to the receiving line, he had not time for more than a brief explanation of the attack on Liverpool, but when that gentleman appeared, Francey tendered her sympathies with a warm smile which overcame him. He was not one of her favorites, since he opposed Tony's attempts to bring some relief to the poor souls suffering from the depressed state of the economy. By nature a kindly man, Liverpool nevertheless had the *arriviste's* scorn of compromise and a stubborn resistance to change. He had been in France during the fall of the Bastille and the Reign of Terror which followed and had never forgotten the horrors perpetrated by the enraged mob. A worthy man, respected more than admired, the rival Whigs called him and his ministers, "Mouldy & Co." He was not the man to entertain Tony's views with any enthusiasm although he was honest enough to admit the justice of them. Francey knew that her husband thought Liverpool had a strong sense of duty and Tony hoped to persuade him to soften his resistance to the growing democratic spirit of the people.

Not long after Liverpool's arrival, Francey and Tony were able to leave their post and open the ball.

"You are a rare one, Francey. No other hostess in London could throw off the Liverpool affair and remain cool, while looking so beautiful, too," Tony praised as he twirled her through the opening strains of the waltz, watched by the guests lining the walls.

"Poor Lord Liverpool. I do feel for him, although he should take this attack as a warning that the populace will not meekly obey his stringent reign," Francey returned. "Do you really want to become one of the Mouldy Company?" she teased, looking up at him with a flirtatious smile.

"Yes, indeed. They need to be unmoulded, and I think I might be quite effective at that. But I am the veriest nodcock to discuss politics while dancing with one of the season's incomparables," he bandied. If he was still annoyed about Oliver Fanshawe, he had decided to postpone that criticism, for which Francey could only be grateful. They were soon joined on the floor by the company, and the evening proceeded without any further incidents.

Francey, some hours later, looked about her as she waited for Fitz to bring her a champagne cup. Really it was going quite well. The décor of the ballroom had been hailed as a startling innovation, for she had eschewed the fashion for baroque Egyptian schemes, so favored by the Prince Regent and his slavish followers, and decked the room with tubs of lemon trees and banks of white and yellow roses against white trellises.

Four gleaming French chandeliers with their hundreds of white tapers lit the scene, a kaleidoscope of beautifully gowned women whose jewels sparkled beneath the lights. The women were complemented by their partners, dressed formally in white satin knee breeches, and well-fitted black coats designed by master tailors. Certainly, Francey admitted with a bit of complacency, if Tony had married her for her ability to produce entertainments which drew the *ton,* she had more than succeeded. But somehow, in the midst of all this revelry she felt lonely and depressed. Her mood was not improved when Oliver Fanshawe interrupted her troubled thoughts.

"Ah, the charming Lady Everely viewing her success." Oliver appeared before she could take evasive action, which he had expected and forestalled. "I fear you are avoiding me, dear lady."

"I don't recall inviting you, Sir Oliver," she replied, refusing to acknowlege his compliments.

"Yes, well, I must apologize. I rather suspected you would not want to receive me. A certain embarrassment after so cavalierly scorning my respectful proposals, and the rather acerbic interview I had with your noble husband," he responded snidely, not a bit put out of countenance.

"If you suspected that, you were correct, and it was not the act of a gentleman to intrude where you are not wanted," Francey said severely, scanning the crowd for her rescuer. Where was Fitz?

"I had no recourse. Dear Lady Sefton asked me to fill in at dinner for a sudden refusal, and I had not the temerity to deny her. Of course, knowing of our former friendship she had no idea I had not received an invitation," he explained, in what Francey considered

116

an oily manner.

"This is hardly the place to discuss our differences, Sir Oliver." She would have liked to ignore him but Fitz arrived with her drink, and courtesy demanded she appear to be having a casual chat with her former escort.

"Ah, good evening, Fanshawe. Jolly ball, what? I do hope you have not prevailed on our hostess to desert me. She has promised to sit this one out with me, to rest from her duties, and enjoy her very agreeable party," Fitz greeted Fanshawe easily. If he was aware of any awkwardness he chose not to acknowledge it. Fitz was a past master at avoiding uncomfortable situations, and he knew that Francey and Oliver had once been quite intimate. Oliver seeing that no further conversation was acceptable made his bow and wandered off in search of more entertaining company.

As she listened to Fitz's gentle stream of gossip, she wondered what Oliver had in mind. Somehow she doubted that he intended to take her rebuff easily. Surely he must have been impressed with Tony's threats if he were to continue to try his blackmail ploy. Tony had not, of course, told him who the real author of the damning Byron letters was, and Francey wondered if Oliver still believed she had penned them. What a mountebank the man was! And she knew that he was in the hands of the moneylenders, about to be rolled up. Well, he could not look to her for rescue. Tony might not love her the way she wished, but at least by marrying him she had been spared Oliver Fanshawe's despicable attentions.

She smiled a bit cynically. Not the best reason for marriage but better than many, perhaps. How few of the couples twirling around her ballroom felt real affection for one another. In their world such an emotion was considered not in the best of taste, a bourgeois emotion, and not to be considered where prestige, property and wealth were at stake.

"I'm afraid, dear Francey, that you are not attending to my clever remarks. Have you taken me in disgust?"

Fitz quipped, noticing her *distrait* air.

"Not at all, Fitz. You are a great comfort. I must be a little tired from all this hectic entertaining. Pay no attention," Francey soothed him, feeling slightly ashamed. Fitz was such a good friend, and she would not offend him for the world. Before she could continue to reassure him, Wellington appeared to claim his dance and for the moment she must return to her duties as hostess.

Chapter Ten

Later that evening, after the lavish supper of lobster patties, cold pheasant, York ham, jellies, comfits and syllabub, several private conversations took place in various rooms of the Everely mansion. These talks, at such an unlikely place and time, were to have a devastating effect on the state of the country, on Tony's political career and not least on the progress of the Everelys' marriage.

Liverpool, Castlereagh and Wellington chose to conduct their conversation in the library. Despite his sangfroid under the attack by the enraged millworker, Liverpool took the matter seriously as an indication that England was in the grip of a dangerous mood. Of a steady but obdurate mind, he asked Wellington about the temper of the troops.

"Well, the veterans are dependable but there are some new recruits I am not too sanguine about," the hero of Waterloo reported. Remembered for his remark about the "infamous army" which had won that famous battle, his companions were not surprised that Wellington had little good to say about the steadiness and morale of the men he had recently commanded. The rank and file had been lured into service by the shilling offered at enlistment, many of them from the stews and slums of London and the Midlands. Discipline was strict, and

Wellington depended on his officers to see that the men they commanded would obey orders. But would they fire on desperate hungry people? He was not convinced.

"Then there is that Hunt, a choleric orator, who stirs up the people to demand what we cannot give them, cheap bread and higher wages," Liverpool admitted. "He has a large following."

"All this talk about the repeal of the Corn Laws by Cobbett, Broughham, Canning and the rest does not help," Castlereagh added gloomily. "I think young Everely has a bright future before him but he has some radical ideas about placating the masses."

"Sidmouth wants him to take over the Home Office when he retires," Liverpool advised. "I am not sure his ideas are sound."

"I always found Everely sensible and quite clever," Wellington insisted. "He will soon see the error of his charitable inclinations. Giving in to these firebrands will not mend matters. Everely will see this. He's a good man."

If Castlereagh and Liverpool were not convinced, they had to be impressed with Wellington's assessment of Tony. The Iron Duke was extremely loyal to the young men who had formed his staff at Waterloo and later at the Congress of Vienna. He believed they would do their duty when called upon by their leaders.

"The mood of the country is ominous. Steps will have to be taken. Parliament must see the wisdom of some coercive legislative acts to put down this ugly situation," Liverpool concluded. And the trio adjourned, in accord with each other, if not entirely at ease with the steps that must be taken.

In one of the upstairs sitting rooms two other gentlemen were discussing the ugly mood of the people, but with no good intentions. They were concerned with how the disturbances could be turned to their advantage. One of them was Oliver Fanshawe.

"This attack on Liverpool was most fortuitous," he

ecided. "There is a conspiracy afoot, and money to be
made from it, as I am sure you are wise enough to see."

"My God, Fanshawe, you would not condone assassi-
ation," his companion protested.

"Of course not, my dear fellow, but handled properly
e could manage to wrest a few guineas from the affair,
nd I could get my revenge on Everely. I have a score to
ettle with that gentleman," Fanshawe insisted bitterly.
He had not forgotten the humiliating interview with
Tony.

"Well, I will have to find some money somewhere, but
I draw the line at conspiracy. I have no wish to end my
days at the Tower, or wandering around the Continent,
igging it in some nasty watering place like poor
Brummel."

"You have to take a few risks to win out, old chap. But
I have a foolproof plan." Fanshawe explained eagerly,
seeing that his companion was indeed desperate beneath
his casual facade. And so the partnership was formed.

Tony Everely had just finished dancing with the
vivacious Countess Lieven and was chatting with that
doyenne when the lady surprised him with an un-
welcomed confidence.

"Have you see Moira Stacy-Long since your return
from the Continent, Lord Antony?" the Countess asked
archly.

"No, and I have no wish to," he replied a bit
brusquely. Countess Lieven, a haughty, dark-haired
patroness of Almack's, and a born intriguer, could not
resist dabbling in affairs better left ignored. Not content
with believing she knew how to manage politicians and
strategies better than those in power, she liked to meddle
in the romantic liaisons of the society in which she was
such a prominent figure. But she was not to be
discounted.

"Ah, but she wishes to see you, and I think would like
to renew your previous relationship. She was most
disappointed at your marriage." The Countess would

121

not be gainsaid.

"Lady Stacy-Long no longer has any part in my life,
Tony said decisively, silently damning the Countess and
her attempts to stir up trouble.

"Poor Moira, and she did care dreadfully, you know,
the Countess murmured, casting Tony a soulful glance
from her dark eyes. She obviously found the situation
amusing.

"Nonsense, Lady Lieven. That brief flirtation should
be relegated to the past. The lady will find more
complaisant men to entertain her, I think." Tony was
furious at the arch comments of this *enfant terrible,* but
he remained coolly polite.

If the Countess Lieven liked intrigue, she knew just
how far she could presume. She sensed that Tony had not
received her remarks about Moira Stacy-Long with any
enthusiasm, and she was quick to retreat. "Ah, I am
forgetting you are so recent a bridegroom. Naturally, you
would rebuff the advances of any woman, no matter how
attractive. The lovely Lady Everely puts us all in the
shade."

"Quite, Lady Lieven. I see you understand. My wife is
more than satisfactory." Long accustomed to dealing
with the Countess, he did not make the *bêtise* of showing
his anger, which she would have found enjoyable. But as
he surrendered her to her next partner, he barely
repressed a few hearty curses. And damn that Stacy-Long
woman!

The story he had told Francey about his involvement
with her, the misunderstanding which broke up their
engagement, had been correct as far as it went. He had not
seen the necessity of explaining that previous to their
engagement he had carried on a rather torrid affair with
the lady. However, they had broken off the business well
before he had asked Francey to marry him. Francey, no
doubt, would accuse him of misrepresenting matters,
that is if she cared enough now to take him to task. He
often wished for the return of the tempestuous spirits of

the girl who had shown her love for him with such passionate enthusiasm. This more mature Francey had learned self-control and the ability to hide her feelings. But he had no doubt that she would not relish Moira Stacy-Long's reappearance on the scene.

Recalling his duties as host, he went off in search of his next partner, not at all in charity with females. Fortunately his quarry was Lady Cowper, a gentle merry woman capable of soothing the most irate male. She was also an astute observer of both the political and social scene.

Meanwhile Francey was dancing with her brother-in-law, Philip Everely, who was regaling her with more details of the attack on Lord Liverpool. Philip was fond of his sister-in-law and had every hope that she would be increasing before too long. He liked Francey for herself, having known her for years, and enjoyed the way she treated him in a friendly matter-of-fact manner, designed to set him at ease.

Philip suffered from comparisons to his dashing brother, and had become inured to such criticism. Since he had no interest in London social life, did not game or drink too much, disliked politics, and preferred the country to the town, he spared himself much aggravation by remaining in Dorset. Only his father's strongest arguments had brought him to London for this ball. Francey appreciated his support.

"I must thank you, Philip, for lending your presence to this evening. I know how you despise all these affairs, and most of us rackety types who enjoy them," she said, with every sign of sincerity. Philip worried her, because he so often appeared unhappy, unable to fulfill his father's ambitions for him. Francey believed the Duke handled him badly.

"Well, I don't despise you, Francey, and I think you have done a bang-up job in arranging all this. But it does make me wonder, in view of the attack on Lord Liverpool, if it is wise for people like us to flaunt our advantages.

There is so much discontent, and real tragedy too—hunger, poor wages, lack of work," he complained a bit diffidently.

"Yes, I know, Philip. It's especially bad here in London and in some of the Midland towns. Conditions are always better in the country. I know all our people in Dorset are far less burdened. You do a fine job of taking care of the estate, Philip, and I know your father is grateful."

"Perhaps it is easier to manage matters down there, but I had no idea people were so aroused here. And with some justice. I hate all this crowding poor souls into factories and down mines. They would all be healthier and happier on the land," he complained, puzzled and distressed, for which Francey could only applaud him. How many peers in his position cared?

"Tony feels as you do, Philip, which is why he entered politics. He hopes to persuade Liverpool and the others to institute some changes," she explained.

"It seems a hopeless task to me. They are all so hidebound in Whitehall. But they had best beware. The mood is ugly and real violence could erupt before they make any move to assist these poor devils. Dreadful, dreadful," Philip sighed. Francey warmed to his feelings but could not help thinking that sighing and moaning did not accomplish much. Philip would never bestir himself to try to alleviate the conditions he deplored. Fortunately Tony did not share his indolence.

By the end of the evening Francey, tired but triumphant, bade the last stragglers farewell with a sigh of relief. Except for the Liverpool fiasco and Oliver Fanshawe's snide remarks, the evening had been a success. She hoped Tony had found it so, and she knew the Duke was delighted, but Philip's laments had left her with a sense of uneasiness.

Well, she thought, wiggling her toes in her scuffed satin slippers, there was little she could do about these large and depressing issues this evening. She had her own responsibilities, and remembering all who had helped to make the evening a success, she did not retire to her bedroom without thanking Jepson and his staff for their care and skilled attention.

Francey's regard for her servants had earned her their devotion, for few mistresses in her position bothered overmuch with the feelings of those who served them. Below stairs Lady Everely was hailed as an unusually considerate and kind mistress. If the staff were wondering about her marriage, or had heard the gossip about her earlier relationship with Lord Antony, they did not discuss it, and Jepson quelled any speculations with firmness. As a result the Everely house ran smoothly and efficiently. In these troubled times its employees knew when they were well-off.

If Martha considered herself among the more fortunate, she seldom showed any indication of it. Having attended Francey since she was a small child, Martha stood no nonsense, and often Francey felt she would be the one to be dismissed if she failed to give satisfaction. Having told her abigail not to wait up for her, as she knew it would be almost dawn before she sought her bed, she was not really surprised to find Martha nodding before the fire when she finally gained her chamber.

"Oh dear, Martha, I did ask you not to wait. It's much too late for you, and you must be tired to death with all you have done the past few days to help me," Francey scolded, knowing it was to no avail. Then giving Martha one of her heartwarming smiles she thanked her. "But I must say, I appreciate your being here. It has been a most successful ball, although I am a bit fagged now it is over." And then with a sigh she prepared to answer Martha's inevitable host of questions, accompanied by acerbic remarks.

"Well, it would have been a scandal if Lord Liverpool had suffered any harm from that crazed man who attacked him," Martha grunted as she helped Francey off with the silver gauze ball gown and into a cream silk

125

nightgown and matching silk peignoir.

"Fortunately, Lord Liverpool suffered no injury, bu
that poor man must have been beside himself.
understand he is an unemployed millworker, probabl
with a wife and children going hungry. I feel for hi
situation," Francey reproved.

"Bah, no doubt worked up to his attack by tha
varmint Hunt, who goes about stirring up law-abidin
folk who should know better. I have no patience with an
of it," Martha replied, as she bustled about the roon
setting it to rights. "Now, sit down here and let me brusl
your hair," she ordered, after Francey had washed he
face. Too tired to argue, Francey did as she was told
lulled by the rhythmic strokes of the brush an
wondering if she would fall asleep where she sat
Although she was half expecting him, Tony's arriva
through the connecting door startled her. He spoke
pleasant good night to Martha, who as usual sniffed, an
departed in a dudgeon.

Settling himself in a chair before the fireplace, whicl
was bare on this rather warm night, he said in a gentl
speculative tone, "That abigail of yours rather despises
me. I can't think why. I am always painfully polite tc
her."

"She dislikes most men, for she thinks they are all the
most dangerous, disreputable creatures, and we frai
womenfolk need protection from them," Francey
quipped, turning around on her dressing table and
viewing her husband with mild amusement.

"More the other way about, I think. Women are the
very devil," he replied with a grin.

"Am I to take that personally? I believe I have behaved
with the utmost charity toward you, except perhaps in
giving you Lady Wellington as a dinner partner, but that
could not be helped," she apologized. "And I am sure you
charmed her with your usual skill. I fear her husband
does not find your political views to his taste. He implied
that I should use my influence over you to persuade you

to become more acquiescent to his coercive measures."

Tony was not deceived. He knew that Francey agreed with his political views, but he played her game. "Well, let me see how you would go about it. I am quite willing to be influenced by my beautiful wife." He stood up and walked over to her, pulling her to her feet and looking down at her with an expression she could not fathom.

"Too tired tonight. All I want is my bed," she replied, refusing to be drawn.

"With me in it, I hope," Tony gathered her closer into his arms. "And I must show my gratitude for your skills as a hostess. Truly, Francey, the ball was a great success, and all admired your aplomb after the contretemps with Liverpool. I think you are a wonder."

Francey was surprised by the depth of his sincerity. Rarely did Tony probe beneath the surface in their daily encounters. He preferred to keep their relationship on a light, amicable plane. But for some reason tonight he appeared grave and disturbed.

"What was that fellow Fanshawe doing here? He was certainly not on your guest list," Tony's tone was casual but with a hint of anger beneath the easy question. And he held her gaze with an unusual intensity.

"I certainly did not invite him. He came with the Seftons' party, asked to fill in at the last moment for some defector, and I suppose Lady Sefton assumed he was invited. He did not disabuse her," Francey explained sharply, not liking the tenor of the conversation. Surely Tony was not going to play the jealous husband. She was much too tired for that foolishness and she was offended that he could believe she had any interest in Oliver after his scandalous behavior.

"Now, don't get into one of your tempers, Francey, although you do look especially tempting when you are in a pet. Of course, I knew you had not invited him. The man's a poltroon, barging in where he knows he is not wanted. There is something about him. . . . He will bear watching."

"Oh, pooh! He's the veriest straw figure, not worthy of anyone's notice. Since his fangs have been drawn, as you so cleverly effected the operation, he has no power except as nuisance value. And why are we bandying words about Oliver, when we both need our sleep," she argued a bit crossly, removing herself from her husband's arms and going toward the bed. But he caught her up before she reached it.

"I may be tired but I am not comatose, and I expect to experience some of that influential treatment the Duke desires you to practice on me. Wellington must be obeyed, you know. It's your patriotic duty," Tony insisted, laughing, and placing her carefully beneath the sheets, turning only to douse the candles, before joining her.

"I am a great admirer of the Duke's," she murmured, before Tony's actions made further conversation unwelcome and unnecessary.

4 FREE BOOKS

TO GET YOUR 4 FREE BOOKS WORTH $18.00 — MAIL IN THE FREE BOOK CERTIFICATE T O D A Y

Fill in the Free Book Certificate below, and we'll send your FREE BOOKS to you as soon as we receive it.

If the certificate is missing below, write to: Zebra Home Subscription Service, Inc., P.O. Box 5214, 120 Brighton Road, Clifton, New Jersey 07015-5214.

FREE BOOK CERTIFICATE

4 FREE BOOKS

ZEBRA HOME SUBSCRIPTION SERVICE, INC.

YES! Please start my subscription to Zebra Historical Romances and send me my first 4 books absolutely FREE. I understand that each month I may preview four new Zebra Historical Romances free for 10 days. If I'm not satisfied with them, I may return the four books within 10 days and owe nothing. Otherwise, I will pay the low preferred subscriber's price of just $3.75 each; a total of $15.00, *a savings off the publisher's price of $3.00.* I may return any shipment and I may cancel this subscription at any time. There is no obligation to buy any shipment and there are no shipping, handling or other hidden charges. Regardless of what I decide, the four free books are mine to keep.

NAME _____

ADDRESS _____ APT _____

CITY _____ STATE _____ ZIP _____

TELEPHONE (____) _____

SIGNATURE _____
(if under 18, parent or guardian must sign)

Terms, offer and prices subject to change without notice. Subscription subject to acceptance by Zebra Books. Zebra Books reserves the right to reject any order or cancel any subscription.

GET
FOUR
FREE
BOOKS
(AN $18.00 VALUE)

ZEBRA HOME SUBSCRIPTION
SERVICE, INC.
P.O. Box 5214
120 BRIGHTON ROAD
CLIFTON, NEW JERSEY 07015-5214

Chapter Eleven

It was two days after the ball, and Tony had come to Francey's bedroom while she was having her breakfast. Usually they met in the dining room for that meal, but this morning she had overslept and she felt a bit vulnerable receiving him in such a manner. He looked unusually grave.

"I am off for the House, but wanted a word with you before I leave. Father and Philip are leaving for Dorset tomorrow and I think you should go with them," he said, sitting on the side of the bed and regarding her with worried eyes.

"At the height of the season, Tony? You must be mad! We have a host of invitations and then there are my at-homes, which you tell me are becoming popular and quite helpful to you," she protested, putting down her cup suddenly. Then, thinking he might imagine her the most frivolous of women, unwilling to sacrifice some pleasure, she added, "I thought one of the reasons for our marriage was that you needed a hostess. If I am in Dorset I can hardly advance your career."

For a moment she thought he would give free rein to the temper she saw flaring in his eyes, but he took a firm grip on his emotions and replied gently, "I do not think you are foolish or frivolous, Francey, and this is not the time to discuss our marriage. The attempt on Liverpool

129

the other evening was a warning, and several members of His Majesty's government have received ominous threats. It's your safety I am concerned about."

"Have *you* received any threats?" she asked, surprised, her irritation vanishing.

"Well, you may not know it, but that violent agitator, Arthur Thistlewood, has been released from gaol, and he has written some very abusive letters to Sidmouth, whom he hates immoderately. And you know there is talk that Sidmouth may be retiring. I would then be considered for the post of Home Secretary, a rather fraught part to play in these troubled times. I do not agree with the coercive measures taken against the rebels, especially the suspension of the Habeas Corpus Act, and I am trying to restore that right. But irrational creatures like Thistlewood are not amenable to persuasion. He and his cohorts want to overthrow the government, and that cannot be allowed. If he thought I was among those advocating sterner measures, he would include me in the list of ministers to be dispatched," he ended with some humor. "Of course, then you would be an interesting widow."

"This is not a funning matter, Tony, and I think your remark in the worst of taste. But I will certainly not countenance the attempt by some rascally varlet to intimidate me and make me flee to the country, where for all I know, some other disgruntled character could just as easily attack me. But I hardly think that's in the cards. Surely you exaggerate," she scoffed.

Tony sighed with frustration, and said, "I might have known you would take that attitude. I cannot force you to go to Dorset, and I admit, I would miss your lively presence. You are quite a challenge, you know, Francey," he concluded enigmatically. "It was just a suggestion. But I must say I appreciate your loyalty and courage. They are among your most appealing qualities."

"And what are the others?" she asked roguishly, quite intrigued with the idea of wringing from her husband some admission that he cared for her.

"That is a matter we must discuss at some more appropriate time. Tonight, perhaps, in bed," he suggested outrageously.

Francey was too skilled at *badinage* to rise to his bait, but she smiled. "I can make no promises. But you will remember we are going to the theater tonight. I do hope you are not intending to cry off. I so rarely have you as an escort," she added lightly, hoping he would not think she was begging for attention.

"I will not fail you. If I do not escort you my place will be taken by someone more exciting," he mocked. "Fitz, for example."

"I will not add to your consequence by admitting that you are more exciting by far than Fitz, but I welcome your escort," she countered, rather intrigued by the direction of the conversation.

"You are the most interestingly provoking female. We will continue this later," he promised, leaning over and giving her a brief hard kiss. Francey's arms went around him but he shrugged her off. "Sorry, no time now. I must be off," he grinned wickedly and strolled to the door, leaving her embarrassed by his knowledge of her response.

What a devil he was, one moment the stern mentor, the next the alluring beau. And she was annoyed at her own reaction to his lovemaking, allowing him to see how much she was attracted to him. She appreciated his fears for her safety, but she thought he was exaggerating the gravity of the danger. Sighing for all her confused emotions, she rose and rang for Martha. Best to put all these muddled thoughts aside and get on with her day.

Tony had not exaggerated the threats to ministers of state. Even the Prince Regent, now more unpopular than ever due to his gross extravagances, had suffered menaces. Lord Sidmouth was an especial target, and was contemplating retiring from office, his temper and health both tried by the recent events. Most of the disturbances had occurred in the North, but even in London dissidents were becoming more vocal. And the government was under attack by the Whigs for fomenting troubles by employing subversive agents to infiltrate the rebellious groups which were increasingly active. If only the Tory leadership were not so hidebound, Tony thought as he walked down the Mall toward Parliament. For his own part, he was discouraged.

Affairs should never have reached this impasse. Repeal of the Corn Laws, a decent Poor Relief Law and some intelligent direction of the economy would have prevented the ugly mood in the country. And who could blame the poor devils, denied work, paying a shilling a loaf for bread, forced off the land and into the cities' slums. This was not the England he wanted to serve. For all his arrogance, Tony had a strong sense of noblesse oblige, but the Tory allegiance was making it very difficult to implement that sense.

And then there was the vexing question of his marriage. He had little to complain of, he knew. He had a wife other men envied, beautiful, charming, well-bred, intelligent. Francey possessed every asset any man could want. How ignoble of him to want her love as well, and to want her to confess it before he revealed his own. Were they to go on this way, a pleasant relationship with no real depth, no commitment?

But perhaps he was mistaken, and Francey had no vestige left of that warm, endearing love which had attracted him and won him years ago. On both fronts, political and personal, his life was proving a disappointment. Probably it was his own fault, and he was a sapskull to complain when so many others followed paths filled with suffering and tragedy.

Shrugging off his black mood Tony lengthened his stride and hurried on his way. The least he could do was to make his objections known about this projected Coercive Bill.

Tony would have been surprised to know how closely his wife's thoughts echoed his. When the season was over, and Parliament recessed, she and Tony would be returning to the Compton estates in Dorset, and there in the comparative peace of the countryside they might be able to sort out their marriage.

She had hoped by this time to be pregnant. That would surely bring them together. She knew Tony wanted children, as she did, but she refused to be relegated to the status of a brood mare for the Compton title while her husband followed his pleasures elsewhere. She had observed her own circle and recognized the plight of many a wife, abandoned in the country while increasing, while her husband was enjoying the favors of mistresses and generally behaving without any regard for the mother of his children. *She* would not be treated thus, although she recognized she had few options if Tony decided to behave in such an odious fashion.

This was her day to volunteer at the refuge for abandoned women and children. Dressed in her plainest gown of gray muslin she set out in her coach for St. Martin's Lane, a situation as far removed from Grosvenor Square as could be imagined. Although not the worst slums of London, these streets off the Strand were a far cry from the fashionable avenues of Mayfair and broad new Regent Street which the Prince had commissioned.

Lady Elizabeth Austell, much influenced by the publication of Mary Wollstonecraft's *Vindication of the Rights of Woman,* some twenty-five years earlier, had seen a crying need to offer lower middle-class women some refuge from the brutality and desperation of their lives. These were not the wretched poor sent to the workhouses—like so many residents of Seven Dials and Spitalfields—but women who had some claim to respect. The refuge, a rather grim grey stone building in the shadow of the church of St. Martin-in-the-Fields, could house about two dozen women with their children. Here they were fed, clothed and given some useful work—sewing, scrivening if they were capable of it—or training

133

as clerks in suitable establishments.

Lady Elizabeth spent a great deal of time at the refuge, and had enlisted several staunch volunteers, among whom Francey was one of the most devoted. She had begun working at the refuge soon after she had come to London following Archie's death, and she found her contribution satisfying, a much-needed respite from the social round which was expected of her, and which she had to admit she usually enjoyed.

Today she intended to spend some time with Maddy Scanlon, a fragile and unhappy woman who had been at the refuge for a fortnight. She decided first to have a word with Lady Elizabeth to discuss Maddy's progress. Lady Elizabeth received her warmly in her austere office to the left of the rather imposing entrance hall. The refuge had once been the home of a merchant, who fell upon evil days, and who had been induced to part with it for a modest sum.

"Good morning, Francey. I am pleased to see you. You are so faithful in your attendance—which is more than I can say for some of my volunteers. The responsibility of this refuge falls heavily on me at times," Lady Elizabeth admitted as she greeted Francey.

"You need a holiday, Lady Elizabeth. You take your work here too seriously," Francey ventured. She admired the valiant little woman, sitting so straight behind her desk. Lady Elizabeth must be in her sixties, her hair was quite white and her face a bit lined, but her blue eyes sparkled with dedication and determination.

"Alas, I do not feel I can delegate this responsibility to others. There are so many poor souls begging for admission and we have no room for them. I do wish we could secure another suitable building," Lady Elizabeth admitted. "Well, what can I do for you this morning? Such a lovely day, and I think we should all be the better for the fresh air, not least our pathetic inmates."

"I want to talk to you about Maddy Scanlon. I have become quite attached to the woman, and hope to secure

134

her a position as housekeeper, with some friends in Dorset. It would be good for her little girl, too. That child looks so delicate," Francey confided.

"Well, it is always a problem, aiding a woman to leave her husband, no matter how badly he has treated her. The law favors the man in these instances, as you know. If you think Mrs. Scanlon is unhappy enough to take the drastic path of desertion, she must be warned of the consequences. If her husband discovers where she has gone he can force her to return to him, or take custody of their daughter. And you know that is why she is here, because he attempted to molest the little girl," Lady Elizabeth sighed, for this problem like so many others seemed insoluble.

"He knows she has come here, and has made several efforts to force his way in and see her, which she has bravely refused. For a man with some education and a respectable job he has a strangely violent and unstable nature," Francey said, wondering if she knew the real story behind this pitiful tragedy.

"Well, I will support your efforts to spirit Mrs. Scanlon away to the country, but you must be careful, my dear. Aiding a woman to leave her husband is apt to cause you personal difficulty."

"I am prepared to cope with that," Francey insisted in determined tones.

"Of course, the Duke of Compton is a powerful man. He would not allow you to suffer any penalty. How unfair it seems sometimes that rank and privilege give such advantages."

Francey agreed but felt that to mention that rank and privilege also imposed duties sounded too prosy and pretentious. She nodded her head and after a few more words from Lady Elizabeth took her leave to seek out Mrs. Scanlon.

She found her in one of the reception rooms, which had been converted into a work area. Several of the women were sewing, but Maddy Scanlon sat apart, a delicate linen blouse crumpled in her lap, her eyes staring into the distance. She was not ill favored, having a mass of light brown hair, bundled into a loose knot, pale complexion, and huge brown eyes which sought constant reassurance. She could not be more than twenty-five, and although worry and ill usage had taken their toll, she still retained a modest suggestion of youthful attractiveness.

"Maddy, I have come to tell you of a plan which I believe will help you, if you have definitely made up your mind to live apart from your husband," Francey said gently, sitting down quietly across from Maddy and putting a hand on the woman's as it lay flaccid in her lap.

Maddy, bringing her eyes and her mind back as if from a great distance, looked in vague surprise at Francey. She appeared to have difficulty in concentrating on her surroundings.

"You are too kind, Lady Frances. It is Mary who concerns me. Whatever happens to me is of little importance," she admitted wearily.

"Where is Mary today?" Francey asked, hoping to lighten the atmosphere, for Maddy Scanlon appeared so *distraite*.

"Doing sums and writing on her slate, upstairs, with the other children. She has become quite a good reader too, for only seven," Maddy said with pride and a certain energy which had been lacking a moment before. Only when concerned with her daughter could she rouse herself to participate in any conversation. She had told her story to Francey in only the sketchiest fashion, but Maddy had implied that she would never have left her husband if it had not been to save her daughter. Francey wondered, not for the first time, if the child was not his, and the marriage a convenient way out of a dilemma which had frightened Maddy beyond bearing.

"I think I have a solution for you. I have found a nice family, gentry, in Dorset, my own neighborhood, who need a housekeeper, and would be willing to take you on

136

trial. They will accept Mary gladly. Mrs. Pettigrew, the present housekeeper, is an invalid and not up to running the Adamsons' manor house, which is a comfortable establishment. I do believe you would be safe there, and Mary would benefit from the country air." Francey did not make the mistake of promising that Maddy would be happy. She thought that state impossible for this beset woman.

"Could my husband find me there?" Maddy asked with a little more animation.

"I doubt it. Unless he is watching this refuge every minute, he would not know when you left, and certainly only Lady Elizabeth and myself would know your direction. And he must go to his work in the Inns of Court every day, I suppose. We would send you off during those hours."

"I greatly fear he has lost his situation. His opinions are so radical and he has such a temper. I have not mentioned this to anyone, Lady Frances, but you have been so good to me, so understanding, not blaming me or mouthing stupid advice. I think Fred has become involved with Arthur Thistlewood."

Francey bit back an exclamation. Thistlewood was the most dangerous agitator in London, a man of violent habits and intemperate speech, who was determined to overthrow the government and introduce general revolution and anarchy. He had already been imprisoned in connection with the Spa Field riots, and he now was threatening the Home Secretary. If Maddy's husband were to find out that Lord Sidmouth's deputy's wife was aiding Maddy to escape his clutches, who could say what his revenge might be. But Francey could hardly refuse to help Maddy now. She had gone too far.

"Well, I think the best thing is to get you and Mary away before he can take any action. I will arrange matters with Lady Elizabeth if that is what you want to do," Francey spoke with decision. This was no time to temporize, and Tony would have to know about this latest news on Thistlewood and Fred Scanlon.

"Yes. We can be ready immediately. We have not many possessions to pack," Maddy agreed rather pathetically. Francey knew that Maddy had suffered greatly, and was sincerely afraid of her husband, but she wished Maddy had more spirit. Francey could not imagine allowing herself to be victimized by her husband, but she thought ruefully, how do I know that I would act differently in her position?

After a conference with Lady Elizabeth to work out the arrangements to transport Maddy and Mary, Francey spent some time interviewing more recent arrivals among the inmates. Far from depressing her, the stories of these women angered her. That a man could have the power to make their poor lives so miserable raised her ire.

Of course, Parliament had the economy, the radical agitation, the debates on the Corn Laws and the reform movement to worry about, but surely some law could insure that women were not at the mercy of these domestic tyrants. If women had any vote, affairs would be different, but there was not much hope of that when the majority of the population, whatever their sex, were disenfranchised. At least Tony realized the inequity of the current conditions, but his fellow members did not seem to share his concern, and Francey feared that the whole country would suffer from their intransigeance.

So aroused was she by the plight of Maddy and her companions in similar situations, that Francey was too distracted to notice any loiterers when she left the refuge some hours later. Her coachman and two grooms provided plenty of protection and she never gave a thought to her own safety. But as she entered her carriage she was observed by a tall burly man, roughly dressed, who spat on the ground and muttered obscenities as the richly dressed nob drove from the refuge. Fred Scanlon blamed women of her sort for his wife's desertion and he intended to have his revenge.

Chapter Twelve

True to his word, Tony returned from the House to escort Francey to the theatre that evening. Concerned as he was with the state of the country, he was equally worried about the state of his marriage. Their relationship was not progressing the way he had hoped. Fitz's constant presence was annoying—and who knew what Francey was thinking? He had been a fool to allow his pride to gain the upper hand, not to admit that he cared for her. But she made it difficult to break through those defenses she had raised. Well, he must change all that. Persuade her that she mattered to him, that he loved her.

He was not pleased on his arrival at the house in Grosvenor Square to find among his correspondence a scented note from Moira Stacy-Long plaintively asking him to call upon her. He had no interest in renewing his regrettable relationship with that lady and he would tell her so if she persisted. He threw the note in the scrapbasket, regretting that, because of the warm weather, there was no fire where the incriminating letter could be destroyed. Combined with the latest rumors about the radicals, this added annoyance was just a pinprick, but it was one he must not ignore.

When he joined Francey for dinner before the theatre he was quick to pay her a fulsome compliment on her appearance. She did indeed look charming in an apricot gauze tunic over a cream silk shift, with triple bands of lace decorating the hem. Tonight she was wearing a simple topaz necklace with matching earrings and she looked the very picture of elegance.

Francey had the enviable quality, once gowned, of paying no attention to her appearance, intent on more important business. She was eager to tell Tony what she had learned about Fred Scanlon and Arthur Thistlewood, hoping he would not take this information as further proof that she should leave London. She appreciated his concern for her safety, but she was determined not to go.

"Tony, I learned that Arthur Thistlewood might be up to some mischief. It was my day for the refuge and one of the women, abused and threatened by her husband, told me in some desperation that he had become involved with Thistlewood and she is sure they are planning some coup against the government."

"That does not surprise me. Thistlewood was released two months ago after serving a few weeks' sentence for breach of the peace. He claims to have learned his lesson and wants to work with ministers toward reform, but we suspect he is working secretly to foment trouble. Fortunately we have an agent in the confidence of these conspirators and he keeps us informed, but there is no denying that Thistlewood hates Sidmouth and would do anything to bring about his downfall. Wellington wants to call out the Army to quell civil disturbance. I think it is unwise, only adding fuel to the violence. But I don't want you involved in these matters," he concluded with some force.

"What could happen to me?" Francey asked, not impressed with his arguments.

"There have been anonymous threats against Sidmouth, and now I believe they have been extended to me, since I am taking over many of his responsibilities. You could be in jeopardy."

"Nonsense. Henry Sidmouth is an old woman, easily

terrified, but I thought you were made of sterner stuff," she scoffed.

"Francey, you don't understand the nasty mood of the populace. I agree that most of the trouble is brewing in the Midlands, but His Majesty's ministers have the responsibility for keeping the peace. I cannot persuade the cabinet that a conciliatory attitude would abate some of the danger. I admit I am worried."

"If you see your children hungry and your wife in rags, I can imagine you want to take action, violent action, but I agree that such a course solves little. Why can't Sidmouth and Wellington see that?"

"Because they are afraid of revolution. They remember only too well what happened in France. Many of our poor countrymen are desperate."

"Yes, I know that. And what do we do? Go to the threatre, give balls, and generally add to their discontent. Who can blame them," Francey said somewhat bitterly.

"I agree, but we must not show fear. What we must do is try to relieve their suffering. But tonight we have an obligation to our hosts. If you are finished toying with that pudding we must be on our way." Tony appreciated Francey's concern but her stubbornness about her own safety disturbed him. If anything happened to her through his involvement with the government he would never forgive himself. Somehow he must make her realize the danger.

"Please consider removing to Dorset. It will relieve my mind."

Francey did not agree, and she was now beginning to wonder if he wanted her out of the way to conduct some liaison about which she knew nothing. Chiding herself for her suspicions, she abandoned discussion, and they left for their engagement, at Drury Lane.

Their hosts that evening in the box were the Lansforths, among the starchiest of the noble families of the *ton*. The Everelys arrived too late for the farce which had preceded Edmund Kean's appearance in *Rule a Wife*

141

and Have a Wife, by John Fletcher, not perhaps the best production to soothe Francey's irritation with her husband's demands that she leave London. And her mood was not improved by the arrival before the first act of the play of Moira Stacy-Long, escorted by Fitzhugh Lennox.

The luscious brunette gave Francey a cool greeting, but rewarded Tony's brief salutation with a languishing glance, implying shared secrets. Tony refused her overtures by sitting down decisively at his wife's side and ignoring the lady. He only hoped his attitudes reassured Francey that he had no interest in Moira, but he doubted it.

Too clever to show her annoyance at this contretemps, Francey chatted brightly with her husband about the performance when the curtain fell on the first act, but she refused his invitation to stroll in the hall. She was determined not to betray her annoyance, but inside she was seething with emotion. Why had Fitz brought the woman tonight? Had she known that Tony would be among the Lansforths' guests and somehow secured an invitation? Fitz might not have known of Moira Stacy-Long's previous relationship with Tony. Surely he would not have been so maladroit as to introduce the woman into their midst if he had known. Tony appeared impervious to Moira's allures, but that might just be a ploy. Francey silently reproved herself. She was behaving like a jealous shrew.

Tony's irritation was not improved when Lord Lansforth drew him away to the back of the box to quiz him about the government's efforts to quell the growing violence in London.

"Damned rabble should be put in gaol, the whole lot, and then transported." Lord Lansforth, a choleric man was noted for his abrupt manner and impatience with any reform. "The Duke should call out the Army."

Tony demurred tactfully, but Lord Lansforth was well on his favorite topic and would not be gainsaid. Moira took the opportunity to sidle up to the two men and exercise her wiles.

"I am sure Tony agrees, Lord Lansforth, and he has the ear of the Prime Minister," she cooed, batting her eyes at Tony in what Francey considered a disgusting display of her charms.

Tony, not wanting to be impolite to his host, could not, nevertheless, let such notions go unchallenged. "I do not agree that meeting force with force is the answer," he protested sharply. "I could not condone using the Army."

Moira, not deterred, put a cajoling hand on Tony's arm, and changed tack. "Of course, you know best, Tony. The government is fortunate to have your services."

Francey, who heard but soft murmurs, was in little doubt that Moira was making advances to her husband, which he did not seem reluctant to receive, and Francey's temper rose. Before she could unwisely give rein to it, Fitz slipped into the seat beside her, and she had to give him her attention.

"I see your husband consented to escort you this evening, Francey. He has been very dilatory in his duties lately, but he is wise to keep an eye on you," Fitz teased.

"Oh, do you think I am casting my eyes about to a complaisant *cicisbeo*, Fitz?" Francey replied in quelling tones.

"Of course not, Francey. Very bad *ton* for a new bride. But he is very occupied with his ministerial duties. I hear Sidmouth intends to retire. Then Tony would become Home Secretary, no doubt, and be even busier than he is at the moment."

"Not too busy to flirt with the likes of Moira Stacy-Long," Francey blurted out, and then—confused and angry at her gauche remark—made matters worse by railing at Fitz. "Why did you bring her this evening? I did not know she was among your *inamoratas*."

Fitz grinned. "Don't get your dander up, my dear. I am innocent of your suspicions. The lady requested my escort. I understand the Lansforths were persuaded to invite her, and she needed a knight errant."

"She is a hussy." Francey was ashamed of displaying her jealousy but could not help herself. Fortunately Fitz was to be trusted with her confidences.

"Don't be a pea-goose, Francey. She represents no threat to you." Fitz was surprised at Francey's reaction.

Francey laughed a bit feebly, then recovered her aplomb. "I know, but at one time she and Tony were quite intimate. She is the reason I broke off our engagement," she confided with candor.

"I had heard some talk of that, but believe me, my dear, you have Tony's utter devotion." Fitz abandoned his lighthearted air and spoke with a tone of sincerity which impressed Francey.

"You are right, as usual, Fitz. I am rag-mannered to be behaving thus. The curtain is about to rise. Just as well, as you must be bored to tears with all my silliness," she insisted with more insouciance than she felt.

Fitz patted her hand, a movement not unnoticed by Tony, who crossed the box to resume his seat, which Fitz abandoned with a certain relief. At times women could be puzzling. Surely, no man who had Francey as a wife could be attracted to Moira Stacy-Long, whom Fitz considered a trifle full blown and too obvious for words. He hoped he had calmed Francey's fears, and she knew that her confidences were safe with him.

The rest of the evening passed without further incident. Francey, embarrassed by her disclosures, spent the next interval talking with her hostess, a plain woman with little conversation, subdued by years of living with her intemperate husband. Before the final act Tony insisted she stroll about the theatre and she managed to behave in unexceptionable fashion, although she had not entirely banished her suspicions. Dear Fitz. He was a good friend and quite right to reprove her for her behavior. Moira Stacy-Long, subdued by Tony's obvious indifference, abandoned her attempts to lure him into a flirtation and the company went on to supper in some harmony.

Tony had been careful not to pay any attention to Moira during the supper of champagne and lobster at Grillon's, and Francey observed that he seated himself at a distance from the lady despite her best efforts to secure him as a supper partner. Fitz was no doubt right and she had made a cake of herself over nothing.

Tony was relieved to see that her manner toward him had softened by the time they left the hotel to seek their carriage. If he had not been so concerned with the undertones of the evening he would have noticed that their exit from the hotel was observed by a dark figure, sidling behind a convenient pillar. As Tony stepped forward to assist Francey into their carriage, the man darted out and raised a cudgel, intent on delivering a crippling blow to Tony or to Francey. Fortunately their footman cried out and Tony turned, so the blow went glancing off his shoulder. Before either Tony or his minions could apprehend the fellow he had rushed off into the night, muttering obscenities, his evil purpose thwarted.

Tony's inclination was to chase after the ruffian, but his first duty was to protect Francey and he bustled her into the carriage and ordered his coachman to hurry home. Turning to soothe his wife he was amused to note that she was more angry than frightened.

"How dare that man attack us!" Francey cried.

"Possibly the man saw some fashionably dressed nobs leaving that impressive establishment and his anger got the better of him. No doubt he was some poor wretch, a veteran of the Army who cannot find work, and believes any well-off lord fair game," Tony explained trying to put as good a face as possible on the distressing incident.

"Nonsense. I heard him call your name. 'Everely,' he said," Francey argued. "He wanted to harm you."

"Or you, Francey. So now you can see my warnings have some foundation," Tony insisted. They were still arguing when they reached Grosvenor Square. But at least the incident had distracted Francey from her annoyance with Moira Stacy-Long. Tony wondered if he should try to plead his innocence of the lady's overtures or if such an approach would raise Francey's hackles.

He was still undecided when they retired for the night. Pressing her hand gallantly he bowed at her bedroom door. "I will leave you to get changed, my dear, but you have not seen the last of me this night," he promised with a meaningful glance, before repairing to his own chamber.

Francey smiled, with an invitation in her eyes she could not repress, despite her best intention not to welcome Tony to her bed while this business of Moira Stacy-Long lay between them. But the frightening encounter outside Grillon's had banished her jealousy and she craved the comfort that she experienced in Tony's lovemaking.

Hurrying into her nightdress, she dismissed Martha rather abruptly, eager for her husband's presence. Her blond hair brushed and unbound, she walked to the window and pulled aside the heavy silk curtains to allow the air to cool her feverish cheeks. What an impossible evening it had been, culminating in that attempted attack. She hoped Tony had suffered no ill effects from the man's blow. He had appeared to discount it, but for the first time since Tony had issued his plea for her to escape to the country she felt some apprehension. Was he in danger? Were they both to become the subject of further attempts? As she looked into the square she thought she saw a shadowy form behind a tree, watching the house. Could the man have followed them home? If so, that meant he knew their direction as well as their names. They were the targets of his attack. As she continued to watch the street, the connecting door between her bedroom and Tony's opened and he entered, crossing the room to where she stood, transfixed at the window.

He put a gentle arm about her and asked, "What are you dreaming of, loitering here by the window, when you should be awaiting your lord and master in bed," he asked mockingly.

Francey settled gracefully into his protecting embrace. "Tony, there is a man outside, watching the house, just there behind that tree in the square."

"Nonsense, my dear. I see no one," he insisted, thinking she was seeing danger where none existed.

And when Francey peered anxiously again, she, too, could see nothing. "A shadow, perhaps. I might have imagined it. But it has been an upsetting evening. Are you sure you feel no pain from that man's blow?"

Her tender concern was a balm, but Tony hastened to reassure her. "It was just a glancing blow. No harm done." He wondered if in this softened mood, she would listen to his pleas for her to travel to Dorset.

"I suppose you suffered far worse in the war," Francey said a bit tartly, masking her concern.

"Yes, indeed. But you are unaccustomed to such violence, my dear. Naturally it frightened you."

"And made me angry. I am not such a tender flower that I do not know there are people out there hoping to harm us. And, in a way, I do not blame them, poor souls," she said with remarkable forbearance.

"Yes, it's difficult not to feel great sympathy for some of them, but violence will not answer. If these heinous Coercive Acts pass the House, more trouble will be caused than averted," Tony fumed.

"Well, you are doing all you can to avert the trouble," Francey acknowledged, accepting generously that Tony was more occupied with the state of the country than with their personal concerns. She, too, had the plight of the people constantly on her mind, although she often felt that perhaps women cared more than men about the personal welfare of families, for men claimed to take the wider, less compassionate view. Bread for hungry children was an immediate necessity, the rights and wrongs of government action less compelling to her.

"You must be weary of my constantly bemoaning the government's policy, and my unavailing efforts to change the stubborn minds of Liverpool and Sidmouth," Tony said, caressing her with a warm wandering hand.

"I knew of your determination when I married you," Francey answered more shortly than she meant.

"I wonder. The conditions which brought about our marriage were not the best," Tony answered, in a distracted manner, his passion rising.

"Perhaps Moira Stacy-Long might have been your choice in different circumstances." As soon as the words left her mouth Francey regretted them, but somehow she had to bring her fears out in the open.

"In no circumstances would that lady have been my choice. Neither six years ago nor now. Her appearance tonight was none of my doing. I think she's a dead bore, a selfish, grasping harpy, if you must know." Tony protested in a decisive manner, happy to make his feelings known. "No sensible man would prefer Moira to you, Francey," he concluded.

"Ah, but most men are not sensible when they fall in love," she countered.

"True, and I am not feeling sensible now. You are too distracting, with the moonlight shining on your hair, and er, other attributes," Tony replied, sweeping her into his arms and carrying her over to the bed. "I will show you what I mean, my temptress."

And he did, all talk of political matters and Moira Stacy-Long forgotten in the heat of the moment. Francey made no further argument but gave herself up to the delights which Tony always made her experience, responding in the grip of their mutual passion.

Chapter Thirteen

Francey, much cheered by Tony's opinion of Moira Stacy-Long, awoke the next morning to a feeling of well-being, enhanced by seeing Tony still lying by her side. Could they at last be achieving that true partnership of mind, heart and body which she craved?

Sitting up, propping the pillows behind her, she regarded her sleeping husband with some complacency. He looked much younger, less formidable, his dark hair mussed, his bared shoulder revealing the strength which was hidden by the fashionable coats he wore so casually. Really, he was a most compelling man, and she was in danger of losing all sensibility when he exerted his charm upon her unresisting body. He might have reassured her about Moira Stacy-Long, but he had not really confessed his love. His actions certainly gave proof of his passion for her, but she wanted the words. Was he waiting for her avowal? She remembered with shame her early, callow obsession with him. If he was expecting that kind of uncritical devotion now, he would be disappointed. She recognized his faults—hot temper, arrogance, stubbornness—but equally she appreciated his virtues—intelligence, determination, a sense of responsibility toward the less fortunate, and a real devotion to his duty as he saw it.

But, of course, she was deluding herself. His paramount appeal was his ability to make her feel the passion he evoked when he made love to her, those compelling grey eyes avid with desire, that skilled expertise which roused her to a frenzy. Surely these feelings could not endure, but must be tempered in the years ahead by friendship, trust and a steady affection.

Her musings were interrupted by Tony's stirring, and casting a slumberous eye upon the picture she made. "What an enticing sight to greet me," he murmured, reaching up an arm to draw her down to him. It was at least an hour later that they finally left their bed.

If Tony's obvious interest had lulled Francey's suspicions, and strengthened her own devotion, it had not altered her resolution to remain in London and pursue her plans to rescue Maddy Scanlon. She had written to some neighbors in Dorset who had promised Maddy a place, and all that remained was to dispatch the poor harassed woman and her daughter.

Parliament had recessed until November, but Tony appeared loath to leave London, although he continued to urge Francey to visit Compton Towers, where Philip and the Duke were eager to receive her, and her own parents complained of her absence. She was tempted to take Maddy herself, but only if Tony promised to follow her to the country. She would broach the matter to him that very evening. She could not see that his remaining in London would serve any purpose with Parliament recessed. Most of the important men in the government had already left town.

Settling to her desk after breakfast she wrote a note to Lady Elizabeth setting out her plans, eager to remove Maddy Scanlon from any danger. That she herself could suffer from her championship of the woman never crossed her mind. But she would be glad to absent herself from the heat, dirt and misery of the city.

Another reason she wished to leave was that the presence of Sidney Portman was a constant irritation to her. No matter what Tony said, she found the man detestable. Moreover she did not trust him, although she had no cause to doubt his loyalty to Tony. She knew he disliked her, but could not fathom the reason, and since his antipathy made her uncomfortable she would be happy to put him behind her.

Luncheon that day only reinforced her intention to be quit of Grosvenor Square. They were alone, as Tony was at White's, and the necessity of making conversation with Captain Portman raised her hackles. Always correct, if somber, he made little effort to charm her.

Desperate to find some innocuous topic to ease the situation, Francey suggested that since Parliament was now in recess Captain Portman might take a holiday.

"I am hoping to persuade Lord Everely to escort me to Dorset in the next few days," she offered brightly as she toyed with some roast chicken, for which she had little appetite.

"I feel it would be injudicious for either Lord Everely or myself to leave London at this time," he replied coldly, his mouth pressed tight and his eyes full of scorn.

"Why? Lord Sidmouth has retired to his estates near Reading. He evidently feels the need of rest and recreation, so he cannot expect his deputy to do less," Francey said, annoyed to find herself speaking in the prosy tones adopted by her adversary.

"Lord Sidmouth was troubled by the attack on Lord Liverpool, and, I believe, feared some reprisals against himself. Lord Everely is not so fainthearted."

"No, not in the least, but still he owes a certain duty to his family. And I should think you would like a respite, too. Tony keeps you hard at it," Francey hoped her tone masked her desire to shake him for his stubbornness.

"Not at all. He is doing worthwhile work. It is an honor to serve him."

Francey gave up. The man was impossible. How Tony could put up with his strictures and his priggish manner, she could not fathom. Well, she would not attempt any more overtures. She waved away the pudding and was

151

about to leave when Captain Portman surprised her by saying, in what she considered a menacing tone, "You would be wise to leave London, Lady Everely. It is a dangerous city these days."

"I can't imagine to what you are alluding, Captain Portman. Your warning is most inopportune and rather presumptuous," she answered in her most quelling tone, and then made her escape. He stood politely but she sailed to the door and was through it before he could offer additional words.

Really, it sounded as though he was threatening her, and Tony should hear about his devoted secretary's suggestion. Then she laughed. She was allowing her animosity to get the better of her. But she decided that she would avoid any future occasions to lunch alone with Captain Portman.

Restless, unable to settle down to Scott's novel or to her tapestry, she called for her horse. A ride in the park at this unfashionable hour would blow away her megrims, and rid her of the nasty taste of Captain Portman and lunch. It was a sultry airless day, and a dull heavy cloud was obscuring the sun when she set out sometime later. Trotting down Brook Street across Park Lane, she felt the oppressive atmosphere begin to lift. The throughfares she rode through were quite empty of people and she was beginning to enjoy her ride, spurring her horse into a canter as she entered the park.

How rare it was to have some moments alone. She had dismissed her groom, despite his protests, and the knowledge that no one was aware of her direction acted as a tonic. How difficult it was to avoid the press of social engagements, the efforts to converse with people for whom she cared little. She felt she had fulfilled her responsibilities as a hostess long enough, and it was time to follow her own pursuits.

When two masked men darted from the shrubbery lining the path she did not at first realize what they intended, but her mare, sensing danger, reared up, and

Francey, taken by surprise, was thrown to the ground. The men hurried to her side, and—winded and stunned—she thought they were coming to her aid, but she was soon in no doubt that their efforts were not kindly. One of them threw a fetid sack over her head, and began to drag her from the path toward the shrubbery despite her struggles. Frightened and furious, she attempted to free herself, but to no avail.

"Give the damned mort a good clout. That will settle her," one of her unseen assailants growled.

"She's got worse coming to her, the bitch," the other agreed. Francey renewed her struggles, when suddenly she was free from the harsh hands, and she heard footsteps running away. Then she was released from the hateful covering on her head, and lay gasping for a moment, barely conscious that she had been rescued. Staggering to her feet, she met the mild gaze of a small brown-suited man in a neat hat.

"Willie Clarke, ma'am, at your service. I am a Bow Street runner," he explained, while trying to dust her off. "Can you stand against this tree while I retrieve your horse?" he asked, as if their encounter were in no way exceptional.

Francey, somewhat steadied by the Bow Street runner's phlegmatic manner, tried to get a grip on her rising panic. Her mind was whirling with questions. How had Mr. Clarke appeared so providentially? Was he following her? And who were these men? She leaned groggily against a tree, helpless to answer these questions and conscious of her bruises and of a rising fear that she might faint.

Mr. Clarke, seeing her distress, placed a respectful but calming hand on her shoulders. "If you put your head down between your knees, I believe your giddiness will pass off. It has been most upsetting, I know, but you are quite safe now. Unfortunately the villains who attacked you ran off, and my first duty is to protect you," he insisted. In his experience ladies of her sort had little stamina, and goodness knows she had suffered a frightening assault.

"Thank you, Mr. Clarke," Francey said after a moment during which she had followed his advice and found her senses steadying. She was rather ashamed of her weakness, having always prided herself on her courage, and now she was in danger of reacting like a trembling fool. "I am most beholden to you. Who knows what my fate would have been if you had not driven those scoundrels off? Who could they have been? This is not the usual scene frequented by such types. They meant to rob me, I suppose. But I don't understand how you were able to come so quickly to my aid."

"Lord Everely hired me to keep an eye on you, milady. I was a bit behind time, not having a horse, you see," he explained apologetically, relieved to see her color returning. "I must try to get you home. Do you think you could possibly remount your horse? I will lead him and proceed with all caution. Can you manage if I help you?" he asked, clearly worried. He indicated her horse, which had wandered off a few paces and was placidly munching on some leaves.

"Never mind about me. Oughtn't you to chase after those men? They might decide to attack some other rider," Francey said, straightening her skirts and realizing that she looked a mess. Martha and Jepson would be appalled to see her in such a state and the thought of all the explanations she would have to make increased her discomfort.

"Can't be done, I fear. They will be well away by now, and I must see you home safe." Watching her with some concern, he decided she looked a little more the thing, and turned away to gather the horse's reins in his large capable hands. He did not seem as worried as Francey about another attack and for the first time, she noticed a heavy truncheon tied to his wrist by a leather thong, a reassuring sight to her.

Throwing off her queasiness she allowed him to assist

154

her into the saddle, fighting off a tendency to shudder. Mr. Clarke grasped the reins, and plodding steadily forward, they made a sedate progress from the park. Francey could only be grateful that they saw no other riders as they left the trail.

On their arrival at Grosvenor Square, Jepson opened the door to the pair, his normal imperturbability disturbed by the sight of his mistress accompanied by a Bow Street runner. That Lady Frances could have been apprehended by such a person was unthinkable, so she must have been rescued from some dire fate. Coming to the proper conclusion, Jepson took charge of both his mistress and Mr. Clarke. He would not demean himself by questioning either of them, but Francey quickly satisfied his curiosity.

"Will you see that Mr. Clarke receives some refreshment, Jepson? He has just rescued me from a nasty predicament. I want to talk to him at length, but perhaps I had best change out of this dirty habit. See to it that he waits, will you?" she asked. Then turning to Mr. Clarke she thanked him, but thinking, perhaps, that he might feel somewhat uneasy in these impressive surroundings, she gave him a tremulous, "Do wait for me, Mr. Clarke. I want to hear more about this—why Lord Everely hired you and what you think those men intended."

Mr. Clarke, not one whit discomposed by the marble-floored hall, nor by Jepson, agreed stolidly. "I must give in my report, milady, but I can spare a few moments."

"Thank you for rescuing me and for all your help. Jepson, see that Mr. Clarke has some ale, or whatever he desires." Francey made her way upstairs, hoping that Mr. Clarke would be comfortable, but wondering a bit what Jepson would think of the truncheon still dangling from that stalwart wrist. Now that the danger was past, she intended to get to the bottom of the problem posed by Mr. Clarke. Halfway up the stairs she heard the front door open and Tony entered. She turned, wanting to see his reaction to Mr. Clarke, and she was not disappointed.

"Clarke, what are you doing here?" he quizzed, ignoring the hovering Jepson, and throwing his stick and hat on a nearby chair.

"I have just rescued her ladyship from an attack, sir. The varmints ran off before I could apprehend them, seeing that I was occupied in restoring her ladyship to her house safely," he reported.

"And is she safe?" Tony asked a bit wildly.

"Of course, I am, Tony," Francey called from midway up the stairs. "But a bit disheveled. I want to talk to Mr. Clarke, so don't try to hurry him away before I have the chance. You might entertain him in the meantime. You'll have a chance to sort out your stories," she said with a wicked glint in her eye, which her husband did not see, although he suspected she wanted a full accounting for this conspiracy to protect her. Now her temper would be up, he knew. Well, the important matter was that she had been rescued. They could go into the rights and wrongs of Mr. Clarke's employment later.

"Are you sure you were not harmed, Francey?" Tony asked, walking partway up the stairs to inspect her. Mr. Clarke sat down patiently in a very unwelcoming chair in the hall, his hat placed carefully on his knees as he waited for the lord and his lady to finish their conversation. It was all in a day's work to Willie Clarke.

"Do not ring a peal over Mr. Clarke, Tony. I am at fault, riding in the park without a groom. Mr. Clarke managed to chase off the two men who tried to rob me, if that was their intent." Francey made light of the episode, but she had begun to wonder if robbery had really been the varlets' motive. Tony had every doubt.

"Hurry up and change, Francey, and meanwhile I will hear what Mr. Clarke has to say. But you have not heard the last of this," he warned sternly. "You could have come to real harm, and it was not just a casual attack."

"Yes, my lord. You may suitably chastise me in a few moments," Francey agreed, sobering a bit, as she realized that Tony was really extremely worried. There was more

156

to this matter than she had at first imagined. What angered her was that he had not told her of Mr. Clarke, or of the possible danger. Well, that was not quite fair, she conceded, as she repaired to her bedroom and let Martha assist her into a clean gown, and helped her to brush her hair, and wash away some of the results of her adventure.

He had wanted her to leave for Dorset because he had feared just such an incident. Her sangfroid had been misplaced. She should have listened to him, but her natural reluctance to take orders from an arrogant husband had made her discount his fears. Most unfair of her.

Francey, when in the wrong, was not averse to admitting her transgressions, and it was a much-chastened Lady Everely who met her lord in the library a mere quarter of an hour after their discussion on the stairway. She was not surprised to see Mr. Clarke seated comfortably across the desk from Tony, his truncheon by his side, but his notebook on his knee.

"I really am contrite, Tony, to have given you and Mr. Clarke all this worry," she admitted in a most winsome manner, but if Mr. Clarke was gratified by her apology, Tony was not deceived. He knew she would not be satisfied with specious excuses.

"I hired Mr. Clarke to keep an eye on you, because I suspected just such an occurrence as happened today. If you will not take the most elementary precautions, someone must do it for you. You are fortunate, and so is Mr. Clarke, that no harm resulted," Tony said, still not appeased.

"Well, you must have had more evidence than the general threats you told me about. And I suppose that business at the theatre the other evening raised your hackles, but I cannot think who would want to single me out for such treatment," Francey confided, her brow wrinkling. The idea that she had such a vengeful enemy was not a happy one.

"There are more than several malcontents who would be pleased to mount an attack on one of His Majesty's government, and I have a feeling that your championship of those poor women at Lady Elizabeth's refuge has not made you popular," Tony explained. Then, turning to Mr. Clarke, he asked, "Have you any idea who the attackers were?"

"No, my lord, it all happened so quickly, and I was a bit behindhand in catching up with her ladyship. It was a close-run affair. A few minutes later and they might have made off with her. It was not robbery, I believe, but kidnapping that the villains had in mind."

"Yes, I rather suspected that. Once they had her, they would probably have tried to extort a handsome reward for surrendering her," Tony agreed.

Francey, a bit annoyed at being discussed as if she were a purloined piece of baggage, protested, "That's ridiculous. They would never get away with such a plot. Certainly not with the vigilant Mr. Clarke on their trail," and she gave that gentleman a blinding smile, which appeared not to affect his stolidity.

"Yes, Clarke, we are very grateful," Tony said shortly. He was not prepared to tell Francey that her fate might have been much more hideous. Her attackers might not have been interested in ransom but in vengeance. And to that end they would have had no compunction about killing her. But that was not an outcome he would suggest, not even to put her on her guard.

Mr. Clarke was again thanked and then he sped on his way, but not dismissed from the case, Francey noted. Francey wondered what he would do now—perhaps take up a position near the house, prepared to repel any other accosters. She had great difficulty in regarding the whole affair as seriously as Tony wanted, but the idea of an enemy dedicated to harming her was difficult to comprehend. Still, she was a bit shaken by the whole business, and had to agree that Tony might have some justice in his concern. And it was too bad of her to cause him this worry when he had so many other grave matters on his mind.

"I know I was foolish to venture out alone, Tony. I find it so constricting always to be shadowed by a groom, but I admit I behaved like a pea-goose. You have every right to be angry."

"You know how to disarm a chap, Francey. Six years ago you would never have admitted you were in the wrong," Tony replied mildly.

"Six years ago I was not in the wrong," Francey said sharply, then regretting her reference to their past differences, she tried a conciliatory approach. "I am mean to try you so, when I had almost decided to give in to your urging and leave for Dorset. But Captain Portman made me angry at luncheon. Why, he almost threatened me! Tony, that man dislikes me. For all I know, he might have attacked me if he had thought of it."

Tony scoffed at such a ridiculous idea. "Portman may be a bit stiff but he is neither a fool nor a villain. You really have taken an aversion to the poor man, and I can't see why. He is most diligent and devoted," Tony reproved. Dismissing Captain Portman as of no account, he returned to the vital matter. "I am relieved that you will go to Dorset, Francey."

"Yes, but only if you come, too. There is no reason for you not to, with Lord Sidmouth away, and Parliament in recess. Please say you will." She came up to him and placed a pleading hand on his arm, glancing into his eyes with a melting look.

"And how will you reward me if I do?" he asked, taking her into his arms and looking at her with ardent eyes.

"I will give you your heart's desire, sir," she replied, teasing, but a blush rose to her cheek despite her effort to speak lightly.

"That is a promise no man could refuse. I will hold you to it, madam. And now put temptation from me. If I am to accompany you to Dorset I must make some arrangements. I will not subject you to the disapproval of the

159

estimable Portman, so begone. I will claim my reward this evening," he promised with a friendly leer, and a laughing kiss, before patting her insolently on her backside and waving her away.

"Oh, la, sir, you put my heart atremble." She gave a *gamin* grin and made her way to the door. Then she paused and looked back at Tony, waiting patiently before her final sally.

She paused, then demanded saucily, "But all bets are off if the wretched Portman accompanies us. Give him a holiday. It might improve his temper."

Before Tony could reply to this demand she whisked through the door leaving behind an amused and rueful husband.

Chapter Fourteen

The wretched Portman did not accompany the Everelys to Dorset, but a large entourage wended its way to Compton Towers. Maddy Scanlon with Mary had a coach to themselves, well guarded by several outriders. They had been spirited from the refuge in St. Martin's Lane from the back of the premises the night before the Everelys' departure, the dark flitting arranged by the invaluable Mr. Clarke. If any interested parties had been observing they would have seen little but the usual exodus of domestics from the premises, but Francey was not completely reassured. Somehow she suspected Fred Scanlon or his cohorts had learned of her interest in Maddy and she feared they had not heard the last of that dangerous unstable man.

Tony had emphasized the legal position, which Lady Elizabeth had corroborated. Coming between a wife and husband was serious business, but a Duke's son had influence with the magistrates that an average citizen did not possess. Francey thought the law unfair, but agreed that they had undertaken a hazardous mission in aiding the beset Maddy to leave her husband. Francey's hope was that the violent Fred Scanlon would be apprehended for plotting against the state and be imprisoned. Only then would Maddy feel safe.

Tony saw the justice of her rescuing the woman from

Scanlon's brutal treatment. Although he could not but wonder what Francey herself would have done if she had found herself in a like situation. He conceded, although only to himself, that Francey would certainly be more than a match for a vicious and cruel husband. He wondered what his own reaction would be if Francey took him in dislike and decided she had endured enough from an unwanted mate. He must see to it affairs did not reach that impasse, he concluded wryly. Marriage to Francey could be an exhausting business.

Maddy was delivered safely to the Adamsons, the Dorset family who had agreed to employ her, and the cavalcade continued to Compton Towers where they were welcomed eagerly by the Duke. If he hoped for some news of an expected heir he did not voice his disappointment when nothing was said of that much-wanted arrival.

The late July and early August days drifted by lazily with the usual country pursuits. Tony might have been restless, away from the onerous government duties he enjoyed, but he did not complain. He was determined to use this holiday to cement his relationship with his wife, and she did not repulse his efforts.

Picnics, dances, dinners, expeditions to nearby Poole where he consolidated his position with his constituents, and the renewal of ties with the Duke's tenants occupied their days pleasantly. The disturbances in the Midlands and the North had not penetrated into Dorset where the people were busy with their crops and village occupations. The Duke and Philip were good landlords. No satanic mills or grimy factories darkened the landscape, and the violence of London seemed an evil dream.

The absence of the ubiquitous Portman was another boon, and Francey plotted to have that efficient if unattractive secretary replaced. If neither Tony nor Francey expressed their contentment with the marriage which had been forced upon them, the result was evident. All was peace and harmony among the chalk downs and fertile valleys of south Dorset.

Francey thoroughly enjoyed the freedom of unescorted rides around the countryside. Sometimes Tony accompanied her but more often she rode alone. That she was in any danger in somnolent rural Dorset never occurred to her. She reveled in the solitude and release from the restrictions of her London life. So she was quite unprepared when the blow fell.

One afternoon, returning from an impromptu visit with an ailing farmer's wife to whom she had delivered some delicacies, she decided to take a shortcut through the densely wooded acres which divided the Compton estate from her father's lands. She had set out later than she had intended, and she was to be back for a dinner to which the Duke had invited a small company. She had roamed these roads as a girl with her brother Robert and with Tony, and knew them well. They held no terrors for her, and she entered them confidently. Midway through she thought she heard the stealthy sound of a horse's hooves behind her, but she dismissed it as her imagination.

As she rode down the narrow path bounded on both sides by heavy oaks and beeches, suddenly from the undergrowth four masked men burst forth, startling her horse, which reared in fright throwing her to the ground. Before she could regain her feet two of the men had grasped her in strong arms, and one of them pushed a noxious smelling rag against her mouth, holding her easily despite her efforts to wrench her head away. That was the last she knew as she sank insensible to the ground, to be picked up and carried away by one of her assailants.

Twilight fell slowly over Compton Towers, the fading sun lingering to cast a benign glow on the grey stone turrets of the imposing estate. Tony, who had accompanied his brother Philip into Poole that afternoon, reached home quite late, eager for a bath and a drink, knowing that his father's guests would be early, for the Comptons did not keep late dining hours in the country. So he hurried his preparations and it was near six o'clock when he entered his wife's room, expecting to escort her to the drawing room. He was greeted by emptiness and silence. Could Francey have gone down before him? He hesitated, and before he could follow her, her abigail, Martha, entered the room.

"Ah, Martha. Has Lady Everely gone down yet?" Tony asked cheerfully.

"No, sir, she has not yet returned from her visit to Farmer Reade. I was a bit worried, for she had said she would be back long before this. Could she have decided to stay? We have received no message in the servants' hall," Martha confided, her concern evident.

"I doubt it. She knew the Duke had invited guests for this evening and he was expecting her to act as hostess. Lady Everely is not that inconsiderate," he spoke a bit sharply, for the maid's news was disturbing. Could she have suffered some mishap, thrown from her horse, perhaps?

"She rode alone, I presume," he asked, knowing the answer.

"I suspect so, my lord. She usually did, stubborn she is, and no use asking her to use any care," Martha fussed.

"Well, I am sure she is all right, delayed somehow, although it is not like her to forget to send a message." He tried to temper his apprehension. No point in sending the gloomy Martha into hysterics. She was an old and valued retainer, but apt to look on the black side of things and she always feared the worst. "I will inquire into it. Meanwhile ask downstairs if any word arrived from her," he ordered calmly, hiding his disquiet.

In the drawing room, Tony found that his father and Philip were also concerned. They greeted him with questions which he could not answer.

"We will have to mount a search party. She must have had an accident," the Duke said. "And damn it, our guests are arriving. I just heard a carriage roll up. What shall we tell them?"

Before they could give orders to send out a party, the first of the guests had arrived, a magistrate and his imposing wife, a most august pair who had to be greeted with composure. Tony left that task to his father and hurried into the hall to make the needed dispositions. He was now almost frantic, convinced Francey had come to some harm. Returning to the drawing room, he excused himself to the gathering company, and informed them that he must ride out and search for his wife.

Stopping only to change into riding gear, he rushed to the stables, where he learned to his consternation that Francey's mare had just returned to the barn, winded and riderless, her sides scratched by brambles, neighing and snorting in fear. It was as he had thought, Francey had been thrown, good horsewoman that she was, and she was lying out there somewhere unable to seek help. Ordering his horse and marshalling some grooms to ride with him, he set off toward the Reade farmhouse, hoping to retrace Francey's path and find her before he reached the farmer's.

Francey was nowhere near the Reade farmhouse, or even on Compton property. Her captors had taken her to a mean house in Bere Regis, a small sad village shrouded in yew trees and dominated by its overlarge Norman church. The villagers, an isolated brooding lot, took little notice of the outside world, but protected their own with a fanatic loyalty. They kept to themselves and did not welcome interference from the outside. Among Francey's captors was a Bere Regis man, who had been chosen for his very allegiance to the village.

Of course, Francey, coming slowly from her drug-induced sleep, knew none of this. When she first

165

regained consciousness, she was aware only of a muddled hazy view of a darkened shuttered close room.

She was lying on a rude bed on a straw mattress, which puzzled her, for she had expected to see the familiar four-poster with its silk hangings, in her chamber at Compton Towers. Then she remembered. She had been attacked, drugged, abducted, in the forest on her ride back from Farmer Reade's.

With an effort, Francey struggled to a sitting position—it was difficult because her head throbbed and her whole body felt bruised and feeble. She recognized the effects of the drug, and although she felt weak and groggy, her immediate reaction was confusion followed by anger and the rueful realization that she had ignored Tony's warnings. Now, she found herself in an unenviable position with no idea of what lay in store. She was not long to remain in ignorance. As she tried to gather her wits together she heard footsteps and then the door to her prison opened.

"Ah, my fine lady is awake," sneered the man who entered. Beyond his height and a certain swaggering air, there was little to observe of his appearance for he was masked.

Francey braced herself, determined not to show fear, but she could not but be intimidated by the tall figure looming over her. The mask, which was in reality a black hood covering his whole face down to his shoulders, somehow made the confrontation more chilling. Two eyes were peering from the holes cut in the material, fearsome eyes unblinking but filled with hatred and cold satisfaction at her plight. Somehow she marshalled her scattered wits and returned his stare with disdain.

"What is the meaning of this attack and abduction?" she asked, keeping her voice steady with an effort.

"You've led us a fine chase, madam. But we have you now and intend to hold you until you provide the information we need," the man answered. Francey was surprised at his speech. If not cultured it was certainly not the crude argot of the streets, nor the soft burr of rural Dorset.

"I have no idea what you want of me, but I must warn you that this day's work will cost you dear. Do you think there will be no search for me? You shall suffer the full penalty of the law when I am rescued," she said bravely, concentrating on not showing her fear. Somehow the man's speech and confident air did not encourage her to think she might bribe or gull him to secure her freedom.

"I want to know what you have done with my wife. You could end up in prison yourself milady, abetting the flight of a wife from her husband. I know you have spirited Maddy and Mary away to some secluded spot, and I intend to get them back."

"You must be Fred Scanlon," Francey replied, seeing that there was no use in evasive tactics. "You tried to abduct me in Hyde Park," she accused.

"Yes, and would have succeeded, if that pesky Bow Street runner had not turned up so handily. He will not rescue you now. And if you don't want to feel my fist you will tell me Maddy's direction without delay. I have no compunction in hitting a lord's lady."

"Yes, I have no doubt you would have no compunction in hitting me. You certainly have practice. Poor Maddy was forced to leave because of your brutality, and I was pleased to aid her." Francey might have been a bit more cautious in her dealings with the violent and unstable Fred Scanlon, but her anger was fast mastering her fear.

Scanlon laughed, a reaction more terrifying than curses or threats. "I have to admire your spirit, madam, but it will avail you nothing. I will leave you to think about your position, and perhaps after a few hours of hunger and darkness, you will see the sense of giving me the information I want."

"Why should I do that? You would not let me go. I could testify against you and you could find yourself in Newgate or worse. The law is quite severe against abduction of a Duke's daughter-in-law." Francey knew he could not afford to release her even if she did give him Maddy's direction, and she would have to suffer untold indignities and disabling injury before she would do that. What a vindictive cruel thug he was. Even more appalling was the realization that he had some education, had once held a respectable job, and now was reduced to terrorism and menaces against women to satisfy his frustration.

Furious and amazed at Francey's temerity in standing up to him, accustomed as he was to Maddy's shrinkings and pleas for mercy, he lost the tenuous hold on his rage, and, raising his hand, struck Francey a stiff blow to her cheek, causing her to fall back on the bed. She did not cry out or beg him to stop, but gave him such a look of scorn and contempt, that he turned away, baffled by her attitude. Not the way women were supposed to behave. But he was not done with her yet.

"If you don't tell me where Maddy is, I will loose my men on you, and your fine husband would not dirty his hands with you after they have finished." He strode from the room, in a foul temper, slamming and bolting the door behind him, leaving Francey to brood on her possible fate.

She knew that by leaving her alone to contemplate what he had threatened, he hoped to weaken her resolution, so that she would be eager to exchange the information he wanted for her release. Francey had courage but not enough to resist rape. Still, she wondered if betraying Maddy would save her. She doubted it. She knew Fred Scanlon was her abductor. That information would insure his arrest, transportation or even death. He certainly had considered that when he kidnapped her. That meant he had no intention of releasing her, whatever she told him. No, if she were to survive, somehow she would have to escape from this prison.

Dusk had fallen, and looking out the one filthy window Francey could see nothing familiar. She had no idea how long she had been unconscious. These men could have traveled some distance from the woods in which she had been apprehended. She saw nothing from the window to give her hope. Obviously this derelict cottage was in an isolated spot, removed from any neighbors. If she succeeded in escaping from this cell where could she find help? She did not have much time. She could not sit here wringing her hands, praying to be rescued.

Shaking off her fear, Francey tried to think of a plan. If she were going to get free it must be by her own contriving. She looked about the room with some misgiving. There was little in it that she might use as a weapon. The window from which she had viewed the gloomy prospect was small. Even if she managed to break the glass without her captors' discovering it, she doubted she could wriggle through the opening. Aside from the bed and a rickety bureau and spindly chair there were no furnishings in the room. Francey crossed to the bed, and lifted the mattress, made of coarse linsey lining stuffed with lumpy fetid straw, much of it protruding from the ragged covering. But Francey cared little for that. What she was looking for was the roping that supported the mattress on the bed.

Yes, it was as she thought, stout leather thongs were laced between the slats to hold the mattress. She bent to her task, wrenching a good section of the leather thongs from the frame of the bed. She knew she had little time, and she felt her heart pounding, and her hands became wet as she hurried. When Fred Scanlon returned she wondered whether he would be alone or accompanied by his allies, those men who had captured her. If she had heard the angry words being exchanged below stairs she would have been much encouraged.

Scanlon, drinking deep from a mug of ale on the table in the room which served as both parlor and kitchen, wiped his mouth with the back of his hand and looked at the trio around the table with disgust.

"What a bunch of mealy-mouthed clodpolls. You rant

and rave about the toplofty nobs and when one drops into your lap you take fright. Their day of lording it over us is finished. When the revolution comes, useless bitches like that one upstairs will be shot, or better yet, guillotined. That's what the Frenchies did with their aristos, and a good thing too." He spat out the words in a fever of rage.

"I don't hold with that guillotine. Nasty," replied a grizzled older man who was beginning to doubt the wisdom of allowing Fred Scanlon full license. It had seemed a simple job, kidnapping a weak woman, holding her for ransom, for that was what Fred had promised. Bert Sowers, who boasted of his radical political leanings and had a grudge against the local magistrate, had agreed to Fred's plan, and enlisted his two sons, who were much too awed by their father to demur. But one of them, a youngster, spoke up now, aware that his father had misgivings.

"I don't hold with threatening women, either," Matt Sowers said boldly. In a fight he could hold his own with Fred Scanlon, and he knew his brother and father would come to his aid. Just enough ale had been drunk to make the Sowerses, normally rather stolid men, provoked. They had been inveigled into this kidnapping by Scanlon, whose sister had married beneath her, into the Sowers family. Radicals more by laziness than by conviction, they spoke grandly against the gentry in the pub, but when it came to harming a Duke's daughter-in-law they were not so certain of their position.

"You're a mouldy lot, chicken-hearted, and weak," Scanlon stormed. "I should shoot the lot of you."

"Hear, now. None of that. I don't hold with murder, either ours or that fine lady's," Bert cried, his fists tightening, confident that the odds were in his favor.

Scanlon, aware that he had gone too far in his contempt, tried to mend matters. "Do you think it was right for that toplofty bitch to wrest my wife away from me? If someone stole your wife, you'd be mad and determined for revenge."

If young Matt thought Mrs. Scanlon had just cause to escape her violent husband, he kept his peace. There was some power about Fred Scanlon which impressed him. He didn't hold with all his ideas about revolution, but the Sowerses, like many agricultural laborers, were beginning to express their discontent at low wages, poor food, and no relief from grasping landlords. They had heard of the rebellion in the North and although not ready for such violent displays in this Dorset backwater, they were more than discontented, a factor that Fred Scanlon had relied upon in enlisting their support.

Although Scanlon dominated his colleagues by his force of personality, and his sharper intelligence, he knew he could only drive them so far, and without them he would find his task impossible. He set about to assuage their concerns, meanwhile plying them with ale. The malt did not seem to affect him but the more he drank the deeper and more rancorous became his grievances against Lady Frances. After an hour or so, he threw down his mug in a fever of impatience, and stood up, pushing back his chair.

"I have let the chit stew long enough. I will learn Maddy's direction now or she will suffer for it. No haughty touch-me-not quality is going to hide my wife from me." He strode off leaving behind a trio who nodded owlishly in agreement but were fast becoming insensible from the bounteous servings of ale. They were unaccustomed to quantities of free drink and could not deny themselves the pleasure. The ale sapped their energies and their purpose. Fear began to cloud the prospect of enacting vengeance. If Fred Scanlon had reason to call upon them for assistance in subduing Lady Frances he would find himself burdened with doubtful allies.

Chapter Fifteen

Francey had made her preparations, alert for any sound that meant her hateful captor was returning. She had little difficulty in wresting the leather thongs from the bedstead, where the wooden supports had rotted. She only hoped the leather strips would be strong enough for her purpose. At first she had planned to stand behind the door and when Fred Scanlon entered, throw a loop of leather about his neck and try to strangle him, but further reflection had caused her to reconsider. She doubted she had the strength to pull the noose tight enough, or the inclination. She did not really want to kill the man, only to disable him so that she could make her escape. Even taken by surprise he looked strong enough to tear the noose from his neck and then overpower her.

No, a different plan had a certain simple efficacy. She tied one end of the thong to the door post, with some difficulty. Then, with the nail pulled from the bedstead, she secured the other end to the opposite post, creating a trip wire, a method used by the gamekeeper on her father's estate. Scanlon would not be expecting such a snare, and while it would only impede him for a moment, she hoped it would be long enough.

Francey sat down gingerly on the bed and removed her riding boots. Really, she was not feeling at all the thing. The drug's effects had not entirely worn off, and her cheek throbbed where Scanlon had struck her. She took a deep breath and then another, refusing to panic. If her attempt to escape were to fail, she knew it would be the worse for her. Scanlon was a man in the grip of an irrational rage, stirred up by the flight of his wife, and by the wrongs he imagined he had suffered from an uncaring group of heedless politicians. In the latter case Francey had some sympathy for his anger, but his brutal treatment of his wife and child she could not justify. And she had no illusions about what he intended for her. He could not allow her to go free. What she would do if she managed to subdue Scanlon and elude his cohorts baffled her. Well—she gave a slight grimace—she would have to wait upon events.

She crept to the door on her stocking feet, holding the boots. She waited, thinking she had heard footsteps. Yes, Scanlon was returning.

Now all depended on whether he would open the door without due care. She stood behind it, a boot raised. He must have been gone more than an hour, although it seemed much longer. Was she ready? She prayed that her somewhat dubious plan would succeed. She heard him pause at the door, and held her breath, then the bolt slid back and he threw open the door, entering the room in a rush, to fall immediately over the leather strap. She did not hesitate but dealt him a resounding blow with the heel of her boot, and then when he tried to regain his feet, hit him again. Fear made her react with more force than she realized. With a groan, he subsided.

Francey did not wait to assess the damage, but stole out the door and onto the dim landing. Ahead of her was the staircase, steep and shrouded in darkness. Creeping soundlessly down the stairs on her stocking feet, her heart pounding, she did not know what to expect when she reached the bottom, but she would not be recaptured without a struggle.

She heard no voices, but paused peeking around the corner of the doorway to spy out the scene. Three men had collapsed at the scarred table before the fireplace, two of them snoring loudly. The third, little more than a boy, appeared befuddled. Before the trio lay overturned tankards, evidence of their downfall. Sidling around the edge of the room, she made for the door, and reached it in safety. As she drew back the latch, the boy raised his head and looked at her in amazement. He tried to struggle to his feet, but the effort was beyond him.

"Here now, what's this. Where are you going?" He fell against the side of the table, and Francey did not wait for any further reaction, but clumsily pulling the door open, sped out into the night, heedless of the cry behind her. Terror lent speed to her feet and she ran blindly, not knowing where to go, but hoping to put yards between her and her possible pursuers. She knew that Scanlon would not be immobile for long, and then the chase would begin.

On she ran, reaching a lane which led from the cottage. Panting, stumbling in her stocking feet, for she could not stop to pull on her boots, she rushed on toward what she hoped was a village or a friendly house. Dusk had fallen and heavy beech trees lined the lane. Behind any one of the trees there could be an adversary. Her imagination quailed before the idea of capture, but she ran stubbornly ahead. She must have covered at least half a mile, when suddenly a figure loomed up before her, grasping her arms. She cried out in fright and frustration.

"Come now, milady, gently does it. Willie Clarke will help you," came the reassuring tones of the Bow Street runner.

How he had discovered her, she had no clue, but relief poured over her. She stopped, crying, "Mr. Clarke, Mr. Clarke, please save me."

"That is my intention, milady. Can you manage a few more yards. I have a horse and cart hidden just beyond here," the imperturbable Mr. Clarke urged.

Francey took a deep breath, her courage rising. "Of course. But do you suppose I could rest a moment, pull on my boots. I'm afraid my feet are in sad shape," she subdued the quaver in her voice and tried to gather her wits. Now that the immediate danger was fading, she realized that she felt faint and her feet hurt.

"Yes indeed, milady. But we must not waste time. I suspect your captors will follow quickly." Willie Clarke guided her to the edge of the road, pulled her boots from her unresisting hand, and with all the dexterity of a lady's maid, prepared to assist her in putting them on.

"You are a wonder, Mr. Clarke," Francey praised him as together they succeeded in restoring the boots. She stood up gingerly, feeling much more able to face any pursuit. "How in the world did you happen upon me so opportunely?"

"I will explain it all later. Let us find the horse and cart." Willie Clarke put a comforting and respectful hand on her arm and led her rapidly up the road, swerving left to a coppice of trees some yards from their meeting place. Francey limped along as best she could, rapidly regaining her natural spirits. Within moments she was established in the primitive cart, and Mr. Clarke had untied the horse and whipped him up. They were on their way to safety, she hoped.

"My husband and my relatives must be frantic, wondering what has happened to me." At last she summoned the energy to remember her family's concern. Surely several hours had passed since her abduction. What would they be feeling, and what were they doing? No doubt, scurrying about the countryside, mounting search parties, and all to no avail. Tony would certainly ring a peal over her when he discovered she had ridden out without a groom.

His anger would be formidable once he knew she was safe. Well, once again he had been right in his suspicions. She would receive his strictures with meekness. Her recent adventure had dampened her enthusiasm for lonely rides, and her belief that she could manage her life without aid.

"How did you know my direction, Mr. Clarke? And were you prepared to tackle my abductors alone? I am amazed at your temerity. There were four of them, you know," she confided as they trotted along.

"I would have contrived somehow, milady. Some days ago, when I first got down to Dorset, on Lord Everely's orders, I learned that Fred Scanlon had followed you. I had been watching him, and when he left London I was right behind him. He made for this village, where he recruited some allies. They're a closemouthed surly bunch in Bere Regis, but I was able by a few bribes to learn a little of what he meant to do. The folk about here are not very friendly to great landlords, but they have a healthy respect for the Duke of Compton. I learned he had secured this cottage, and was convinced he had some fell purpose in the matter. He had to find a wagon and horses for the abduction. I stayed close by here, not attempting to follow him to Compton Towers. I thought he might have a reason to hole up here, and so he did."

Mr. Clarke, normally laconic, seemed quite weary of this account of his doings, and Francey did not press him. As each mile lengthened behind her prison, she felt more reassured. She thought Bere Regis must be at least twenty miles from the Towers and she settled back to savor her rescue.

Oddly enough, Mr. Clarke did not appear interested in how she had effected her escape and she was too tired to explain. Her head drooped. She could have fallen asleep as they traveled, despite the rude cart and rutted road. In less than an hour they reached the boundaries of the Compton estate, and her fear diminished. She began to wonder about Fred Scanlon and how he learned that hers was the hand which had wrested Maddy and Mary from him.

She could not contain her curiosity, so she asked, "How do you suppose Fred Scanlon knew his wife had left with us? We took the utmost precautions."

"I suspect he had some confederate inside Lady

Elizabeth's refuge, some gullible maid perhaps who believed his lying tongue," Mr. Clarke explained with more fervor than Francey had ever heard from that stolid man.

"Yes, that is possible. I wonder if he has spies elsewhere. He is a dangerous man."

"A threat to the realm, indeed," Mr. Clarke replied. "But we have our methods of dealing with a scurvy cove like that one." Obviously Mr. Clarke had no patience with agitators or disgruntled rebellious citizens. As they rode up the road within a mile or two of the Towers, Francey saw a cavalcade approaching them. She recognized Tony on his black stallion and Philip not far behind riding his usual chestnut. Mr. Clarke pulled his tired horse to a stop and waited for their approach.

Tony checked sharply, causing his horse to rear, and then jumped down tossing the reins to Philip, and rushed to Francey's side, reaching up to grasp her tightly, and help her alight.

"Oh, Francey. You are safe." He held her in a comforting embrace, running his hands over her as if to reassure himself that she had suffered no harm. He bit back a curse when he saw her bruised cheek, but he asked no questions.

"Thanks to Mr. Clarke, here." Francey subsided gratefully into Tony's arms, impervious to the curious stares of Philip and the three grooms in the search party.

"Good job, Mr. Clarke. You will not go unrewarded. Come on up to the Towers and we will hear your story. But now I want to get my wife home." Tony picked up Francey and carried her to his horse. Leaping astride he reached down for her and gathered her up before him. "Explanations can wait," he added tersely and galloped away, leaving Mr. Clarke, Philip and his entourage to follow.

The rooms of the Towers were ablaze with light. Francey realized belatedly that the carriages waiting before the entrances signified that the dinner guests were still inside. She had forgotten that the Duke had invited a dozen or so people for dinner. What would they be thinking?

"Tony, you cannot drag me into the house with all the guests present. And my parents are here, I expect. They will be quite alarmed at my appearance."

"Damn the guests. They would be more alarmed if you had not been rescued. We have all been frantic with worry. And I have some harsh words for you, milady, but they will wait until you are yourself again," he growled.

She grimaced. She was not in the mood for a set-to with Tony, although she recognized that fear had sharpened his tongue, and now that she was safe, his reaction was expected.

Ignoring the Duke and the group of concerned guests gathered in the hall to meet them, he strode with Francey in his arms up the stairway, not pausing for any explanations. He did not stop until they had reached her bedchamber, where he reluctantly delivered her to the hovering, worried Martha.

"See that her ladyship has a bath and some ointment for that bruise on her cheeks," he ordered the abigail in peremptory tones, depositing his burden on the bed. "I will send up a tray. You must be hungry. But I will return shortly to hear an account of this evening's doings. Right now I want to hear Mr. Clarke's tale. He has some explaining to do, too."

Francey, knowing there was no arguing with Tony when he adopted this hectoring arrogant stance, wisely did not argue beyond saying, "Do be kind to Mr. Clarke, Tony. He was a Trojan." Then she subsided, willing to allow Martha to repair the damages of her adventure. Tony stalked to the door, gave her a burning look, and without a thought for the presence of the maid, returned to clasp her in his arms and give her a hard kiss.

"You are a menace to my peace of mind, Francey, but I am so relieved. I cannot spare you. You mean too much to me," he spoke impulsively. He could not tell Francey

178

of his love before her abigail, but he vowed not to let the night pass without admitting his feelings. His pride had fallen beneath the awful contemplation of what might have happened to her. He strode out, leaving behind a pleased if exhausted wife, who was deciding that perhaps her wretched experience would yield great benefits to them both. If her brush with the brutal Fred Scanlon had shaken Tony out of his detachment it had been worth it.

Francey's natural resilence surfaced after a comforting bath, and a light meal. Only her throbbing cheek and painful feet reminded her of the frightful crisis she had been through, and her imagination, always active, supplied her with some lurid pictures of what might have happened. That she had managed to thwart her captors gave her a great deal of satisfaction, but she admitted that without the timely arrival of Mr. Clarke her escape might not have turned out so well.

Dressed in a warm peignoir she dozed before the fire, finally dismissing Martha after allaying her irate maid's concern and giving her a much-edited account of the night's doings. She knew Tony would not be content with such a sketchy disclosure, but she hoped that the revelations he had made about his feelings for her would not be swamped by his justifiable anger at her carelessness.

Downstairs, the Duke and Philip, having reassured Francey's parents, and the other guests, sped them on their way. Tomorrow would be time enough for the Lawtons to visit Francey and hear of her experiences. Tony was closeted with Mr. Clarke, listening to the Bow Street runner's account of the matter and the role he had played.

Willie Clarke, refreshed by some beef, cheese and ale, embarked on his involved tale of discovery. His story was much as he told it to Francey, but he added some questions of his own.

"I admit, my lord, that without Lady Frances's own foresight and courage, affairs might have turned out badly. I could have arrived too late to rescue her from real trouble. And the odds were not in my favor, four to one. I should have called up reinforcements, but the villagers were not friendly. It might have been disastrous. I have no idea how she effected her escape from her incarceration," he admitted with some chagrin.

"Yes, well, she is a resourceful lady, but she has gone a bit too far this time. I shudder to think what that villain had in mind for her. And I would never have searched as far afield as Bere Regis. Tomorrow we will have to investigate that village, but I suppose Fred Scanlon will have left, and returned to London to further his conspiracy. He is hand in glove with the most violent of the agitators against the government."

"True, my lord, but I believe this escapade was entirely inspired by vengeance against Lady Everely for removing his wife and child from his clutches. I doubt the larger purpose came into it."

"Well, he shall be brought to justice." Tony's expression boded no good for the miscreant.

"Yes, sir. He is a dangerous man." Mr. Clarke awaited further orders, and when he had received them he took his leave under the auspices of Jepson who would provide him with a bed for the night.

Tony, impatient to speak to his wife, gave his father and Philip only the briefest of explanations of the abduction, but promised a fuller account the next day, and despite their concern he tore himself away. He had to see Francey.

He promised himself he would deal gently with her, but fear fueled his anger. He might have lost her, and all because she would brook no restraint on her actions. If warnings had no effect perhaps a confession of his love might prevent her from riding heedlessly into danger. He knew he had dropped his pride and his facade of aloofness. She would not let him retreat behind that convenient cloak again. And he did not want to.

He smiled kindly as he entered her room, determined

not to lose his temper.

"Are you feeling better, my dear?" he asked.

"Almost restored, although my feet ache a bit," she confided ruefully.

"And what were you doing running away in your stockings?" he asked, barely hiding his amusement. Really, she was the most amazing woman. Any other fine lady he knew would have succumbed to the vapors, crying and moaning, but not Francey.

"Well, I had to remove them to hit Scanlon after he tripped over the snare I laid at the door of my prison," she explained with a chuckle. Now that the danger had passed she was more than pleased with her resourceful efforts to escape. "I hope I have not killed him," she added with some compunction.

"That hardly matters," Tony replied callously, not one whit concerned with Scanlon's fate. God, she had been in the most frightful danger and all her attempts to pass off the episode as a trifling affair did not convince him otherwise. "I want a full account of what happened. Mr. Clarke confessed that you had dealt quite handily with the villains before he appeared." Tony's reactions to her adventure gave her a thrill of satisfaction. It must mean he cared for her more than he wanted to admit, she thought.

"Without Mr. Clarke, I might have been recaptured," Francey conceded, honesty forcing her to admit that she had not been quite so valiant as she appeared. Then she gave Tony a bald account of her kidnapping, not wanting to relive the nightmare, but convinced that Tony would not be fobbed off with a sketchy tale. She wanted to return to Tony's admission. If he really loved her, that was far more exciting than the danger she had just experienced.

"You said you could not go on without me. If I had been dispatched by that murderous crew would you have pined, I wonder?" she mocked not entirely in jest, but afraid of pleading for an answer he did not want to give.

181

"Damn you, Francey, I have never been so frightened in my life, not even on the battlefield. You are an obstinate baggage, with no proper regard for my feelings. Of course, I would have pined, you shrew," he said angrily, a flush rising to his face as he watched her warily, still not willing to let down his guard.

"That's comforting," Francey replied, turning her face away to hide her disappointment. If she had expected more she would not let him see her eagerness. But, as if he had lost any small remnants of control, he grabbed her angrily into his arms and began to kiss her with feverish intensity. Despite her bruises and weariness, her heart pounded and she responded with all the warmth she had hidden for so long.

Forgetting her sore feet, her throbbing head, and any other injuries, Francey was conscious only of the rising passion overwhelming them both. Tony's hands roamed beneath her dressing gown, finding the inviting flesh, and winning a gratifying response from his heightened caresses.

"I shouldn't do this, but I can't stop. Don't ask me to," he pleaded roughly, laying her on the bed. "If you want me to confess I love you, have always loved you, will always love you, and I don't give a curse for anything else, there it is," he growled, furious at losing his control but unable to subdue the emotions which had been stirred by her danger and her incredible return to him when he had thought her lost. "And you love me, too, don't you?" he pressed, struggling out of his own clothes, while keeping her pinned to the bed, denying her attempt to escape.

"Oh, Tony, what fools we are," she murmured, winding her arms around him and surrendering to his insistent ardor. She could not help herself as his passion flowed over her and her own rose to meet his demands. "Don't stop," she pleaded, beside herself.

"Admit you love me, admit it," he urged, continuing his assault on her senses. A shiver of desire pulsed through her body, and desperate for release she cried.

"Yes, of course, I love you, Tony," she cried, forgetting doubts, pride and anger, everything except the craving for the release only he could give her. She shook with frenzy as he plunged into her, both of them responding to the rising crescendo of their pounding senses. They reached the peak of fulfillment together, and together collapsed as their desire was satisfied. They drifted off to sleep soon after, replete and content. Whatever questions remained could be answered later but for now they were united together in whatever the clouded future promised.

Chapter Sixteen

The days following her escape from Fred Scanlon proved to be among the happiest Francey had ever experienced. She was to recall them later with gratitude. As Tony had suspected, by the time Mr. Clarke directed them to Bere Regis and the derelict cottage the next day, their quarry had flown. Scanlon, no doubt, had disappeared into London's hidden streets, and the villagers of Bere Regis professed to know nothing of the trio who had abetted him, although neither Tony nor Willie Clarke thought they were ignorant of the affair.

Francey, with only her painful feet and the purpling bruise on her cheek to remind her of her near disaster, soon forgot even these mementoes in the halcyon August days which followed. Once Tony had declared his love and received an equally sincere avowal from her, he lost all his former reticence, and much of his mocking manner. Nothing would ever rid him completely of that haughty air, but Francey was no longer the victim of his arrogant dictates. The Duke smiled benignly, seeing the lovers at peace with one another, and he believed it would not be long before his wish for an heir became a reality. If the rest of England was troubled by disgruntled workers, high prices, starvation wages and rumbles of rebellion, this small corner of Dorset appeared to have escaped the general discontent.

A week or so after Francey's rescue, she and Tony rode to the furthest boundaries of the Compton acres, to a secluded glade bordering the Channel, where they picnicked on cold chicken and fruit, lazing afterwards in the dappled sunshine.

"It will be difficult to wrench ourselves away from all these bucolic pleasures to take up our London duties again," Tony sighed, packing up the remains of their food, and then throwing himself on the ground, pillowing his head in Francey's lap.

"I suppose we do have to go back, but London seems a continent away now," Francey sighed toying idly with Tony's chestnut hair.

"Would you be content to live down here most of the year and give up your London life?" Tony asked idly, not really caring what Francey decided, for politics, economic woes, and the intrigues of society seemed far distant, to be ignored if possible.

"Not really. It is blissful to be here now, but you would soon be bored, and I might, too, until we set up our nursery," Francey mused, a bit shy. Then, as if determined to take the plunge, "Are you disappointed that I am not yet *enceinte?*"

"Of course not. But if we go on the way we have been, I don't doubt that an heir will be making an appearance before too long," he teased, then sensing Francey's worry. "Are you afraid that you cannot have children, Francey?"

"Sometimes I think about it. The Duke would be so unhappy, and then you might rue this marriage."

"I could never do that. I did not marry you merely to have children." He sat up suddenly, and looked deeply into her eyes. "Surely you do not doubt my love, Francey?"

"No, of course not. But I know you want children, and so do I." She frowned. "It has been much on my mind. when you have given me time to think of it," she mocked a bit hollowly.

185

"Are you complaining about the ardor of my attentions, milady?" Then seeing that she was indeed concerned, he took her hand and said with deep sincerity, "Please brood no more on it, Francey. Your life lately has been full of danger and worry. Once this business of Scanlon is settled and the country settles down a bit, we will both be more relaxed. I believe there will be a full quiver of Everelys to occupy us before long."

Relieved by sharing her doubts, and comforted by Tony's attitude, Francey smiled and agreed. "It is certainly not for lack of application on your part, my lord."

"True. I seem not to be able to concentrate on anything but my delectable wife these delightful summer days." He took her in his arms and gave her a lingering kiss, reveling in her unrestrained response and for a time all else but their lovemaking was forgotten. They were content to bask in this rural retreat where cares of the world could not intrude.

But later, as they prepared to return to the Towers, Francey could not but voice her disquiet. "Soon you will have to return to London, when Parliament reconvenes. Will Fred Scanlon continue to threaten us? And do you think that the earlier attack in front of the theatre was his doing? Could there be another enemy out there intent on harming us?"

"Perhaps. But you will be well guarded by the redoubtable Mr. Clarke. I think the theatre incident was not Scanlon's work. He may be involved with the odious Thistlewood, a schemer and agitator if ever I met one, but I think his attempt to capture you was entirely personal. He wants to find his wife and child, poor devil, unwilling to admit he drove them away with his own brutality. But I believe his fangs have been drawn. The first attack puzzles me. It may just have been a frenzied unemployed laborer, like Liverpool's assailant, but I wonder if we have some unknown villain who has a personal grievance against us. The man called our name, I remember."

Tony frowned, recalling the incident, then realizing he was not relieving Francey's worry, smiled and said lightly, "I have every confidence in your efforts to escape from any other rogues. You are quite an opponent, able to bash a strong man with your boot, and transform a cynical rake into a pattern card of a husband."

"Hah, pattern card indeed! Time will tell sir, if you deserve that accolade." Francey replied with spirit. Even though neither of them had been completely satisfied with Tony's explanation, they did not want to pursue the matter, content to enjoy the peace and rapport their confessions of love had induced. Whatever evils lay ahead, they would meet them together.

It appeared that Tony had assessed the situation correctly. No further attempts were made against either of them in Dorset. Mr. Clarke was dispatched to London to continue his investigations. The men sent to Bere Regis to follow up on the Scanlon attack met a firm wall of resistance. No further information was forthcoming from the sullen villagers. Although Bere Regis was not among the Duke's holdings, his status as the shire's leading landowner was such as to frighten the hamlet's citizenry into outward obedience. There was not a man among them prepared to challenge the anger of the Duke of Compton.

Francey, reluctant to remember the details of her abduction, did try to tell the authorities all she could, but for the time being little could be done to bring the miscreants to justice. In musing over Tony's explanation of the various attacks, she wondered fleetingly if Oliver Fanshawe could be involved, his motive revenge, and she recalled Sidney Portman's menacing tones to her at that last luncheon.

She had told Tony of her distaste for the man, and Tony, in his first abandonment to love's dictates, had promised to think about giving Portman his *congé*. But he had warned that it might be difficult, as the man was a bang-up secretary and had his finger on the pulse of politics. Francey, trying to be generous, had agreed that if he was so useful perhaps he must remain. Her only stipulation was that he not appear at her luncheon table again. She realized that Tony did not take her suspicions against his secretary seriously, and in their current state of accord she did not want to press the matter.

With their personal problems settled in so promising a fashion, and the weather so obliging, Tony and Francey, at the Duke's urging, had decided to spend some additional weeks at Compton Towers. Nothing appeared pressing in London with most of the government enjoying a holiday. However, if London was quiet, the Midlands were not. "Inhabitants of Manchester! The eyes of all England, nay of all Europe, are fixed upon you," cried Orator Hunt announcing a meeting to be held in St. Peter's Field to argue for radical reform of the government.

Radical meetings of workers had become commonplace in the Midlands, but as yet agitators had not penetrated Dorset nor much of the Southwest, where farm wages were depressed but villagers rarely starved. In the factory and mining towns of the Midlands conditions were far more savage. Hunt's personal magnetism combined with a sense of real grievance brought more than fifty thousand people to St. Peter's Field on a hot and airless August 16, in the year 1819.

Twenty minutes into his invective, the magistrates ordered out the yeomanry to disperse the peaceful assembly. The part-time soldiers, excited and undisciplined, tried to force their way to the hustings to arrest the leaders. When the crowd impeded them, they unsheathed their sabers, slashing indiscriminately at men, women and children. In the panic which followed, nine men and two women were killed, hundreds were injured, and the vast meadow was reduced to a bloody battlefield, strewn with torn and gory clothing, women's bonnets and shawls, groaning victims, drooping banners, broken flagstaffs—the aftermath of a massacre.

Tony and Francey heard of the "Peterloo Massacre" from a London newspaper enclosed in a message sent posthaste by Lord Sidmouth, requesting Tony's immediate return to London. Within twenty-four hours of the debacle all of England was aroused.

"This has torn it," Tony groaned, reading an account of the riot to his wife, father and brother. "The government could fall, and perhaps, there is justice in turning such people out of office. How could His Majesty's ministers condone such a murderous attack on what this journal calls 'unarmed and distressed people.'" Turning to his father he explained, "I must return at once. I greatly fear Lord Sidmouth's reaction. He must be persuaded not to do something foolish."

"I will accompany you, Tony," Francey said firmly. She would not remain here in the country, isolated from events, and she hoped that her presence and support would be of some assistance to Tony.

The Duke promised to follow his son and daughter-in-law within a few days. He was intent on seeing that the country's general discontent did not penetrate his own acres, where conditions until now had not inspired any hatred againt landowners. All of that could change as a result of the aroused mood of the countryside. Within a few hours, Francey and Tony were on their way to London. Their coachman had orders to drive straight on, not stopping except to change horses. Francey could sense Tony's impatience and his eagerness to reach the Home Office, so that he could try to restrain his chief and other rigid Tories from enacting coercive measures that would only exacerbate the situation.

Tony had assessed the position of the government correctly. Determined to stand by the Manchester magistrates, the Lord Chancellor, Lord Eldon, railed, "Can any man doubt that these meetings are the overt acts of conspirators, to instigate . . . to specific acts of treason. I cannot doubt it." Yet even the rigid diehard

Lord Eldon admitted that the freedoms of Englishmen were at risk. The people had a right to assemble, and most observers admitted that the Manchester demonstrators had offered no violence.

Wellington, like Tony, was appalled at the undisciplined reaction of the troops. He might excuse the yeomanry, but the 15th Hussars had been involved. He believed in force, but complained that any fool could get ten thousand soldiers onto a field but only a real general can get them out again. "Lord Sidmouth," Wellington protested, "the Radicals will impeach you for this. By God they will."

Tony, who admired the Iron Duke, although he did not always agree with him, could only urge Sidmouth to calm the aroused tempers, so as to discourage further violence which might not only impeach Sidmouth and the rest of the Cabinet, but turn the government out of office, and touch off the very revolution the Tories so feared. But Liverpool was adamant. He said the House was filled with "an evil temper and disposition."

The Whigs and other independents were urging reform. Even Wellington's joining the cabinet had not soothed the unrest in the country, which was beset with hunger, joblessness and distress among the common people. Sidmouth drew up the Coercive Acts and was determined when Parliament reconvened in November to see them pass. The Regent was worried. Never had he been more unpopular, his gout was causing him pain, his wife was disporting herself on the Continent in an unseemly manner, and his father, George III, was sinking rapidly toward death. He might not last through Christmas.

Tony was in despair, cursing the shortsightedness of both the Regent and the Tory government, but only Francey heard his concern. She tried to comfort him, but since she shared his view, it was difficult.

"You could resign and make the reasons public," she advised as they sat in her bedroom having a quiet coze one fall evening.

"Yes, and then any effectiveness I might exert would be finished, as well as my political career. And if I changed parties, neither the Whigs nor the Tories would ever consider me reliable again," sighed Tony.

Francey, hating to see him so disturbed, did her best to ease his worries, but she could see that he was not calmed by her soothing words. It was too bad, just when their personal affairs were so blissful, to have this distraction. Of course, Francey was aware that her life lay along pleasant lines, and she could not be so ungrateful as to discourage Tony from helping his countrymen, but it all seemed so hopeless.

"And this business with the Regent. At times I groan over his selfishness. Now he wants Parliament to foot the bill for extensive repairs to Buckingham Palace. He couldn't have broached the matter in a worse climate," Tony complained. Then, throwing off his cares, he clasped Francey's hands in a warm grip. "But I am a cad to burden you with all this. And Francey, I am more than grateful to have your love and support. How could I manage without you?"

"You don't have to. And I feel quite guilty, also, that I am so contented and happy when the country is so miserable. I don't deserve it."

"Yes, you do. But I worry about you. Scanlon has gone to ground, and no further attacks have been made upon either of us. But I don't trust Thistlewood. He will not allow the Peterloo tragedy to go unpunished, I know. I believe he is planning some coup."

"I thought you had an *agent provocateur* who was keeping you informed of his conspiracies."

"We do, and he is playing a dangerous role. Those madmen would wreak horrible vengeance upon him if they were to unmask him. He's a brave fellow."

"Well, we can do no more tonight about all this. Let us be off to bed," Francey suggested, smiling temptingly.

"You are insatiable, madam, but I am more than

191

willing," Tony agreed with commendable promptitude and a wicked glint in his grey eyes which made shiver run up Francey's back.

"I suppose I will eventually get accustomed to the pleasures of your lovemaking, and become bored with the whole business of marriage," she teased as they made their way to bed.

"Hah! I should be a poor husband and lover if I were to allow that to happen," Tony scoffed, and set about proving to her how foolish were her fears.

Francey continued to work at the refuge, despite Tony's concern for her safety. She was much more agitated about Tony's own situation. And there was still the problem of Sidney Portman. His manner toward her had not altered, although if he blamed her for being banished from the luncheon table, he did not voice his displeasure. When he met her in the hall, which was seldom, as Francey took pains to avoid him, he was always polite. But beneath that correct facade, she realized he viewed her with contempt, and appeared to be waiting for some occasion to get his own back on her. She knew she was a goose to bother about Portman, but his brooding presence in the house did not quiet her unease. She felt as if they were all holding their breath, waiting for some disaster.

She was not reassured when one afternoon in Gunther's, where she was having tea with Letty Colgrove, she noticed Oliver Fanshawe at a corner table, an odd place for that sophisticated man-about-town. Surely White's, the gambling rooms of Crockford's or the ambience of Kate Argyll's rooms would better suit his temperament. Francey could barely repress a giggle. She was not supposed to know about Kate Argyll, the most elegant of madams, who presided over a very provocative stable of light skirts, much patronized by the *ton*. Her hopes that Letty would not notice Oliver were in vain.

"What is that man doing here? The last place one would expect to see him. Probably some assignation. How thrilling!" Letty exclaimed, titillated by the thought of Oliver's dallying with some matron among their acquaintances. "Aren't you glad you accepted Tony and not Oliver? There is something quite swarmy about that man."

"There was no question of my marrying Oliver Fanshawe. He was only interested in my money," Francey protested shortly. She disliked talking about the man. And she wanted to leave before he saw her. "Hurry up, Letty, and drink your tea. I must be home for we are going to the Esterhazys' for dinner and I have to rest before changing. I have had a most exhausting day."

"Nonsense, Francey. Of course, I know you find me exhausting. Henry tells me I quite wear him out. But I do want another ice. They are so delicious," she sighed, knowing that Gunther's ices would only add to her increasing pounds.

"You don't need another ice. You have already had two," Francey argued, and settled the matter by calling for their bill. Hurry as she might, with Letty pouting and preening, unwilling to sacrifice her ice, they did not escape without gaining the attention of Oliver Fanshawe. He rose and approached their table.

"How lovely to see you, Francey, and you, too, Lady Colgrove," he bowed and let his eyes roam suggestively over the two women.

"Good afternoon, Oliver." Francey accepted his fulsome greetings as briefly as politeness allowed. "I did not know you were in town."

"I only returned yesterday. Had to go on a repairing lease to some cousins in Shopshire, so tedious, my dears, you would not believe. But can I not prevail upon you ladies to have some more cakes or perhaps an ice and chat a bit? I need to catch up on all the news."

Letty, seeing the promise of the denied ice materializing, was about to agree, when Francey forestalled her.

"We are late already and must leave. Come, Letty. You greed will be the death of you," she insisted, brooking n further delay, and rose to her feet.

"Yes, of course, Francey. So nice to see you, Oliver," Letty said nervously, for she feared Francey would los her temper. She scurried about, dropped her gloves which Oliver politely restored to her, and she prepared t run after Francey who was sweeping toward the door.

"I fear Lady Everely is displeased with me. Do try t assure her that I am not a bad chap," Oliver urge persuasively as Letty prepared to follow.

"Yes, of course, Oliver," Letty agreed, completely overset. She hated scenes and feared that Francey woul create one if she lingered. Not that Francey would be s gauche, but it was obvious that she wanted nothing to d with Oliver Fanshawe. As she joined Francey at the doo they were almost brushed aside by Moira Stacy-Long who was just entering.

Politeness demanded that Francey greet the lady with some attempt at cordiality.

"My apologies, Lady Everely. I am afraid that in my haste to make my appointment I was a bit careless. How nice to see you, Lady Colgrove," Lady Stacy-Long effused. It was obvious she did not include Francey in this last pleasantry. Letty, sensing uncomfortable undercurrents, murmured a suitable rejoinder.

Moira added, addressing Francey, "I do hope Tony's duties are not taxing him unbearably? When I saw him the other day he looked quite haggard." Moira was trying to insinuate that she had spent some time with Francey's husband.

But Francey did not receive her remark with any appearance of dismay, although she lifted a haughty eyebrow at the familiarity, as she replied, "Tony appears quite able to cope with his government responsibilities, Lady Stacy-Long. How kind of you to inquire." Unwilling to continue the conversation she turned to Letty, "We must not keep the carriage waiting, Letty." And that young woman, sensing difficulty, hurried to comply. Francey sailed through the door, but Letty's curiosity would not be gainsaid, and she turned to see whom Moira Stacy-Long was meeting. She was not surprised to see that it was Oliver Fanshawe.

"I had no idea that Lady Stacy-Long and Oliver Fanshawe were intimate," Letty offered, her nose for gossip twitching.

"They are well suited," Francey replied shortly. She would not confide in Letty. "Now, Letty, tell me about my godchild. You haven't mentioned little Henry all afternoon." She knew this would distract Letty from further questions and so it did.

As Letty prattled away about the virtues of her son, Francey wondered about Moira's allusion to Tony. Could he still be meeting the lady, and if so why had he not mentioned it to her? Was it conceivable that Tony was deceiving her? She tried to dismiss the idea, remembering their own new happiness, but the idea lingered to trouble her.

Chapter Seventeen

"Rather unfortunate, your meeting Francey just
then," Oliver greeted his guest as he seated her.

"I don't see why, Oliver," Moira replied, rather
annoyed at the remark. "Surely I am entitled to meet
you. Unless, of course, you still entertain prospects of
returning to Lady Everely's good graces," she said
waspishly as she bestowed her gloves on the table and
unclasped her pelisse.

"No chance. And I owe that lady a bad turn. She
treated me very badly."

"I am not overfond of her myself," Moira replied
spitefully, recalling Tony's rejection and properly
believing Francey responsible. "Now why did you want
to see me? I doubt you intend setting up a flirtation, and
for anything more serious I must say we cannot afford
one another."

"Quite right, my dear. But I think we both owe the
Everelys a set-down, and I believe you will join me in a
little plan I have to accomplish that," he replied suavely.

"I admit I would like to see the lady's downfall, but
tangling with Tony might lead to all kinds of trouble for
me."

"Not if you follow my suggestion. There is no danger
to you. And I think my idea will win your cooperation."

He said no more as the waiter appeared to take their orders. But they spent some time over their ices, and when they parted, Oliver's suggestion had won Moira's reluctant assent.

Oliver and Moira believed that Francey's knowledge of their meeting was of no significance, but they both would have been delighted if they had known how much Moira's remark concerning Tony disturbed Francey. She tried to put it from her mind, hoping it was just an attempt by Moira to cause her the very disquiet she was feeling, but she could not completely discount it.

She wanted to challenge Tony with the possibility that he was still seeing Moira, but somehow she knew she could not do it. The nagging suggestion took root, however, and would not be abandoned. Much refreshed by a bath and short rest, Francey dressed for dinner at the Esterhazys' in a distracted manner. Her pride would not let her entertain the idea that Moira was a rival for her husband's affections. She was determined to look her most enticing and to that end she donned her newest and most daring gown, a low-cut black lace, of simple design which showed off her figure to advantage and served as a perfect foil for the Compton diamonds.

"You take my breath away, Francey. I will have to spend the evening fending off your admirers," Tony said enthusiastically as he greeted his wife. But she averted her cheek when he tried to kiss her, much to his surprise. Now what ailed her? Had he incurred her anger by some untoward action?

"Thank you, my lord. But there will be few exciting types to lure me in tonight's guest list. I hardly think Prince Esterhazy or Lord Eldon will make a push to become one of my flirts." Her tone was mocking but cool, causing Tony to wonder at her distant air.

"You relieve my mind. But I understand Uxbridge will be among the guests and his reputation is *formidable* with the ladies," he insisted with a wry grimace.

"I think since he lost his leg at Waterloo he has become less of a rake and more of a benedict. Lady Charlotte sees to that, although schooled womanizers rarely lose their inclination to flirt," she said, annoyed at herself for the innuendo but unable to prevent the dig.

The Earl of Uxbridge had managed to survive a terrific scandal, Francey recalled. He had abandoned his wife and numerous progeny, and eloped with Wellington's sister-in-law, Charlotte Wellesley. The two had eventually married and produced their own children, eventually being received again into society. It appeared that Wellington, although he was angry at his brother-in-law, realized that he was the best cavalry officer in the Army, which he subsequently proved at Waterloo.

"I wonder if the Iron Duke will be there, too?" Tony asked, ignoring Francey's reference, but wondering at the reason for it. Surely she could not doubt his devotion and love.

Francey, feeling ashamed of herself, hurried to pursue the distraction. "Princess Esterhazy is too tactful a hostess to invite those two together, but it would be entertaining," Francey agreed with a grin, determined to respond to Tony's overtures. Much as she enjoyed the *on dits* of society, and her position as a reigning hostess, she had no malice in her heart and lacked the inclination to intrigue which engaged the energies of so many of London's most exclusive *doyennes*.

"I want to talk to Uxbridge about the Army. This will be a perfect opportunity," Tony informed her, then as they entered their carriage, and settled against the squabs, he bent over and kissed her gently on her neck. "You really are the most enticing creature, Francey, and I should not be wasting time discussing politics and escorting you to dull dinners but I should behave in romantic fashion—abduct you to Venice where we could make passionate love in a gondola."

"Sounds lovely, but a bit impractical. We must just

imagine that Grosvenor Square has its own mysteries."

"And the Esterhazy dinner party not a duty but a delirious delight?" Tony scoffed, suddenly tired of all the intrigue, the political arguments, and clash of temperaments which he had been enduring.

"Quite right. And we are almost there, so compose your expression or our hosts will be shocked, thinking you have been making love to your wife, when you should be pondering weighty matters. Shame on you, sir!" Whatever had caused her pique, she seemed to have forgotten it.

"You shall pay for those words, madam, later this evening," Tony laughed into her sparkling eyes, and thought not for the first time what a fortunate man he was to have not only an intelligent, elegant, and witty wife, but a passionate and loving one.

The evening went as might be expected, although the conversation, sprightly and knowledgeable, surprised Francey somewhat. Happily, Tony's chief, Lord Sidmouth, was not among the guests, as Eldon, the Lord Chancellor, was quite outspoken in his criticism. He blamed Sidmouth for the disaster at Peterloo and spoke harshly of the Army's behavior. Lord Uxbridge, Francey's dinner partner, as Tony acknowledged with a wry lift of his eyebrows, took umbrage at any slur on the troops.

"My dear Eldon. It was an impossible situation. You cannot blame the Hussars. If the yeomanry, untrained and badly disciplined, had not lost their heads, L'Estrange could have managed the matter with dispatch."

"Perhaps, but the Hussars and the 31st Foot should not have been there, or if they were entrusted with the job why call out the specials?" Lord Eldon, usually a mild-tempered man, was rapidly becoming in danger of disrupting the Esterhazy dinner table.

Francey, out of sympathy for her hostess, intervened with a winning smile, "I am sure you have every reason to be dismayed, Lord Eldon, but surely you agree with

199

Lord Uxbridge that the regulars are a fine body of men, experienced and brilliantly commanded. We must yield to the superior knowledge of one of the heroes of Waterloo, on which field Lord Uxbridge made such a sacrifice for his country," she soothed.

"Humph, I suppose you are right, Lady Everely. My Lord," he called across the table to Tony. "Your wife is quite a diplomat. The Foreign Office could use her, what with Castlereagh's bumbling about."

Tony wisely did not take exception to this very cavalier description of the Foreign Secretary and leader of the House of Commons. Prince Esterhazy, Austria's ambassador to England, was close to Metternich, who endorsed a firm stance toward any agitation. Esterhazy would not approve of a guest's taking issue with the Lord Chancellor. "I have always found her so, my lord. She has to be the soul of tact to deal with me," Tony explained lightly, defusing what might have become an awkward situation. The other guests laughed and conversation continued on a more amicable plane.

"You are a clever puss, Lady Everely," Lord Uxbridge murmured giving her a glance of admiration.

"Not at all, my lord. But since the Princess has provided us with such a fine dinner, I would not want any of you to suffer from indigestion due to rancor."

Having safely negotiated this pitfall, Francey relaxed a bit. Really, these dinners where social and political maneuvering was so prevalent, taxed her patience. How much more enjoyable were the simple country parties in Dorset. It was at times like these that she yearned to return to the scenes of her childhood.

Later in the drawing room, Princess Esterhazy thanked her profusely for her intervention. "I only hope the gentlemen behave themselves over their port without your calming presence, my dear."

"I am sure they will. This business of Peterloo has put them all in a pet. But it was most unfair of Lord Eldon to twit Lord Uxbridge, not at all like him."

"I find him a most difficult creature, not at all *comme il faut,* but what can one do? These duty dinners must be held," the Princess sighed mournfully, but Francey knew her hostess really relished such set-tos. She lived up to her reputation for enjoying mischief.

As they were going home in the coach Tony congratulated Francey on her handling of Eldon. Then, suddenly somber, he added, "This is all so trying, Francey. I wish we were home in Dorset, for I can see nothing but trouble ahead. I have half a mind to resign."

"Our last visit there was a bit tempestuous. No, Tony, you must stay and do your best to calm matters." The evening and Tony's unstinted approval had improved her spirits and she would not allow vagrant thoughts of Moira Stacy-Long to intrude.

"I think you would make a better minister than I do. My patience is sorely tried by all these machinations, and the obduracy of such hidebound types as Eldon."

"Nonsense, you love it. The government needs cool heads and calming influences."

"At which you are a master, my dear, but fortunately these are not your only admirable qualities," Tony insisted, putting a warm and comforting arm about his wife, which she received, though not eagerly—at least she did not rebuff it. She almost mentioned the encounter with Moira but decided that if there were any substance to her fears, no good could come of admitting her jealousy. Francey believed that husbands strayed because their wives were unreceptive, and she would not make that mistake. But events were to prove that she had erred in not confiding to Tony that she had observed a meeting between Oliver and Moira, two characters who intended no good to the Everelys.

The next few days passed with no more untoward

incidents and both Francey and Tony tried to dispel the slight shadow in their relationship. For the most part they were successful. Francey had dug her heels in about Sidney Portman, whose manner toward her had become increasingly abrasive. Their relationship had deteriorated to the point where it affected the whole atmosphere of Grosvenor Square even though she tried to avoid him whenever possible. Finally, she decided Tony must approach him and try to discover why he disliked her so and warn him that his attitude was making it impossible for him to continue in Tony's employ.

"Really, Tony, he is quite the most disagreeable man I have ever encountered. Surely you can at least find out why he dislikes me so? He is poisoning the whole place," she insisted a bit extravagantly.

Tony sighed, anticipating an unpleasant interview, but he had to appreciate Francey's point of view.

"All right, my dear. I really don't think it is you he dislikes personally, just women in general. And he is naturally of a dour nature, I fear, but it does not affect his work."

"Thank you, Tony. Sorry to be such a burden," Francey said, happy to have gained her point. She might just be creating additional difficulties for Tony, and some of her mood could be put down to the suspicion that she was pregnant, a condition apt to inspire all kinds of fancies. She was not prepared to tell Tony of the possibility that they would become parents until she was sure, and in view of all the pressures on him she hated adding to his troubles. But the Portman situation must be settled, one way or the other.

Tony called Portman into the library early the next morning, deciding to get the affair over with before the day's business intruded.

"You wanted me, my lord," Portman said, appearing as usual calm and efficiently prepared.

"Yes, Sidney. Put away your pen. This is a personal

matter which I hesitate to mention, but alas, must solve. Lady Everely is disturbed by your attitude toward her, which I must say I have noticed myself. You seem to hold her in aversion, which I cannot understand, for she has always treated you kindly."

For a moment an ugly gleam rose in Portman's cold eyes, startling Tony with its fierceness, but he thought he must be mistaken, as it was quickly masked.

"I am not much of a man for the ladies, my lord. I have never been very comfortable in the circles in which Lady Everely is such an ornament. I fear she is accustomed to a more appreciative audience than I am able to offer. I regret that she finds me unacceptable," he explained in measured tones, somehow giving Tony the impression that the fault lay in Francey's frivolous social expectations, not in Portman himself.

"Yes, well, it creates an awkward dilemma. You must try to treat Lady Everely with more forbearance. I cannot have her disturbed by unhappy undercurrents, especially when there is little reason for them," Tony spoke more severely than usual. He paused and then continued, since he had won no response, but he was conscious of Portman's disapproval. "You have served me most efficiently and loyally, Sidney. I would dislike exceedingly having to dismiss you just because you cannot appreciate my wife. Do try, that's a good fellow, to treat her with a little more courtesy. I am sure I can rely on your good sense to see the advantages of a more friendly manner on your part." Tony was vastly uncomfortable with that warning speech, and felt he had really achieved very little. He had not discovered why Portman disliked Francey, and he feared he had even made the man's obvious resentment worse. Oh well, he had tried. And he would have to get rid of Portman if the man would not cooperate.

"I regret to have caused you any annoyance, my lord, when you have so many important matters on your mind," Portman replied, but making no promise. If he was offended he did not show it, but Tony was aware that he had not won any concession. As a result he dismissed him curtly and wondered after Portman departed just what he had achieved.

But his curiosity was aroused. Obviously the man had some maggot in his brain about Francey and would not reveal it. For the first time since Francey had mentioned the matter he began to see that Portman's animosity was not to be ignored. If the man did not heed his warning and improve, he would have to go, a damned nuisance right now. Tony turned to the papers on his desk, feeling uncomfortable and irritated by the distraction.

Francey, unaware of the interview below stairs, was having a lazy morning, indulging herself after a bout of nausea. On her breakfast tray was the usual post, an assortment of invitations and from her *modiste* a bill which rather shocked her by its total. Among the letters was a strange envelope, which when opened proved to be a note from Fitz, written on White's stationery, asking her to ride with him that afternoon. Having not seen Fitz in some time, Francey was pleased to accept, penning an answer immediately and ringing for a maid to see that the missive was delivered posthaste. Scrawling a word or two on the rest of the post, to be answered by her secretary, she dressed for the day.

After conferring with her chef, a Frenchman of mercurial temperament, about a forthcoming dinner and lunching off a tray in the morning room to avoid Sidney Portman, she changed into a dress suitable for a drive in Hyde Park. The day had turned cold and windy and if it were not that she had seen so little of Fitz recently she would have cried off. He arrived at three o'clock, prompt as always, and greeted her with his usual insouciance.

"Francey, my dear, you look especially blooming. I heard that you saved Princess Esterhazy's dinner from

204

becoming a brangle bath last evening. What an asset you are to Tony," Fitz remarked, as he took up the reins and they traveled at a spanking pace toward the park.

"How you manage to hear the latest gossip I cannot fathom. Much exaggerated that tale, believe me. But it seems to me that our Cabinet is becoming more than a bit testy," she confided, tying her bonnet more firmly. The day had turned grey and threatening, not at all pleasant for a tool about the park, and very few vehicles could be seen at this usually fashionable hour for a promenade. Fitz chatted somewhat perfunctorily. He did not seem his usual cheerful self although she was conscious that he was making a valiant effort.

"I greatly fear for the government," he said with rare solemnity. "I hope Tony is taking care."

"What do you mean, Fitz?" Francey replied, worried by Fitz's serious manner. It was not at all like him to be concerned with the government. His forte was gossip, fashion and light persiflage.

"Just a word of warning, Francey. Despite Tony's efforts to force the Tories into a more moderate stance, there is little doubt that they will refuse to listen to reason. And whatever Tony's feelings may be, he is associated in the agitators' minds with the government and its repressive measures. His very life could be in danger."

Francey, thoroughly alarmed by Fitz's abnormal concern, looked at him in surprise. "What have you heard, Fitz? And who are your sources? It is unlike you to worry about such matters."

"I fear there is a conspiracy afoot, and both you and Tony could become victims of some attack."

"Surely you exaggerate. And, at any rate, since that imbroglio in Dorset, we take the utmost pains to be on guard. Although that episode was one of personal vengeance, and nothing political was involved," she assured him. "You know I was abducted because I had

rescued a poor woman from a brutal husband? Perhap
Tony told you."

"Yes, he did. And he is not as sanguine as you seem t
be. I am disturbed. Be on guard, Francey. I have tol
Tony that affairs are coming to a boil," he urged.

"But, Fitz, what do you know? Have you some specifi
knowledge? If so, you must tell me."

"I can say no more. But I have reason to believe that
conspiracy is afoot."

"Oh, Fitz, I trusted that you would not become a
alarmist." Then, as a few light drops of rain began to fal
and the horses began to shy, Fitz turned his attention t
controlling them. "We had best return you to Grosveno
Square. I would be the veriest nodcock to allow you to ge
a wetting." And he would say no more. When he brough
his phaeton to the entrance of the Compton house
Francey invited him in for some refreshment, but h
would not come in. She wanted to quiz him further but h
showed an uncharacteristic stubbornness to be ques
tioned, and they parted.

Francey went up to her room, much troubled. How di
Fitz come by his information? And why did he give he
that gypsy warning and refuse to explain? Why th
secrecy? Surely if he had some definite information h
would tell Tony, even if he were not willing to confide i
her. She felt an ominous cloud settling over her life. I
Tony were in danger from some crazed assassin, Fit
must alert them. It was so unfair to hint at trouble and
then not tell them whence he had learned the news. Wer
they harboring a traitor in their midst? Sidney Portma
immediately came to mind, but Francey persuade
herself that her instinctive dislike of the secretary had n
real basis, and she was unfair to lay any mischief at hi
door.

Oh dear, she had awakened this morning feeling s
hopeful and pleased. She had almost decided that Moir
Stacy-Long's sly remark at Gunther's had merely been a

attempt to upset her, and that it had no foundation. Tony had been especially loving and attentive these last few days. Surely he was not playing a part.

But now mysterious and perilous events were darkening her happiness and she did not know whom to trust. Could Fitz's friendship mask some other motive? She would not believe that he intended harm toward her. He would not have warned her if that were so. But she suddenly yearned to be away, out from under this fog of doubt and suspicion. Francey lay back on her bed, exhausted by her thoughts, praying for some answer to her premonition of danger.

Chapter Eighteen

Tony had decided to make one more herculean effort to soften the Cabinet's attitude toward repression. He knew Liverpool had agreed to the Coercive Acts. Such an agenda prevented the type of drilling which had gone on in Manchester, permitted magistrates to seize arms, restricted the right of citizens to hold public meetings, taxed newspapers in an effort to gag the press, and strengthened the Army. Liverpool insisted that when the old King died and a change of regime was instituted, serious unrest might break out. He would be prepared.

Tony protested in vain, but he decided that he might make more progress in an informal atmosphere. He talked it over with Francey and they decided that dinner at the Grosvenor Square house might put the Cabinet in a more receptive mood. No women would be invited and the men could discuss the current situation without bothering about the social amenities. A date was decided upon and most of the men—including Eldon, Sidmouth, and Wellington—accepted.

Francey's responsibility was to order a plain but nourishing dinner to, as she put it, "soothe the savage beasts." To that end she conferred with her chef, who naturally took umbrage at dishing up some ordinary fare as baron of beef and partridges with cheese to follow. It allowed him little scope for his Gallic culinary talents.

After calming him, Francey was in no mood to suffer any more complaints when she set off for her *modiste* to challenge her latest bill and to order a new ball gown, but only if the price were reasonable. There would be a huge state dinner following the convening of Parliament and she was determined to look her best and be a credit to Tony. As yet she had not told Tony about the expected baby, and among her calls that day would be a visit to Sir Richard Croft, the preeminent *accoucheur* of the day, although he had not been able to save Princess Charlotte when the Regent's daughter was brought to bed with a child.

Mme Héloïse's emporium in Bond Street was quite crowded when Francey arrived and she was not pleased to see Moira Stacy-Long among the clients. She nodded coolly to the woman and began her business with the *modiste*, satisfactorily adjusting the outrageous bill and deciding upon a figured apricot silk gown. Preparing to leave, she was surprised when Moira approached her with Mrs. Lipton, a hanger-on in society and an intimate of Moira's.

"Dear Lady Everely, what a fortuitous meeting. Do come back and have tea with us. It is so stupid for us not to be friends, and I want to make amends for any disquiet I have caused you. Please say you will," Moira pleaded, joined in her invitation by Msr. Lipton, who much wanted to attach herself to the Everelys.

"I have an appointment later today which I cannot cancel," Francey insisted, not wanting to accept, but unwilling to create a scene in Mme Héloïse's with so many of the *ton* listening to their exchanges.

"I will send you on in my carriage. Please do relent," Moira cooed.

Seeing no way out of accepting the invitation, and with her curiosity aroused, Francey gave a grudging consent. They left the establishment together, trailed by the fawning Mrs. Lipton, and causing an outburst of speculation behind them. Most of the ladies present were well aware of Moira Stacy-Long's previous attachment to Tony and they wondered at her approaching his wife with the invitation.

Dismissing her coachman, she entered Moira's carriage, feeling distinctly put upon, and condemning her own weakness in assenting so easily. But perhaps she could clear up this business of Tony's supposed meetings with the lady and that would be all to the good.

Upon returning from the Home Office, Tony's first instinct was to search out Francey, his normal reaction upon entering his house. But before he could rush upstairs both Jepson and Sidney Portman checked him.

"Lady Everely has gone out, my lord. However, the carriage has returned." Jepson appeared worried, for he was not unaware of the dangers to his employers after the abduction in Dorset. Such secrets were not kept from the upper servants and the encounter with Scanlon had not gone unremarked below stairs.

"You mean she dismissed John?" Tony asked, becoming worried.

"So I understand, my lord," Jepson answered, uneasy at Tony's concern.

Before the butler could offer more information, Portman intervened. "My lord, a memorandum has just arrived from Lord Sidmouth requesting your immediate presence at the Home Office."

"Damn the man! I just returned from there. What could have happened that requires me to return?" Tony said in exasperation. Really, his chief was becoming unhinged. "Well, there is no use in speculating. I suppose I had better answer his summons posthaste. Who knows what maggot he has in his head?" Tony admitted. Sidmouth had proved unusually intransigent lately, threatening to retire, and putting an undue burden on Tony.

"Jepson, find out from John just where Lady Everely

went. I will return as soon as possible." Donning his driving cape again, Tony hurried toward the door, a nagging sense of unease settling on him. Of course, Francey had probably accepted some harmless invitation from a friend. Surely she would not have been abducted again. She was on her guard and would never relax her vigilance. He was just seeing danger where none existed. Still, he paused and turned to Jepson, who was standing by, uncertain and confused.

"I will see John before I leave," he insisted.

Portman protested, "But Lord Sidmouth sounded most adamant, my lord."

Tony wondered fleetingly why Portman was so anxious to send him off to the Home Office. "Lady Everely's safety is my paramount concern at the moment. Sidmouth can wait." Tony stood, knocking his whip against his side, and Jepson hurried to obey his command. John was not tardy in arriving. An old retainer, he had known both Francey and Tony since their childhood, when he was an undergroom at Compton Towers. Grey-haired and weather-beaten, a Dorset man of few words and phlegmatic temper, he was not easily alarmed, but on being questioned by Tony, he began to share his concern.

"A fashionable dark-haired lady, and another pawky type, came out of Mme Héloïse's where I was awaiting her ladyship and dismissed me, saying her ladyship was going on to tea with them, and would be sent home in her carriage. I was to return to Grosvenor Square."

"And I am sure that is what happened, my lord," Portman intervened smoothly, giving John an impatient look.

"Well, I am not. You know perfectly well that several attempts have been made to injure Lady Everely, Sidney, and this may be just such another. On the other hand it may be as you say, but that is a chance I am not willing to take. Please send a note to Lord Sidmouth that a family emergency prevents me from honoring his request,"

Tony ordered brusquely.

"But, my lord, I am convinced you are alarmed to no purpose and her ladyship will arrive home safely. Lord Sidmouth must have some cogent reason for asking you to return." Portman seemed unduly determined to prevent Tony from running after Francey, but Tony put that down to his secretary's dislike of his wife, and his great respect for Lord Sidmouth.

"Whatever it is, it will keep," Tony answered shortly. Tony was both frustrated and angry. And he was the more alarmed when he realized that Willie Clarke, who had been retained to keep an eye on Francey, was nowhere to be seen. Surely, if anyone had tried to harm Francey he would have prevented it, unless he, too, had been put out of action.

"I will drive to Mme Héloïse's and get to the bottom of this," he insisted and was out the door before either Portman or John could delay him further.

Driving posthaste to Bond Street, he caused quite a stir in Mme Héloïse's chic shop when he strode in, obviously in a furious temper.

The proprietress, a grocer's daughter from Bethnal Green, forgot her assumed French accent when confronted by this distraught peer.

"My lord, I know nothing. Lady Everely was here to settle a bill and order a new gown, but she has been gone some time. We have been very busy, as you see," she pleaded, seeing the Compton custom disappearing through no fault of her own.

"With whom did she leave?" Tony asked trenchantly, not at all calmed by her fussing, fluttering mannerisms.

"Well, let me see," Héloïse temporized. "Oh yes, I believe she accompanied Lady Stacy-Long and Mrs. Lipton," she offered.

"Ah," Tony appeared to understand. This was the information he wanted, and without a word, he turned on his heel and left the shop, without thanking the agitated Mme Héloïse or offering any explanation.

212

*　　*　　*

Francey's misgivings about accepting Moira's invitation for tea and a cosy chat were not relieved when Mrs. Lipton suddenly clasped her hand to her head and twittered, "What am I thinking of? I must be home immediately. I had completely forgotten that I am interviewing a housemaid this afternoon. You will excuse me for being an utter scatterbrain."

Since that was exactly what Francey was thinking, she could make no demur. Moira replied smoothly, "Of course, dear Maria, we will take you home. It is right on our way." That was not exactly true since they had to make a detour to Mrs. Lipton's somewhat shabby lodging on Wimpole Street, and Francey wondered if this ploy had been planned in advance to leave her alone with Moira, not a situation she relished.

"Perhaps it would be more convenient to postpone the tea party," she suggested without much hope. Moira hastened to reassure her. "Oh, no, Lady Everely, or may I call you Francey. We have quite a bit in common, I think, and it is foolish for such formality to exist between us. Do call me Moira."

Francey felt that she had no choice but to acquiesce. Obviously Moira was determined to have her way, and Francey sensed that she would find the whole affair very distasteful. Still, she was not about to cavil before the foolish Mrs. Lipton who no doubt put her own interpretation on the refusal.

"Yes, of course, Moira," Francey agreed reluctantly, wondering what on earth had impelled Moira to such a pass.

Within moments they had discharged Mrs. Lipton, still twittering, but giving meaningful looks at Moira, which reinforced Francey's suspicion that the whole business had been planned between them.

At the Stacy-Long house in Brook Street, Francey was escorted through the entrance, with Moira's somewhat frenzied grip on her arm preventing any escape. The woman looked absolutely triumphant, and Francey had a sinking feeling that she would rue her acceptance of this mysterious invitation. Once inside the door, where they were received by a balding manservant who reminded Francey of a mangy giraffe, Moira excused herself to remove her bonnet and make some repairs. She directed her man to take Francey to the drawing room, to the left of the hall. As Francey turned to follow him, she caught a glimpse of Moira's vindictive expression, and if she had had any sense she would have left the house immediately. But perhaps she was imagining it, for Moira was all cooing effusion, and Francey allowed the giraffe to lead her to the drawing room.

When she entered the room she saw that her apprehension was justified. Rising from a brocaded settee by the fireplace was Oliver Fanshawe. Francey demurred, and turned to make her leave, only to find the door locked behind her.

"I really must apologize for this stratagem, my dear, but since you would not receive me I had to arrange matters in this rather *outré* way," he drawled. "Please do sit down, and let me have your cloak and bonnet."

"We have nothing to say to one another, Oliver, and I cannot conceive why you have taken such pains to arrange this meeting," Francey said, sitting down in a straight-backed chair, keeping her pelisse firmly wrapped around her, although the room was unbearably warm.

Oliver strolled over and loomed above her for the moment. "I feared you would be displeased, and I greatly fear that what I have to say will make you even angrier, but you will listen." His tone was menacing and Francey subdued a shiver. What an intolerable situation!

Wisely biting her tongue, she remained silent. Let him get on with it, then. He proceeded to do so, and what he said left Francey shocked and furious.

"I have always meant to repay you, Francey, for your cavalier treatment of me. I had every reason to expect you would marry me, and then you went off to Gloucester, and came back wed to that popinjay, Everely. I should have thought your earlier experience would have been warning enough. He treated you in a scurvy fashion, my dear."

"As I remember, Oliver, I rejected your proposal quite firmly before leaving town. And I am in little doubt that marriage to you would have been a huge mistake," Francey replied as calmly as she could, although she sensed that any attempt to gain the upper hand was doomed to failure. How could she have been so stupid as to accept Moira's invitation? "I suppose Lady Stacy-Long conspired with you to arrange this regrettable interview."

"She dislikes you almost as much as I do, my dear, and wants to get her own back. You winkled Tony from her avaricious grasp and she would not let that go unrewarded." Oliver's voice held a malicious enjoyment which frightened Francey more than his actual words. What a cad and mountebank the man was! Worse was to come.

Since she made no rejoinder, he continued. "Your husband's secretary is no friend of yours, either. By the time Tony returns from his useless duties at the House he will find a note from you explaining your absence. It will say, in a very creditable copy of your handwriting that you have run away with me, as you find life with him no longer tolerable." Oliver smirked with satisfaction.

Refusing to be cowed now that she knew what he intended, she asked in a matter-of-fact voice which surprised her adversary, "Am I to understand that you have enlisted Sidney Portman in your nefarious scheme?"

"Oh, yes. He is quite as determined to seek revenge on you as Moira and I are. It seems your late husband, Pembridge, was within an ace of marrying his sister when he heard of your broken engagement and rushed to your side. Harriet Portman was so distraught she went into a decline and succumbed to pneumonia. Portman puts his sister's death at your door. He was quite attached to her," Oliver explained with satisfaction.

"Quite a troika of villains, I see," Francey commented with every appearance of indifference, although her heart was pounding in her throat, and she wondered frantically how to extricate herself from this melodramatic farce. "And just how do you intend to force me to go along with your nasty scheme? You must know I find you repellent, and would never agree to any stratagem of yours."

"I rather thought you might protest. Soon, Givens will be bringing your tea. I would not deny you refreshment. The tea will be drugged, and I will insist that you drink it. By the time you recover consciousness we will be on our way to Dover, and thence to the Continent, where you will be persuaded to cooperate, or your fate will be most unhappy. There are some rather disreputable houses in Paris whose chatelaines would welcome such an addition to their, shall we say, ladies of the night." Oliver's explanation, put in suave decisive tones, was more chilling than any impassioned threat.

"Really, Oliver, you are the most veritable nodcock. Do you think Tony would accept my elopement so easily? He will be after me in a trice, and I think you would find yourself in a very unfortunate position when he caught up with you."

"How naïve you are, Francey. He will console himself with the luscious Moira, who is eagerly awaiting your demise. He has never completely broken with her despite your marriage. Surely you did not believe such a practised rake would become a settled husband content to sample only your charms, bountiful as they are?"

Oliver spoke with an assurance that almost persuaded Francey, but then she took a grip on herself, and stood up. "You are talking utter fustian, Oliver. If you think I will tamely submit to your odious plan, you have

216

mistaken me, which does not surprise me, as you are such a paltry fellow."

Francey was pleased to recognize that she had scored a hit. Oliver flushed, and took a step toward her. She retreated toward the fireplace and reached for the poker. If he meant to force her to accede to his evil plan it would not be without a struggle. He stepped toward her, his eyes glowing with a fervid light, his mouth thinned to an ugly line, but before he could reply, they both heard a disturbance in the hall and then a mighty *thud* upon the drawing room door.

Chapter Nineteen

Upon leaving Mme Héloïse's establishment Tony had driven quickly to the Stacy-Long house on Brook Street. He arrived in a flurry of rearing horses, his chestnuts not accustomed to such treatment, objecting strongly. Tony paid no attention, leaping to the ground and throwing the reins to his tiger who had been silently cursing his master from his perch, hoping not to be thrown to the pavement as they careened wildly down the yards from Bond Street. Rushing up the steps, Tony at first paid no heed to the voice that hailed him, but as he was about to pound on the door, a hand held him back.

"Her ladyship is inside all right, sir. No need to carry on so," repeated Willie Clarke, looking his usual benign self. Tony hesitated, realizing that he had been within an ace of making a cake of himself. And now that he had a moment to reflect, he accepted his foolishness in barging in on Moira, who would no doubt make capital of his appearance.

"I wondered what had happened to you, Clarke, but after that Dorset fiasco, you can imagine how disturbed I was when her coach returned without Lady Everely." He did not want to admit that the image of Francey and Moira having a tête à tête over the teacups was unpalatable.

"Quite so, sir. Perhaps if you called to say you had

218

come to escort Lady Everely home it would be acceptable," Clarke suggested diplomatically. Privately he thought Tony in a pother for no cause.

"Yes, indeed. But there is something havey-cavey here that puzzles me. You had better come inside with me," Tony had no intention of confiding the basis of his apprehension to Mr. Clarke, but he did not like the situation. He doubted that his erstwhile paramour had charitable words for Francey.

Composing himself, he knocked on the door, and after a brief wait, a manservant answered the door.

"I wish to see Lady Stacy-Long," Tony stated firmly to the man, who did not appear very welcoming.

"I regret, sir, that the mistress is not at home," the man replied smoothly, meanwhile blocking the entrance. Somehow the ubiquitous Mr. Clarke had inserted a heavy brown boot into the jam preventing the man from closing the door.

"Nonsense, my man. I have come to collect my wife, who is having tea with your mistress," Tony brushed the man aside and trailed by Mr. Clarke strode into the hall, intimidating the manservant, who did not quite know how to cope with this obdurate nob and his lowbred companion. That was his undoing, for Tony, remembering the layout of the house, walked toward the drawing room. To his astonishment he found it locked. Now he was thoroughly alarmed.

"Open this door immediately," he ordered in his most haughty tone.

"I regret that I do not have the key, sir," the man mumbled, caught between two equally uncomfortable dilemmas. His mistress had been firm. No one was to disturb the occupants of the drawing room, and she was quite capable of throwing a tantrum, dismissing him on the spot. But facing this arrogant peer he had no stomach for an objection.

"Come, Clarke. I think between us we can effect an entrance," and suiting his action to his words, Tony leveled his boot at the door, aided after a moment by Clarke and his truncheon. The door, a stout one, resisted at first, but finally crashed open with a resounding splinter.

There was no sign of Moira but Francey stood in her pelisse and bonnet, her face pale, before the fireplace, a poker in her hand, confronting Oliver Fanshawe.

Ignoring Fanshawe, Tony said smoothly, "Oh, there you are, my dear. I was passing and thought I would escort you home." Crossing to her side he removed the poker from her unresisting hand. "I don't think you need to stir up the fire, as we will be leaving."

Fanshawe, off guard and furious, tried to recover his aplomb, but was not successful. "Good afternoon, Everely. I hope you will not misconstrue this meeting. You seem a trifle put about," he sneered.

Francey, hoping to avoid a scene or worse, recovered more quickly than her adversary. "How thoughtful, Tony. Let us leave immediately. I do not think we need make our adieux to Moira under the circumstances. I am feeling quite fatigued." She placed a placating arm on Tony's sleeve but beneath the driving coat could feel the tensed muscles. She glanced briefly at Mr. Clarke and nodded to him, repressing her surprise. She knew that if she told Tony now what Oliver had threatened he would mill down the man without any hesitation and that would only create havoc in the drawing room. Also she would prefer that Mr. Clarke not witness such a scene. She tugged on his arm in desperation.

Tony was in no mood to worry about Mr. Clarke's impressions, nor to restrain his fury. The sight of Francey clutching that poker, obviously trying to defend herself from Oliver, had done nothing to reassure him. And how had she been lured here in the first place? He wanted to attack Oliver, primitive feelings overcoming any prudence he might be expected to exert. "Fanshawe, I am warning you now that I will not tolerate any attempts from you to contact my wife." He glared menacingly at Fanshawe who summoned a weak sneer.

"Perhaps Lady Everely may not agree." He paid no attention to Francey's gasp of indignation. "She is not the innocent who deserves your protection. If not I, there will be some other, Fitzhugh Lennox, perhaps. He is not the paragon you think." Oliver would have been wise to hold his tongue. Almost before the last words had left his mouth, Tony had landed a flush hit on his chin, and dropped him to the floor.

Stepping over the recumbent Oliver, who made no effort to rise, Tony took Francey by the arm and said, as if nothing untoward had transpired, "Come, my dear. We can sort this all out once we are home. Oh, Fanshawe, you may tell Moira to send the bill for the repair of her drawing room door to me," he said haughtily, looking down at the man who lay at his feet, before striding out of the house with Francey, followed by Mr. Clarke.

Oliver cursed in reply, and managed to struggle to his feet. He staggered to the settee, lowered his head to his hands and groaned. How had his careful plan turned out so disastrously? He must get out of London. He had no doubt that Tony would return, either here or to his rooms, to seek further vengeance and information. Much as he would like to implicate others, he had not the fortitude to face Tony. He would be a laughing stock in White's. Even a Cit's daughter would not have him, if his role in this affair became known. As usual Oliver cared more for the appearance of propriety than for the exercise of it. He groaned in an excess of self-pity, and soon heard a tirade of complaint from Moira, who had crept downstairs to hear the Everelys' departure and confront her co-conspirator.

"Oh, shut up, Moira! You wanted to get Tony into your clutches again, I wanted some revenge, as did Portman, and we've all been unmasked. We'll have to leave town, or become the butt of gossip and humiliation. You can forget about Tony Everely, he wouldn't have you now as a gift," he offered in vicious satisfaction, determined to vent his spleen on Moira, since his real victims had escaped.

"Nor would Francey consider you, Oliver. Your melodramatic plan is a bust, and I am not going to allow you to drag me down with you. Get out of here, Oliver, and don't come back! I will make my own dispositions without any more help from your clever scheming," she mocked. If either felt any compunction for what they had tried to do, it was not evident. Frustration and fury at their failure reigned.

Outside the Brook Street house, Tony hurried Francey toward his phaeton. She was shaking and trying valiantly not to show it. Before mounting himself, he drew Mr. Clarke aside to deliver either instructions or explanations. Francey, tired to death, hardly cared.

"I suspect there is a nasty tale here, Francey, but we will have our discussion in private," Tony said sharply, his recent fear stiffening his tone. Francey, now that she had escaped from Oliver, tossed her head. She would entertain no criticism from Tony.

With Tony's tiger perched behind, able to hear every word, she was not about to express her dismay and disgust at her recent predicament. But neither would she accept any blame for the situation in which Tony had found her. She had been an innocent victim. She still could not believe what Oliver had plotted with the cooperation of Moira and Sidney Portman. She was shocked that any of the three could have hated her that much. Tony had arrived in time to rescue her, but that did not entitle him to rail at her for the near tragedy. Francey was quickly regaining her usual spirits, and she remembered that she had some questions of her own. It was just as well that the tiger prevented either of them from voicing any thoughts just then for both Francey and Tony felt ill used and angry, not emotions suited to judicious explanations.

Back in Grosvenor Square Tony lost no time in quizzing Francey about her meeting with Oliver Fanshawe. She could see he was in a black rage and she hoped it was due to jealousy. But she was in no mood to be conciliatory.

"The whole miserable episode was the fault of your friends," she explained sarcastically, "Moira Stacy-Long and that pillar of rectitude, Sidney Portman. I demand you get rid of him immediately!" Francey rallied, and prepared to take the battle to the enemy's camp. "Moira conspired with Oliver to lure me to her house with an innocuous invitation to tea, abetted by that goosish Maria Lipton. Once there Oliver proceeded to tell me that he intended to dope me and carry me off to the Continent where if I did not submit to his disgusting attentions he would deliver me to a brothel. And you were to receive a note, forged by your estimable secretary, saying that I preferred eloping with Oliver to continuing in my sterile marriage." She stopped to take a breath and a gulp of the glass of brandy Tony placed in her hand.

As Francey's anger heightened, Tony's cooled. He realized she had endured a dreadful experience and he had done nothing to comfort her. In an attempt to temper Francey's indignation, he asked wryly, "And is your marriage sterile?"

"Don't joke about this, Tony. Since I married you I have been threatened, abducted, and almost raped. I am beginning to wonder why I ever accepted you," she stormed.

Tony, seeing that serious measures were called for, crossed the room, took the brandy glass from her hand, and gathered her into a comforting embrace. Looking down into her flashing brown eyes, he suggested, "I hope it was because you love me as much as I love you. Surely you do not doubt that?"

Francey, realizing that she was behaving like a termagant sighed and admitted, "Of course I don't. But I have just endured a dreadful scene with Oliver, and I was jealous, too, thinking you might want to get rid of me to take up with Moira again."

223

"I shall settle that presuming woman once and for all. You could not believe I had any interest in her!" Tony explained with a sorrowful shake of his head. "And Fanshawe will answer to me for his obnoxious suggestion to you. But what is this about Sidney? How did he come into the picture?" Leading Francey to the divan, he settled her down, keeping her within his embrace.

"According to Oliver, and who can believe his lying tongue, Sidney blames me for his sister's death. It seems Archie was paying her some address, and when he heard of my broken engagement to you, abandoned her to propose to me. She went into a decline and then succumbed to pneumonia, fainthearted ninny," Francey scoffed. Tony knew that she, in a like position, would never have behaved in such a witless manner and he barely repressed a smile. He must discover the truth of this accusation.

"And that is the reason for Portman's dislike of you?" he asked, astounded. "He must be unhinged."

"Call him in here and confront him with his infamous behavior," Francey insisted, her sense of justice demanding some satisfaction.

"Yes, of course. He must answer for his participation in Fanshawe's disgusting plot," Tony agreed. Kissing Francey lightly on her brow, he crossed to the bell and pulled it. Almost immediately Jepson appeared. Francey wondered if he had been waiting just outside the door.

"Jepson, tell Captain Portman I want to see him immediately," Tony ordered, in a stern tone of voice.

"Yes, my lord," Jepson scurried to obey him. Francey and Tony waited in silence, both of them appalled at what had so nearly been a tragedy. Francey, who had every reason to remind Tony that she had wanted him to rid himself of his secretary for ages past, wisely kept her peace. There would be time enough for recriminations when the culprit was confronted with his odious conduct.

Portman was ushered into the room by Jepson, who

was brusquely dismissed. If he seemed surprised to see Francey sitting there when he could have expected her to be on the way to the nasty fate he had planned, he gave no evidence of it.

"You wished to see me, Lord Everely?" he asked with assurance, not regarding Francey in any way.

"Lady Everely had made quite a serious allegation against you, Sidney. She says you were a party to a diabolical plot of Oliver Fanshawe's to spirit her out of the country. And that you were inspired to such a heinous action by your belief that she caused your sister's death." Tony spoke calmly but firmly, determined to give his secretary every effort to explain himself.

Portman flushed, revealing that he had been unmasked, and he lost every vestige of his famed control. "She is a jade, a heartless toyer with men's affections, and probably deceiving you with dozens of the beaux who hover about like bees around a honeypot. Fitzhugh Lennox is the latest," he sneered, giving Francey a look of deep loathing.

"Your opinion of Lady Everely is mistaken and offensive. But I want to know if you agreed to forge a note implying she went willingly with Fanshawe?" Tony insisted, not losing sight of his secretary's villainy. If he was shocked by the man's animosity he restrained himself.

"I would do anything to see this scarlet woman receive her just deserts," Portman replied, not ashamed to be caught out in such traitorous behavior by one to whom he owed loyalty and respect.

"You will pack your bags and leave this house within the hour. The only reason I do not have you up before the beak is to avoid a scandal, and I owe you some payment for your devotion to my political work, but you are a shabby creature, and my patience is not inexhaustible. Get out of my sight!"

"You will live to see that this woman will betray you

and cuckold you before your eyes are opened," Portman raged, seeing his comfortable post vanish and knowing there was no relief. "You are besotted by this stupid, vain chit," he concluded, giving Francey a scathing look.

Tony's fists clenched. He would have liked to throttle the rogue, but he kept his temper. "Get out, Portman, or I will have you thrown out!" He stepped toward him, as if prepared to punish him in a manner which would leave no doubt of his feelings.

Portman, paying no attention to Tony, turned to Francey and spat out, "Curse you, you vile woman! You killed my sister, and now you ruin me. But you shall get your deserts, I promise." Then he turned on his heel and strode from the room, slamming the door behind him.

"How could I have been so deceived?" Tony shook his head in wonderment. "I should have listened to you."

"Why would you think he hid such hatred beneath his prim and efficient facade? The man must be sick, to entertain such delusions. And I had no idea Archie had made a commitment to anyone when he proposed to me. I should have known." Somehow Francey should have understood the root of his hatred, but all she was capable of comprehending now was her vast sense of relief, combined with a numbing weariness.

"His insinuations about Fitz. There is no basis to them. You believe that, don't you, Tony?" she asked, worried.

"Of course, my love. Just as you must believe that I have no interest in Moira Stacy-Long. Whatever she implied, I have not seen her alone since our wedding. I suppose she thought with you out of the picture she could lure me back to her arms. Her poor benighted husband died some time ago. I know she intends to wed a comfortable rent roll, but she had no chance of getting me, I promise you."

Then realizing that Francey had endured quite enough for one day, he drew her into his arms, and gave her reassuring evidence of his love and devotion. After a very thorough and warm kiss he patted her on the shoulder and guided her to the door. "What you need is a cup of tea and a bath followed by a long rest. I have some urgent business to attend to, but I will join you for dinner, in your bedchamber, an intimate little meal followed by a very enjoyable interlude which should lay all your doubts to rest."

Francey, aware that he was doing his best to banish the memories of her recent hateful encounter by his teasing promise, agreed with a wan smile and allowed him to escort her to the stairs. She knew he would seek out Oliver and wreak some vengeance on him, but she had little fear that Tony would come to harm. Oliver could not stand up to him and would not try.

Tony later repaired to his study where he had some dispositions to make, but his temper was not soothed when he saw the note on his desk—the forged communication that Sidney had evidently forgotten. Without reading it, he tore it across and threw it in the fire. Then he rang for Jepson and gave him certain instructions before ordering his horses put to again. Sidney Portman, if he valued his safety, would have departed before his return. Tony would not delay his confrontation with Fanshawe, and he had a plan to put Moira in a position where she could do no more harm.

Tony suspected that Francey had a very good idea about what he intended for Oliver Fanshawe. His instructions to Willie Clarke had been to follow the man when he left Moira's. Oliver would not retreat to his rooms in Piccadilly, of that Tony was convinced. Obviously he had made preparations to leave for the Continent immediately and to that end must have a carriage ordered and advance arrangements at Dover or wherever he meant to embark with his unresisting companion. Just the thought of what Oliver had intended for Francey caused Tony a rush of blood to the head and a sick feeling beneath his waistcoat.

He might have a slight sympathy for the deranged and

unhappy Sidney Portman, who had served him faithfully while plotting Francey's disgrace, but for Oliver he had none. Fanshawe's revenge was motivated by sheer spite at having been dismissed by Francey—it was an affront to his amour propre. He claimed to be a gentleman, to embrace the code of honor which that designation implied. He had behaved no better than Fred Scanlon or the rustic brutes who had abducted Francey. Actually his plan was far more horrible, to wrest a respectable lady from her husband and subject her to disgusting intimacies against her will.

Tony's own code of morals was perhaps not as strict as it should have been. In his younger days he had had no compunction in taking advantage of those beauties who had offered him their favors, including the avaricious Moira Stacy-Long. But he did not seduce innocent girls or ravish respectable matrons, nor fail to pay generously for the pleasures various experienced Cyprians had been eager to give him. For all her sophistication, Francey had led a sheltered life, and this latest exposure to man's greed and lust must have proved a dreadful shock to her. He would have to go gently with her, to assure her of his devotion, as well as his passion.

Tony waited impatiently, eager to take some action, but could not move until he received a message from Willie Clarke. Fortunately it was not long in coming. The young street urchin who brought the information was received with gratifying kindness. He had been reluctant to demand entrance to the august mansion on Grosvenor Square, and had appeared at the servants' door, demanding to see "the governor." Jepson, who had been alerted to expect such a visitor, received him in a stately but welcoming manner.

"I'm from Mr. Clarke. He guv me a message for the nob who owns this place and says I must see him and no one else, your Excellency," the undersized ragged boy urged, impressed despite himself by Jepson, whom he at first mistook for the high-toned lord himself.

228

"Yes, yes, come along, wipe your feet, and don't touch anything," ordered Jepson, who had hardly been able to contain his curiosity and frustration at not knowing exactly what had been going on in his domain.

Wide-eyed, but jaunty, the young boy followed Jepson through the servant's hall and past the baize green door into the marbled entrance hall to the library. He had never seen such grandeur and was more than overawed but tried not to gawk. He would have a tale to tell when he left here. He had served the Bow Street runners before, hanging about the Cannon Street headquarters earning a few coppers by running errands, but none of his tasks had brought him to such majestic surroundings. He was received with great patience and kindness by Tony, but there was an aura to his lordship which impressed young Johnnie Banks and he knew he had met a rare one.

"Mr. Clarke says, sir, that the cove you want made off hotfoot in a traveling coach and Mr. Clarke is after him. That what you want, sir?" Johnny Banks asked hopefully.

"Yes, indeed. Good lad. Here is a sovereign. And Jepson here will give you a meal. Off you go." Tony, now that he had learned what he needed to know, wondered if he should take off after Fanshawe. The man, obviously frightened and knowing retribution loomed, had decided to go ahead with his plan to flee to the Continent.

Much as Tony would have liked to follow him and mete out the hard justice he deserved, he saw, after calmer reflection, that there was little point to such a pass, beyond relieving his own anger. Oliver Fanshawe would not dare show his face in England for many months to come and that was probably the best punishment for him. Francey would be spared a scandal and London was well rid of a cad. A clever tactician and a practical operator who knew when to accept a fait accompli, Tony acknowledged that he must forgo his vengeance and accept Oliver's flight.

Willie Clarke would see that the man did actually take

ship for France, but that still left Moira Stacy-Long. Dealing with her might take a bit more finesse, but Tony had little doubt he could persuade her to join Fanshawe on the Continent. Her tenuous position in London society was finished.

As he thought about his next moves, Tony heard a disturbance in the hall, the commotion attendant on Sidney Portman's departure. Tony rose, crossed the room and locked his door. He did not want a further outburst from his fanatical secretary. Sidney had truly blotted his copybook, and if he could find no employment, it was only what he deserved. Tony's mercy had been strained and he was in no mood to listen either to cringing apologies or to raving justifications. The whole business reeked of unsavory wicked conniving and he wanted to put it behind him.

He sighed. All these personal troubles atop the current political worries tried his patience. As soon as Portman had cleared out, he intended to call on Moira, and that should be the end of his deplorable affair. Not that he had played a very heroic role in matters. He had been deceived by Sidney, manipulated by Moira, and he had acted like a jealous fool over Fanshawe, causing Francey unjustified pain. He had always prided himself on his judgment and management of both men and events, but lately he had used precious little of either quality. Well, from now on, he would not be so easily gulled nor tempted from his conscience's dictates. Lately the Everelys had suffered more than their share of calamities, and Tony decided that he would arrange matters more adroitly in the future.

Chapter Twenty

Several days after the flight of Oliver Fanshawe and the dismissal of Sidney Portman, Francey sat in the morning room of the Grosvenor Square house reading a letter from Maddy Scanlon. An outpouring of gratitude was followed by a detailed account of her life in her Dorset refuge. Little Mary was thriving and the family had been most kind to her. She only hoped she was giving satisfaction to her employers. Francey was convinced that the solution to Maddy's problem had been the right one, but she wished she had been able to settle the matter of Fred Scanlon once and for all. He had disappeared successfully into the netherworld of London and attempts to winkle him out had come to naught.

Sidney Portman had been replaced by Leofric Hardcastle, a round tubby man, of engaging manner, and cheerful devotion to Tony's interests. Francey quite enjoyed Leo, as he preferred to be called, and he had settled comfortably into their household. She had managed another appointment with Sir Richard Croft and had her pregnancy confirmed, a fact she had yet to reveal to Tony, keeping that happy news for an appropriate time. Willie Clarke had reported watching Oliver board a packet for Calais, and Francey hoped they had seen the last of that troublesome gentleman for some time.

As for Moira Stacy-Long, she too had earned her just deserts. Francey chuckled as she remembered that sly lady's discomfort on being roundly snubbed by Tony at a recent rout. With incredible brashness she had tripped up to him, intent on cajolery, only to be cut dead, a social snub remarked upon by most of the *ton's* arbiters. He had let it be known that the Everelys would not attend any function to which she was invited. In desperation she had departed for Scotland, where Francey hoped she would succumb to both boredom and frustration in that rugged primitive land. Only Tony's continuing concern for the state of the country marred their domestic tranquillity.

One other troubling question still dogged her. Fitzhugh Lennox's premonition of danger, and her own dismay at the warning he had given her. She hated distrusting Fitz. He had been such a stalwart friend and confidant. Tony thought she was overly alarmed, but suspicion remained.

Later that day she had disturbing evidence that she had every reason to fear Fitz's involvement in some dubious enterprise. As she was leaving the refuge in St. Martin's Lane, an activity she had refused to abandon despite Tony's pleas, she thought she saw Fred Scanlon. As her coach drew away, she retreated into the corner, and watched her former captor swagger down the street. Knocking on the coachman's perch, she instructed him to follow the man. As he shambled down Charing Cross Road then onto the Strand toward Covent Garden she realized she might be courting the very danger that Fitz had cautioned her about, but she was determined to discover Scanlon's whereabouts. He dived into the warren of lanes behind the Garden, and she thought she had lost him, for her coach would have great difficulty in following there without detection.

He seemed to have disappeared, when suddenly he surfaced on the steps of the Opera House, and stopped peering around as if searching for something or someone. To her surprise she saw Fitz swinging along the street, as dapper and insouciant as if he were strolling down St. James's. The two men met, stepped behind one of the pillars and talked briefly. What could it mean?

She dare not linger, and the carriage went on at a leisurely pace. She only hoped that she had not been noticed, that the coach with the Compton crest prominently displayed had not caught the eye of either Fitz or Scanlon. There was little more she could do. She could not stop.

She ordered the coachman to turn back on his traces and reenter the Strand. If only she had been on foot she could have tried to get nearer, despite the danger of discovery. To have Scanlon within her grasp and then lose him was infuriating. She must alert Tony and Willie Clarke immediately. Perhaps the Bow Street runner could track down Scanlon and apprehend him, but she doubted their quarry would be so obliging. She wondered if Mr. Clarke had observed the odd progress of her coach.

Once the carriage had reached the comparative safety of Piccadilly, she ordered John the coachman to stop. Descending from the carriage near Bond Street, she looked about, hoping to catch a glimpse of Mr. Clarke, but he was not to be seen. Could he have deserted his post, secure in the knowledge that she was safely on her way back to Grosvenor Square? Feeling a bit foolish, Francey reentered the coach, ignoring the grimaces of her coachman and footmen, and continued on her way home.

Once back in Grosvenor Square, she wondered what she should do. If she waited until Tony arrived home for dinner, it might be too late to track Scanlon into his hideout. Should she send a message to Bow Street where officers there might know how to contact Mr. Clarke? The whole affair puzzled and alarmed her. Why would Fitz meet with the wretched Scanlon, and not notify them of his whereabouts? How could she face Fitz again without revealing that she knew he had been caught out in some dubious situation. She havered and paced, all her instincts insisting that she should make some move, but she couldn't decide what to do. Finally she summoned Leo Hardcastle. He would know where Tony was. The obliging little man, looking quite like an amiable bear bounded into the morning room in answer to her summons.

"What can I do for you, dear Lady Everely?" he asked all eagerness.

Francey could not but smile at his cheerful earnestness, such a contrast to the dour and devious Portman.

"I wonder if you might know where Lord Everely can be reached? I am quite anxious to give him an important message." She was reluctant to say too much, not knowing if Tony had told his new secretary of the past plots against them.

"I believe he was going on to White's after leaving the Home Office. Should I try to reach him there? I can easily step over to St. James's Street," Leo offered placidly.

"Would you mind terribly? It's vital that I see him before tonight," Francey explained. Perhaps she was making too much of what she had just seen, but she had to do something. Inaction would drive her mad.

"Of course not. Would you like me to deliver a note?" he asked in a most obliging manner.

"Yes, that would answer. Wait a moment while I write a brief line," Francey scrawled some words on a sheet of her note paper, and sealed the message in a crested envelope. "I could send a footman, but you would stress the urgency of the matter much better," she confided, in the easy style which readily won the hearts of those who served her. "Please don't alarm him. He is apt to be overly careful of my welfare."

"Deservedly so, if I may say so. Recent events have been most disturbing, Lady Everely," Leo surprised her by saying gravely. "I will be most circumspect." Then he trotted away, the letter clutched in his hand.

Francey fumed impatiently. How long would it take

Tony to answer her summons, if indeed he was at White's? He could be anywhere, at his tailor's, or back at the Home Office, even at the House. If Leo could not locate him she would just have to exercise some patience but she felt that every moment counted. If Fred Scanlon was to be found, they must not waste time.

And what was she to do about Fitz? She would have to tell Tony of her fears. Was Tony protecting her by not telling her what he knew about their friend's doings? Were the authorities aware of his dubious associates? Surely Fitz could have no honest reason for meeting Fred Scanlon, a known agitator and criminal. From the little she had observed she doubted this was their first meeting. They seemed to know each other well. If Fitz knew of Fred Scanlon's hideout it was surely his duty to inform the authorities. Francey knew Tony had told Fitz something of her treatment at that villain's hands. Fitz had appeared appalled. There was definitely a mystery here. She was determined to solve it.

It seemed hours before she heard Tony return, but actually it was barely three-quarters of an hour. She rushed to the hall, hoping to assure him that she was all right. He threw off his cape and hat, raising his eyebrows at her obvious distraught state.

"What is the matter, my dear? You must be in quite a pother, although Leo informed me you were safe at home." He followed her into her sanctum, eager to get to the bottom of this uncharacteristic summons.

"Oh, Tony, I have just seen Fred Scanlon. He was hanging about the refuge when I emerged this afternoon, and I had John follow him down to Covent Garden. But that's not the worst. He met Fitz there. I cannot believe their business was not suspect," she blurted out in her eagerness to find some answers to this unexpected assignation.

Tony hesitated. He trusted Francey, but he did not want to reveal all he knew. What could he say to calm her suspicions without giving away the whole show? It would never do for Francey to have this dangerous information. She would be in dreadful jeopardy. But he knew he had to give her a serious explanation.

"I suppose I will have to reveal Fitz's secret," he confessed. "Come, sit down here and compose yourself. This may not come as such a surprise." He led her to the divan and sat down beside her, prepared to answer her questions.

"What is Fitz's secret? It cannot be disreputable. I would never believe that of him."

"On the contrary. He has been working for the Foreign Office as an agent in this business of winkling out traitors. He had compiled quite a damning dossier on Oliver Fanshawe, for example, and if that poltroon had not decamped to Europe, he would have been hailed up before the magistrates." Tony spoke with scorn, but eyed Francey cautiously, hoping this revelation would distract her from the scene she had witnessed today.

"Whatever shabby tricks Oliver played would not surprise me. I think he was under the hatches and would have accepted money from anyone." Francey was all indignation, recalling her late duel with Fanshawe.

"Well, he made overtures to Fitz, at our ball, of all places, and suggested that since Fitz had so many friends among the Cabinet he might be willing to confide some of the idle chatter he heard, for a suitable sum, of course."

"But what would Oliver do with this information, even if Fitz agreed? France is no longer our enemy. Who would want to have a spy in our government circles?"

Tony hesitated, then realizing she would not be fobbed off with a lie, admitted, "Metternich. He is absolutely terrified still of revolution, in Austria, in Russia, in England. He has been pushing Castlereagh and Liverpool to clamp down on any radical protest. He brooks no political agitation in Vienna or in the provinces. I think despite the very full bulletins Prince Esterhazy sends him of conditions here he really has no idea of how the average Englishman feels about liberty and personal freedom." Tony hoped that his explanation of Fitz's activities would calm Francey and distract her from more searching questions. He should have known better.

"Well, I am relieved to hear that Fitz has been serving his country, not subverting it, but that does not explain his meeting with Scanlon. I cannot believe that scurvy fellow is of any use to Metternich," Francey protested, cleverly seeing past Tony's sketchy defense of Fitz to the real enigma.

Tony hesitated just a bit too long, unsure of what he should confide to Francey. He trusted her to keep any information sacrosanct, but the secret was not his. "Largely through Fitz's offices, we know of a plot to use violence against the government, and Scanlon is one of the cabal. Scanlon's whereabouts has become known to us, too, but for the moment we prefer not to arrest him. That is all I can tell you now. You will have to be satisfied with that, Francey," he insisted soberly.

"Well, I am not satisfied, but it is obvious you can say little more," Francey conceded. "I am sorry if I dragged you home without cause." She was feeling a bit cross, her information about Scanlon not received in quite the manner she had expected.

"I am always willing to be dragged home by you, my dear, and I understand your vexation. I sometimes wonder if we, and for that matter, the country, will ever return to a peaceful settled existence."

"Well, we personally will not, for I am expecting a baby and I understand they are far from peaceful," Francey said, knowing that her news would cheer Tony, and she hated to see him so despondent.

"Oh, Francey, how marvelous! Are you sure?" Tony asked.

"Well, I have consulted Sir Richard Croft and he tells me we can count on the heir to arrive sometime in early June. Of course, it may be a girl," she added whimsically.

"That would be equally exciting, especially if she takes after her mother. My father will be pleased," Tony observed, but then frowned. "Are you sure Croft is the man to oversee this *accouchement?* And should you be staying in London, now. You might be healthier and happier in the country?"

Francey sighed, having expected this reaction. "I do not want to leave you in London, prey to all sorts of temptations, and I would only fret in Dorset. I have every confidence in Sir Richard, who tells me I am extremely healthy and should have an easy confinement," she finished a bit proudly.

"You still believe I am some kind of practised rake. Really, Francey, you wound me," he answered, only half in jest. Then he smoothed back her hair, and kissed her gently. "I have yearned to become a parent. You will make a splendid mother, and I want no more from life than to head up a thriving family. Perhaps I should give up all this political strife and retire to the bucolic life of a farmer."

"We have been through this before, and that's nonsense. You would be bored to death and get into all sorts of trouble. If we can just settle this question of Scanlon, Fitz and the conspirators, all will be tranquil," she said with more assurance than she really felt.

"Promise me you will take care, Francey," Tony agreed gravely. "And I promise you this whole imbroglio will be settled by Christmas."

"And then there will be another crisis, I don't doubt."

"Probably, but one which won't involve you. For the next few weeks you must be on your guard. Scanlon and his colleagues are an irrational crew. He has no reason to love you."

"Yes, I know that. I can only pray that other concerns occupy him now. So that means you, too, must be on your guard. What do these agitators want?" Francey asked a bit wearily.

"Another French Revolution. They want to destroy the existing system, destabilize the government, regardless of the resulting chaos. And most of them have no idea what should be instituted in its place. They are unhappy madmen, who just want to tear down. They have some justice to their cause, for they represent a whole class of people who are not served well by the present system. And when they see the Regent indulging in gross excess, and he is not the only one, they feel justified in attacking us." Tony spoke with dejection.

"Perhaps Liverpool should be replaced. He has been in office a long time and perhaps has lost the ability to see any urgency in affairs, intent only on securing the status quo," Francey offered.

"No, Liverpool is a calm port in a welter of confusion. Would you see the Whigs and Radicals in, and our lot out?" Tony asked.

"I suppose you know best. All I want is some way to keep you out of the eye of the storm. You know I did not choose all this trouble when I married you. I should have known better. You were always the mercurial type, not at all a reliable man," she teased, determined to lighten the mood.

"The past few months have indeed been tempestuous, but we will come about. And, Francey, despite all the difficulties, one positive result of these past days is that you and I have reached a calm haven. We no longer distrust one another, and I hope our love will weather any adversities," Tony insisted gravely.

"And there will be crises, I am sure." Francey smiled. Somehow discussing all the country's troubles had emphasized her happiness. "We are fortunate. From all this has come personal contentment, and that is a bonus I rather doubted at the beginning."

"Cling to that assurance. We love each other and soon will have a child to care for and that should be our first priority. Believe me, I consider you and any children we might have more important than my political aspirations."

"Thank you, sir. I shall remember. And if you are inclined toward another crusade, either political or personal, please inform me. I am not a hothouse flower to be cosseted and sheltered from trouble." She hoped Tony would take her words seriously, and although she felt greatly comforted, she was not yet completely reassured. Fanciful, perhaps, to think that danger still loomed, that their personal happiness was threatened. However, for the moment, Fred Scanlon, Fitz and the mysteries surrounding their strange alliance could be relegated to their proper sphere. Obviously Tony and the government had matters well in hand. In this conclusion she was only partly correct.

Chapter Twenty-One

On the day of the dinner party which Tony was hosting for the Cabinet, Francey saw to it that all was prepared, flowers, food and décor. She put down her restlessness to her pregnancy, but she could not settle down to any task. Finally she decided she would relieve her state of nerves by accepting an invitation from Letty to luncheon. She had not seen her godchild for some weeks, and she had yet to inform her friend that she was *enceinte*. Letty would be hurt not to be told. And certainly the volatile Lady Colgrove would prove a distraction. She ordered her carriage and prepared to banish her megrims by listening to Letty's budget of scandal.

"I am so pleased you are increasing, Francey. Babies are so satisfying, even if their fathers are somewhat disappointing," Letty said cheerfully.

"Surely Sir Henry is not disappointing?" Francey teased, recalling that rather dull pompous gentleman, and wondering what Letty had expected.

"Oh, Henry is all right, but rather prosy. Right now he is creating a fuss about my losing his mother's sapphire ring, a rather ugly bauble. I quite hated it," Letty complained.

"Did you misplace it on purpose?"

"Of course not. But I have had my eye on a really lovely ruby and Henry is proving most intransigent. He says we cannot afford it."

"Well, in these trying times perhaps he is right."

"Nonsense! He just wants to thwart me. But I will persuade him," Letty insisted carelessly. "It's the least we can do because he is urging me to return to the country. Can you imagine it? At the height of the season! Ridiculous! Sometimes I wish I had married a man with a bit more go. Like your Tony. But then, of course, I would be worried constantly if he was being faithful," Letty implied Francey might have similar worries about her dashing mate.

"If you are implying that I should be worried about Tony, let me reassure you. He is a very pattern card of devotion," Francey said a bit sharply. Really, Letty was too much, always trying to nose out a scandal or create one.

"No trouble from the encroaching Moira Stacy-Long? I hear she has gone to Scotland, and I also heard it was because Tony snubbed her royally," Letty confided eagerly, intent on wringing the last morsel of excitement from the current *on dit*.

Francey, knowing her friend's insatiable desire for gossip, would not be drawn. "Perhaps she felt the need for some bracing air. And if you think Tony had anything to do with her leaving, you are out of bounds." Francey lied with convincing aplomb. Not for the world would she tell Letty what Moira had really wanted.

"If you say so, my dear." Letty, if disappointed, knew just how far she could push Francey and was unwilling to take the matter further. "Now if you are finished with that strawberry meringue, would you like to go shopping? I understand a new shipment of silk ribbons has just arrived from France. If I am to economize I must retrim my last bonnet. It is looking quite limp."

"Of course, just the ticket. I might buy some wool and knit the coming heir a sacque, although I am not at all skilled at that art," Francey agreed laughing. "I must endeavor to become more matronly."

"Not a chance, Francey. You will always be an Incomparable, even when you are increasing. You look blooming now. But come, we will take a peep at little Henry and be on our way. I have ordered the carraige, and will drop you home after our outing," she promised.

But Francey, understandably leery of riding in others' vehicles, insisted they take her carriage, and after a suitable interval spent admiring Master Henry Colgrove, they set out on their expedition to the Pantheon Bazaar. Alighting in Oxford Street beneath the colonnaded portico, they were greeted with affability by the gold-laced beadle and were directed to the maze of stalls, presided over by very superior young ladies. Letty, in her usual indecisive way, agonized over the assortment of ribbons, wavering between a bright magenta and a citron yellow, neither of which Francey thought at all suitable for her friend's hearty complexion. Becoming bored with Letty's havering, Francey drifted away, attracted for the first time to the charming display of children's dresses. Purchasing some knitting wool at yet another stall, she was about to collect Letty, when, to her amazement, she saw Fitz strolling down the aisles toward her. He hailed her with every appearance of enthusiasm.

"Just the person I need, dear Francey. You cannot imagine how intimidated I am by the condescending treatment of these competent ladies behind the stalls. Mere males have no purchase here, I have discovered, and I must accomplish this task that Aunt Amelia has entrusted to me. She's such an old harridan, if I return with the wrong gimcrack it will be all up with me. And no chance of inheriting the old lady's blunt," he sighed in mock sorrow.

"Oh, Fitz, you are the most complete hand. But before we solve your difficulty I must collect Letty, whom I left trying to decide on ribbons, each equally ghastly. Perhaps you can persuade her toward the more flattering shade." As they made their way toward the ribbon stall Francey thought what an accomplished actor Fitz was.

243

From his idle man-about-town pose one would never guess what he was really up to. Fitz had been playing a dangerous game with all his usual insouciance. He never appeared less than obliging, always had all the time in the world to trail about on stupid errands for fashionable ladies, and never seemed impatient or irritated by the frivolous demands of his many female relations, of which Aunt Amelia was the most intransigent.

Letty, somewhat in awe of Fitz's reputation as a social arbiter, gracefully acceded to his suggestion that her bonnet would be improved by some tasteful blue sprigged ribbons instead of the violent yellow she had set her heart on. Then the trio wandered over to the wax flower display where Francey persuaded the clerk to make up a fetching bouquet under glass, ordered by Fitz's aunt.

"I really cannot traipse around with this very elegant object in my arms. What do you suggest, my dear young lady?" Fitz pleaded with the salesperson, a prim-looking woman in a subdued grey silk dress.

"We shall be delighted to deliver it for you, sir," she said, her sternness melting before Fitz's practised address.

"Oh, how kind," he thanked her, adding a guinea to the price for her trouble, and writing out the address plainly. Then, turning to Letty and Francey, he sighed. "I am now at your service, ladies, and I recommend a calming cup of tea or other suitable beverage after this fatiguing commission," he suggested gallantly.

Letty, always eager for confections and pastries, assented happily, but Francey would have preferred to wrest Fitz from Letty's grasp and quiz him about certain actions of his. Still, courtesy must be observed.

"I believe there is a suitable purveyor of cakes and tea in the midst of all this vulgar display," he invited, shepherding them down an aisle.

Letty, never knowing quite how to take Sir Fitz and fearful of committing some solecism, decided she had quite misjudged him. He was not the supercilious dandy she had expected, but a genuinely decent man. Her courage restored, she asked him to relate some of the more fascinating *on dits* of the day over the teacups while managing at the same time to consume three or four cream buns. Accustomed as Francey was to Letty's irrepressible taste for gossip, and fond as she was of her bosom bow, Francey could have shaken her. She was itching to get Fitz to herself and ask him some pungent questions. She contained herself with difficulty, ignoring for the most part their exchange of scandal until she heard Letty mention Moira Stacy-Long.

"Do tell us, Sir Fitz—why did Lady Stacy-Long abandon the season and rush off to Scotland? I am sure there is an intriguing mystery behind her sudden flight," Letty asked avidly, while delicately wiping traces of cream from her mouth.

"I understand some irate matron objected to the lady's overtures toward her husband and took steps to enforce a social ostracism," Fitz confided gravely to Francey's discomfort. Really Fitz could play the most complete hand. Could he be referring to Tony's methods of removing the woman? Just how much did he really know about Moira's and Oliver's intrigue to bring about Francey's disgrace?

"What a lively imagination you have, Fitz! That is sheer embroidery," Francey countered giving him a speaking look.

If her comment abashed him, he hid it well. "I could be wrong. Perhaps she feared the bailiffs in the house, or is having a passionate intrigue with a Scottish laird and could not resist bearding him in his cold and gloomy fortress," he offered outrageously.

Francey was convinced he knew something of the real state of affairs but she controlled her annoyance, and changed the direction of the conversation. Then, after a suitable interval, she suggested to Letty that they might be on their way. Since they had traveled in Francey's carriage, Letty had no choice but to agree, much as she would have liked to quiz Fitz further.

"Can we drop you somewhere, Fitz?" Francey asked, as they made their way through the crystal conservatory toward the Great Marlborough Street exit where the carriage awaited them.

"Too kind, dear Francey. If you could drop me at White's it would be most obliging. I need the solace of some masculine companionship after this exhausting foray into your ladies' emporium," he jested. Francey's carriage was summoned by the beadle and the trio were soon on their way to St. James's Street.

They arrived at White's and Fitz made his effusive adieux, stepping out of the vehicle onto the pavement. The carriage was held up by another just before them, and Francey noticed at once that Fitz was approached by a strange man. Loath as she was to give Letty any ammunition for conjecture, she asked, "Who is that man who approached Fitz? They are on the steps now and he seems to be importuning him strongly."

Letty craned her neck, determined not to miss anything. "Why I believe that is Arthur Thistlewood, you know, the Radical, a really dreadful man. What could he want with Fitz?" she asked naïvely.

Francey, who feared she knew the answer, only murmured, "I cannot imagine. What an odd circumstance! See, they are walking off together." Indeed Thistlewood, if that was who it was, was almost dragging Fitz along St. James's with a hard grip on his arm, admitting of no escape. For a moment Francey was tempted to follow them, but what excuse could she give to Letty, whose insatiable curiosity was already aroused. Just then their carriage started up, and they continued down St. James's Street but Francey noticed that Fitz and his companion had ducked down King Street and she believed they were joined by another figure, but could not be sure. Thoroughly alarmed now, she had the greatest difficulty in hiding her unease from Letty, who prattled on about the strange encounter.

"I can't imagine how Fitzhugh Lennox could have met Mr. Thistlewood. Henry says he is a wicked man, pretending to work for reform through the ministers but secretly plotting behind their backs," Letty expounded with the quaint air of infallibility she always assumed when repeating her husband's pronouncements.

"I'm sure Henry is correct," Francey agreed demurely, a bit amused at Letty's analysis, but more concerned as to the manner of Fitz's disappearance with the suspect Arthur Thistlewood. But the carriage had now turned down Letty's street and she concentrated on bidding farewell to her friend, hoping she would not think her too abrupt.

"Don't forget dinner, Thursday week," Letty reminded her, and Francey agreed absentmindedly. If Letty thought her *distraite* she put her mood down to her pregnancy, and the friends parted with mutual promises to meet again soon. Francey lay back in the carriage exhausted from hiding her unease from Letty. It would never do to reveal anything to that chatterbox. Fitz might be in some danger.

She must alert Tony immediately. She had ordered John to drive to the Home Office, but what if Tony were not there? Should she then try Bow Street and Mr. Clarke? Should she have abandoned Letty and tried to follow Fitz and Thistlewood? She seemed incapable of making any decision. She must leave it to Tony. He would be furious if she tried to interfere.

By the time they arrived in Whitehall she was both confused and alarmed. Sending in a footman to find Tony, she fumed with impatience. Fitz could be in the most terrible danger and here she was hanging about doing nothing, abandoning him to his fate. Within a few moments, although it seemed like much longer to Francey, her footman was back with the message that Lord Everely had gone to White's, where he planned to meet Sir Fitzhugh Lennox.

Hearing these words increased Francey's fears. She

247

must locate Tony. Fashionable and respectable ladies did not enter such a sacrosanct male preserve as a club. She could send a message but that would take valuable time.

"Is Mr. Hardcastle within? If he is would you ask him to please come out as I have an important mission for him?" Francey ordered. She could send Leo to White's, to drag Tony out if necessary. Poor Leo, he was always being sent to soothe the vagaries of a hysterical mistress. But as every moment delayed action, Francey had become convinced that Fitz was in danger. Every insintct warned her that this danger could affect Tony, too. Even now it might be too late. To her relief she saw Leo Hardcastle, his tubby form bundled into a coat, hurrying out of the Home Office, clutching papers and looking benign and unruffled as if being disturbed at his desk by his employer's wife was a common occurrence, not a crisis.

"Is there some way I can assist you, Lady Everely?" he asked, climbing into the carriage and viewing her placidly.

"Yes, Leo. You can accompany me to White's and bring out Lord Everely. A rather worrying situation has developed and I must consult him immediately," she said as calmly as she could, although she was feeling far from calm.

"Are you unwell, Lady Everely?" Leo asked, now worried, but determined not to panic, wondering if her ladyship, whom he knew to be pregnant, might be having some mysterious reaction to that state.

"No, no. It's far more serious. Oh, why won't John drive faster?" Francey tried to take a grip on herself. She knew she was causing poor Leo undue concern. And the last time she had sent Leo to White's to wrest Tony from his sanctum, it had proved to be of little account. Was her condition making her prey to weird fancies? She hoped not, but she was sure that this time she was right. Events were leading to a climax. Not only Fitz, but Tony

248

and even the Prime Minister might be in dreadful peril. At last the carriage turned down St. James's Street and Leo leaped down the steps, not waiting for the footman to open the door.

"I shall be as quick as possible," he promised Francey, throwing the words over his shoulder, by now infected with her sense of urgency.

Francey leaned back against the squabs, hoping not to be seen by any passersby, although she knew her coach was distinctive. It was ridiculous, this shibboleth about women not appearing near any man's club. She felt like a fool, doubts now creeping into the reason for her precipitate action. Tony would probably be furious.

But Tony, when he appeared, and heard of Fitz's meeting with Thistlewood, was as alarmed as she was.

"This is very disturbing. I wondered why Fitz had not turned up for our meeting. Evidently the conspirators have decided on action. I must inform Wellington, and he will call out the Guards. We cannot delay a moment," he spoke curtly, ignoring Francey's questions, and ordering the coachman to drive directly to the War Office. Poor Leo Hardcastle, who had accompanied him, looked as horrified and puzzled as Francey felt, but she knew she must hold her peace. This was no time to behave like a foolish female, badgering Tony with lamentations and queries.

At the War Office, he sent Leo inside to insure that Wellington was there, and when Leo returned signifying the Duke would receive him, he jumped from the carriage, only turning to say in some desperation, "Francey, return home immediately and do not stir from the house until I return. I promise to explain the whole matter then, but you must not delay. Do not try a nonsensical ploy of your own, promise me? You could endanger not only yourself, but Fitz, the whole Cabinet. Do you understand?"

Seeing that Tony was passionate in his insistence, she nodded wordlessly, now frightened, but determined not to give in to her terror. Were they on the brink of revolution?

"I will do just as you say, Tony. Only please come as soon as you can. I shall be dreadfully worried," she promised. He leaned over, and ignoring the presence of Leo, who was standing by his side, and the footman, waiting to close the door, gave her a hard brief kiss. Then he was gone.

Chapter Twenty-Two

It was three hours later before Tony appeared in Grosvenor Square. Francey had passed through agonies of apprehension before she heard his step in the hall, and rushed out to greet him. Heedless of Jepson, who was assisting Tony with his hat and coat, she cried, "What has happened? Where is Fitz? Is he safe?"

"It's all over, a nasty conspiracy, nipped in the bud, and just in time, thanks to your warning. Come, I need a drink. Let us go into the library and I will tell you all about it."

Jepson, overcome by curiosity, but determined not to show it, reminded them, "Are you still expecting the gentlemen for dinner, my lord?"

"Oh, God. I had forgotten all about that. Yes, I suppose so, Jepson. But we still have an hour or so." Tony realized that Francey would not be fobbed off with any sketchy report. And she was entitled to a full explanation. They adjourned to the library, where Tony poured himself a generous tot of brandy and settled Francey in a chair by the fire. She was suddenly aware of a dreadful cold shaking sensation—reaction, of course, and she took a firm grip on herself. She would not give in to timorous fainting.

"We have known for some time that Thistlewood and his cohorts, pretty violent types, working men for the most part, were planning a coup, but we had no idea of the date or just what they intended. Fitz had managed to worm his way into their confidence by telling Thistlewood some folderol about his disappointments and need for revenge against me and the government who would not reward his efforts. Why they believed him, I cannot fathom, but they needed a spy in government circles and thought Fitz an informer. And he played his part to perfection.

"Thistlewood, somehow, learned that the Cabinet would be dining here tonight and decided to strike. He had a cache of guns and grenades stashed in that hideout near Covent Garden. When the guards broke in they discovered the plotters about to take off, intending to come here and kill us all as we gathered about the port. Unfortunately one of the officers was killed and two of the plotters, and Thistlewood escaped. But he will be rounded up and brought to justice.

"Fitz is fine, but the Guards arrived just in time. The gang was beginning to suspect Fitz was a government agent and had tied him up preparing to shoot him before leaving for here. It is a miracle you saw him being hustled away by Thistlewood, for I would never have realized that the date for the assassination was tonight, even if I had worried about Fitz's not turning up at White's. You saved us, my dear, and Wellington sends his heartfelt thanks for your intervention. I am proud of you, Francey."

He paused, not wanting to tell her the bloody truth, that the conspirators had sacks, ready to hold the Cabinet members' severed heads, which they planned to display atop the Mansion House. They were particularly anxious to secure Wellington and Castlereagh as symbols, and one of the plotters, a butcher by trade, was prepared to do the job. Tony spared Francey those details, for the horror of it was too dreadful.

"I felt so helpless. And I can hardly comprehend such evil. What would have happened if they had been successful?" she asked, appalled at the near success of the plot.

"Thistlewood would have proclaimed a republic, with himself as president. He raved that we deserved to be murdered, having failed to relieve the condition of the country. Perhaps he is right. Wellington thinks they were just a group of crazed agitators, and now the country, hearing of the plot, will settle down into its usual condition of apathy and foolishness, his very words. But I am not so sanguine."

"Well, I suppose I am selfish, but I am only grateful that you have been spared, and the others, too, of course," Francey added almost as an afterthought.

Tony grinned. "I don't believe you care a bit about Wellington, Liverpool, Eldon and the rest. You have a one-track mind, and I am happy to be your chief concern. You would have made a lovely widow," he added in an effort to defuse the emotional environment.

"How callous, Tony! I would have been devastated, as you well know. How can you joke about this! It's too terrible to contemplate, that these men, Englishmen, could have planned such a murder!"

"Desperate men, my dear, contrive desperate remedies to their condition. Once the word is out, I think the average Englishman will be as appalled by this attempt as he was by Peterloo. Perhaps we can now contrive to reach a pacific settlement of our differences. I do not have the Iron Duke's contempt for and haughty indifference to the common man. But come, this has all been a most upsetting experience for you. You need not receive the gentlemen when they come this evening if you would prefer not to. I will make your excuses, but the Duke will be disappointed. He views you as a heroine, and wishes to compliment you."

"Well, I am quite at odds with him, but I shall be all graciousness, and then retire to my room and eat my solitary dinner on a tray. I only hope your gentlemen may now come to some compromise about settling the

253

country's affairs. I want my baby born in a less chaotic setting," she returned sharply, now that the crisis had passed, prepared to speak her mind to the intransigent ministers.

"Yes, well, I will look forward with pleasure to the scene of you scolding the Duke. But please, do rest now. I am concerned about the baby, too, you know," he urged gently.

Despite her words, Francey was most gracious to the Duke when he arrived for dinner. Ever gallant, he was profuse in his praise for her prompt action.

"Where we poor men would be without the protection and clever schemes of you ladies, I cannot imagine! You are a heroine, Lady Everely!" he insisted, bowing over her hand later that evening.

"Not at all, Duke. But surely this near escape from tragedy is a warning to us all that we should not despise the populace. We might all end up at the guillotine," she warned sharply.

"I hope such a bloodthirsty answer to our deficiencies can be avoided. Thank goodness that murderous contraption is not a staple of English justice," he replied, not exactly sure how to take Francey's warning.

Feeling she had said enough, Francey retired, leaving the gentlemen to discuss the day's events, and hoping they would see this narrow escape from assassination as a warning to change their tactics.

Feeling exhausted but relieved, she undressed after her light dinner, and waited for Tony to join her. She suspected it would not be a late evening, and that only courtesy and a certain noblesse oblige had impelled them to hold the meeting as if nothing had happened that day. She was right, and it was just before midnight that her husband entered her bedroom.

"Well, have you settled the fate of the country, my lord?" she asked as he took off his dressing gown and climbed into bed beside her.

He smiled at the picture she made, with her unbound

gold hair spread across the pillows, and the sparkle of defiance in her brown eyes.

"You will not believe this, Francey, but little mention was made of the foiled plot. We spent the entire evening talking about the commotion being caused by Princess Caroline in Europe. Prinny has told Liverpool he will insist on divorcing her before he is crowned. And unhappily that could be sooner than we think, as the King is sinking fast. We shall soon be embroiled in the messy conflict between Prinny and his Princess. Neither one of them has any sense of decorum."

"Neither do you, my lord," Francey teased as she felt his hand run up and down her thigh, causing all sorts of emotions. For the moment all thoughts of plots, princesses, and politics vanished under the intense feelings which Tony could arouse. For the Everelys the affairs of state would never replace the affairs of the heart.

Author's Note

The attempted assassination of the Cabinet in this novel is based on the Cato Street Conspiracy, February 23, 1820. The actual plot was engineered by Arthur Thistlewood, who was hanged with his fellow conspirators at Tyburn. Tony Everely was correct in believing that once the plot was exposed, the horrified country, repelled by such villainy, would abandon any thought of rebellion. As employment improved, trade increased and food prices lowered, the anger of the public subsided. Englishmen had no taste for domestic revolution. The people displayed their disgust at the new king, George IV, by championing his wife, Caroline, whom he tried to divorce before the Coronation.

Terrorist plots against the Cabinet continue to this day. John Major and his Cabinet narrowly avoided injury during Operation Desert Storm when a bomb went off in the garden of No. 10 Downing Street. Earlier several of Margaret Thatcher's aides were injured at a bombing incident in a Brighton Hotel on the occasion of a Conservative Party meeting.